The Foreign Classical Romances

Complete in Twenty Crown Octavo Volumes

With Introductory Essays by

HAMILTON WRIGHT MABIE, L.H.D., LL.D.
Co-Editor N. Y. Outlook.
Author of "Norse Stories," "Essays on Books and Culture," etc.

PROF. MAURICE FRANCIS EGAN, A.M., LL.D.
Catholic University of America.
Author of Studies in Literature," "Modern Novelists," etc.

PROF. LEO WIENER
Harvard University. Translator of Tolstoy's Complete Works.
Author of "Anthology of Russian Literature," etc.

BARON GUSTAVO TOSTI
Doctor of Laws, Naples University. Royal Consul of Italy at Boston

WOLF VON SCHIERBRAND
Former Berlin Correspondent N. Y. Evening Post. Author of "Germany," etc.

A. SCHADE VAN WESTRUM
Licentiate Amsterdam University. Literary Editor N. Y. Mail and Express

General Editor: **LIONEL STRACHEY**
Compiler of "Little Masterpieces of Fiction."
Translator of Stories by Balzac, Sudermann, Serao, etc.

Frontispieces and Biographical Sketches

THE LION OF FLANDERS

HENDRIK CONSCIENCE

VOLUME II

FATE

COUPERUS

TRANSLATED FROM THE DUTCH

A FRONTISPIECE AND A BIOGRAPHICAL SKETCH

P. F. COLLIER & SON
PUBLISHERS   NEW YORK

THE LION OF FLANDERS

VOLUME TWO

CONTENTS

THE LION OF FLANDERS
(CONCLUDED)

BOOK THIRD

FATE

3

Contents

THE LION OF FLANDERS

BOOK THIRD

CHAPTER I

Two years had gone by since the foreigner had set foot in Flanders, and cried: "Bow your heads, ye Flemings! ye sons of the north, yield to the children of the south, or die!" Little thought they that there had been born in Bruges a man endowed with large sagacity, and inspired with heroic courage; a man who shone forth as a bright light among his contemporaries; and to whom, as to His servant Moses, God had said: "Go, and deliver thy brethren, the children of Israel, from the thraldom of Pharaoh."

When the desolating bands of the French first trod the soil of his fatherland, and darkened the horizon with the dust of their march, a secret voice spoke in Deconinck's soul, and said:

"Take heed, these are in quest of slaves!"

At its sound, the noble citizen quivered with anguish and wrath:

"Slaves! we slaves!" groaned he; "forbid it, oh Lord our God! The blood of our free-born fathers

5

hath flowed in defense of Thine altars; they have died on the sands of Arabia with Thy holy name on their lips. Oh, suffer not their sons to bear the debasing fetters of the alien; suffer not the temple which they have raised unto Thee to have bondsmen for worshipers!"

Deconinck had breathed this prayer from his deepest soul, and all his heart lay open to his Creator. He found therein all the noble courage and energy wherewith He had endowed the Fleming; and He sent down an answering ray of trust and hope. Instantly filled with a secret strength, Deconinck felt as though all his capacities of thought and action were doubled in energy; and, impelled by a true inspiration, he cried:

"Yea, Lord, I have felt Thy strong and Thy strengthening hand; yes, I shall ward off this degradation from my fatherland; the graves of Thy servants, my fathers, shall never be trodden down by the foot of the alien. Blessed art Thou, oh my God, who hast called me to this!"

From that moment one only feeling, one only deep yearning lived in Deconinck's heart; his every thought, his every faculty, all were consecrated to the great word—my fatherland! Business, family, repose, all were banished from his ample heart, which held but one, one only affection —his love for the native soil of the Lion. And what man more truly noble than this Fleming, who a hundred times risked life and liberty itself for the freedom of Flanders? what man was ever endowed with more ample sagacity? Alone and unaided, in spite of recreants and Lilyards, who would have sold their country's freedom, he it was who baffled the efforts of the King of France —he alone it was who preserved for his brethren a lion's heart even under the chains of slavery, and thus gradually achieved their deliverance.

The French knew this well—well they knew him who at every moment shattered the wheels of their triumphal chariot. Gladly would they have rid themselves of this troublesome guardian of his country's weal; but with the cunning he combined perfectly the prudence of the serpent. He had raised up for himself a secure rampart and defense in the love of his brethren; and the stranger well knew that a dire and bloody revenge would follow any attempt upon him. During the time that the French ruled all Flanders with the rod of tyranny, Deconinck lived in entire freedom among his townsmen; and he was indeed the master of his rulers, for they feared him much more than he feared them.

And now seven thousand Frenchmen had on one day atoned with their lives for the oppressions of two long years; not a single foreigner breathed within Bruges, the victorious and free; the city echoed the joyous lays wherewith wandering minstrels celebrated this deliverance, and from the watch-tower the white flag displayed the Blue Lion on its waving folds. This ensign, which had once waved from the battlements of Jerusalem, and commemorated so many proud achievements, filled the hearts of the citizens with lofty courage. On that day it seemed impossible that Flanders should again sigh in the chains of captivity; for on that day the people remembered the blood their fathers had shed in behalf of liberty. Tears rolled down their cheeks—those tears which relieve the heart when it is overful, when it throbs with too strong and sublime an emotion.

One would have thought that, now his great work was done, the Dean of the Clothworkers would have occupied himself in the reconstruction of his plundered and desolated home. But no; he thought neither of the dwelling nor of the wealth of which he had been despoiled; the welfare and the peace of his brethren were his first care. He knew that disorganization might soon follow upon inaction, and therefore, on that very day, he placed at the head of each Guild, with the concurrence of the people, an old experienced master. He was not chosen to the presidency of this council, no one devolved any duty on him; but he undertook and accomplished all. No one ventured to do anything without him; his judgment was in everything an injunction; and without issuing a single command, his thought was the absolute rule of right to the republic, so transcendent and all-subduing is the way of genius.

The French host was, indeed, destroyed; but it was certain that Philip the Fair would send fresh and more numerous troops to Flanders to avenge the insult put upon him. The greater part of the citizens thought little about this terrible certainty; it was enough for them to enjoy the freedom and the gladness of the moment. But Deconinck did not share the common joy; he had almost forgotten the present in his schemes for averting future disaster. He well knew that the exhilaration and courage of a people vanish at the approach of danger, and endeavored by every means in his power to keep alive a warlike spirit in the city. Every Guildsman was provided with a "good-day" or other weapon, the banners were put in order, and the command issued that all should be ready for battle at a moment's notice. The Guild of Masons began to repair and strengthen the fortifications, and the Smiths were forbidden to forge anything but weapons for the people. The tolls were again imposed, and the city dues collected. By these wise regulations, Deconinck made every thought, every effort of the citizens converge to one object and one aim; and so he warded off from his beloved city the manifold evils which a great insurrection, how noble soever its cause, is apt to inflict on a people. All was as orderly as if the new government had existed for years.

Immediately after the victory, and while the people were drinking in every street the wine of gladness, Deconinck had sent a messenger to the encampment at Damme, to recall the remaining Guildsmen, with the women and children, into the city. Matilda had come with them, and had been offered a magnificent dwelling in the Princes' Court; but she preferred the house of Nieuwland, in which she had passed so many hours of sorrow, and with which all her dreams were associated. She found in the excellent sister of Adolf a tender and affectionate friend, into whose heart she could pour all the love and all the grief which overflowed her own. It is, indeed, a consolation for us, when our hearts are pierced with mortal anguish, to find a soul which can understand our sufferings because itself has suffered: a soul that loves those whom we love, and whose wailings are the echo of our own. So two tender saplings interweave their tendrils, and, supported by this mutual embrace, defy the devastating hurricane which bows their frail heads. To us mourning and sorrow are a hurricane, whose icy breath chills the life and wastes the fire of our souls, and brings down our head untimely to the grave, as though each year of unhappiness were reckoned as two.

The sun was rising in glowing splendor for the

fourth time over the free city of Bruges. Matilda
was sitting in the same room of Adolf von Nieuwland's house which she had formerly occupied.
Her faithful bird, the beloved falcon, accompanied
her no more—it was dead. Sickness and sorrow
had spread their paleness over the soft features
of the maiden; her eyes were dimmed, her cheek
had lost its fulness, and her whole appearance
showed that a deep grief lay, like a gnawing worm,
in her heart.

Those who are visited with long and bitter suffering take pleasure in sad and gloomy dreams;
and, as if the reality were not painful enough,
fashion to themselves phantoms, which appal them
yet more: and thus was it with the hapless maiden.
She fancied that the secret of her father's liberation had been discovered; she saw in imagination
the murderers, bribed by Queen Joanna, mingling
poison with his scanty food; and then she would
shudder convulsively, and tears of agony would
stream down her cheeks. Adolf was dead to her:
he had expiated, with his life, his love and his
magnanimity. These heartrending fancies passed
ever and anew before Matilda's soul, and cease-
lessly tortured the poor maiden.

At this moment her friend Maria entered her
room. The smile which passed over Matilda's
features as she greeted her friend was like the
smile which, after a death of anguish, lingers

a while on the face of the departed; it expressed more of pain and profound sorrow than the bitterest wailing could have done. She looked at Adolf's sister, and said:

"Oh! give me some comfort, some alleviation of my suffering!"

Maria drew near to the unhappy girl, and pressed her hand in tender sympathy. Her voice took its softest tone, and sank like music into the soul of the sufferer, as she said:

"Your tears flow in stillness, your heart is breaking with anguish and despair; and there is nothing, nothing to lighten your heavy burden! Alas! you are indeed unhappy."

"Unhappy! say you, my friend? Oh, yes! There is a feeling in my heart which fills it to bursting. Can you imagine what hideous fancies are ever floating before my eyes? and can you understand why my tears unceasingly flow? I have seen my father die of poison; I have heard the voice as of one dying—a voice that said, 'Farewell, my child; thou whom I have loved.' "

"I pray you, maiden," interposed Maria, "banish these gloomy shadows of your fancy. You rend my heart with sorrow. Your father is yet alive. You sin grievously in abandoning yourself thus to despair. Forgive me these words of severity."

Matilda seized Maria's hand and pressed it gently, as though she would express to her what comfort these words had given her. Nevertheless, she continued her desponding discourse, and seemed even to find a kind of comfort therein. For the wailings of an oppressed soul are, as it were, tears which lighten the burden of the heart. She continued:

"I have seen yet more than this, Maria: I saw the headsman of the inhuman Joanna of France— he swung his ax over the head of your brother, and I saw that head fall on the dungeon floor!"

"Oh God!" cried Maria, "what horrible fancies!" She trembled, and her eyes glistened with tears.

"And I heard his voice—a voice that said, 'Farewell! farewell!'"

Overpowered by these hideous thoughts, Maria threw herself into Matilda's arms; her tears fell fast on the heaving breast of her unhappy friend, and the deep sobbing of the two maidens filled the room. After they had held each other in a long and motionless embrace, Matilda asked:

"Do you understand my sufferings now, Maria? Do you understand now why I am slowly wasting away?"

"Oh, yes," answered Maria, in an accent of despair; "yes, I understand and feel your sufferings. Oh, my poor brother!"

The two maidens sat down exhausted, and without uttering a word. They looked at each other a while with unutterable sorrow; but their tears gradually lightened their grief, and hope returned into the hearts of both, they knew not how. Maria, who was older than Matilda, and more self-possessed in suffering, first broke the deep silence, and said:

"Why should we allow our hearts to be thus crushed by false imaginations? There is nothing to confirm the painful apprehensions which torment us; I feel sure that no harm has befallen Lord Robert, your father, and that my brother has already set out on his return to his fatherland."

"Yet you have wept, Maria! Does one weep at the smiling expectation of a brother's return?"

"You are torturing yourself, noble damsel. Oh! anguish must have struck deep its roots in your heart ere you could cling with such passionate energy to the dark dreams which are overshadowing you. Believe me, your father yet lives; and who can say how near his liberation is? Think of the joy you will feel when his voice, the very voice that rings so frightfully in your disturbed fancy, shall say to you, 'My chains are broken!' when you shall feel his warm kiss on your brow, and his loving embrace shall call forth again the roses upon your blanched cheek. Once more shall the fair castle of Wynandael open its gates to welcome you; Messire de Bethune will ascend the throne of his fathers, and then shall you tend him again with loving care; then you will remember no more the sorrows of the present, or remember them only as sorrows which you endured for your father's sake. Tell me now, Matilda, will you not admit one solitary ray of hope into your heart? Can not these thoughts of joyful promise bring you any consolation?"

At these words a sensible change came over Matilda; a gentle gladness beamed again in her eyes, and a sweet smile played on her lips.

"Oh Maria!" she sighed, throwing her right arm around her friendly comforter, "you can not imagine what relief I feel, what happiness beyond hope you have poured, like a healing balm, into my heart! So may the angel of the Lord minister comfort to you in your last hour! With what soothing words has friendship endowed you, oh my sister!"

"Your sister!" repeated Maria. "This name beseems not your handmaiden, noble damsel; it is a sufficient reward to me that I have been enabled to dispel the gloom of death from your soul."

"Accept this title, my beloved Maria; I love you so tenderly. And has not your noble brother Adolf been brought up with me? Has not my father given him to me as a brother? Yes, we belong to one family. Alas! I pray the livelong night, that the holy angels may shield Adolf on his dangerous journey. He can yet comfort me, yet cheer me. But what do I hear? Can my prayer have been answered? Yes, yes, that is our beloved brother!"

She stretched forth her arm, and remained standing motionless, pointing toward the street. She stood like a marble statue, and seemed to listen eagerly to a distant sound. Maria was terrified; she thought the maiden had lost her senses. As she was about to reply, she heard the echo of a horse's hoofs in the street; and then the meaning of Matilda's words flashed upon her. The same hope filled her breast, and she felt her heart beat with redoubled energy.

After both had listened a while in silence, the noise suddenly ceased; and already was the glad hope deserting their hearts, when the door of the chamber was violently thrown open.

"There he is! there he is!" cried Matilda. "God be praised that mine eyes have seen him once more!"

She ran eagerly toward the knight, and Adolf as eagerly hastened to meet her, when a sudden emotion overcame him, and he well-nigh fell trembling to the ground.

Instead of the youthful blooming maiden whom he expected to see, he beheld before him a worn and wasted figure, with haggard cheeks and sunken eyes. While yet in doubt whether this shadow could be Matilda, a cold shudder ran through him; all his blood rushed to his oppressed heart, and he turned pale, pale as the white robe of his beloved one. His arms dropped, he fixed his eyes intently on Matilda's wasted cheeks, and remained as one struck by a thunderbolt. A moment he remained in this attitude; and then suddenly his eyes fell, and hot tears rolled down his cheeks. He spoke not a word—no lament, no sigh escaped his lips. He would probably have remained yet longer in this stupor of despair— for his heart was touched with too keen a pain to admit of his finding alleviation in words—but his sister Maria, who had hitherto remained in the background out of respect to Matilda, threw herself on his breast, and the warm kisses which she imprinted on the lips of her beloved brother, in the intervals of the most tender words, soon aroused him from his stupor.

The noble maiden beheld with emotion this outburst of sisterly love; she trembled, and a deep trouble filled her heart. The paleness of Adolf's features, the consternation which had so visibly seized him, said to her: "Thou art ill-favored, thy wasted cheeks and thy dimmed and lustreless eyes inspire fear and abhorrence; he whom thou callest thy brother has shuddered at thy look of death." A dark despair overcame her; she felt her strength desert her; only with great effort did she succeed in reaching a couch, and then sank down faint and exhausted. She hid her face in her hands, as though to exclude from her view a spectre that appalled her; and thus remained, still and motionless. After a few moments, all was quiet in the room; she heard no more, and thought that she was left alone in that dreadful solitude.

But soon she felt a hand which pressed hers; she heard a gentle voice, which spoke to her in sorrow and in sympathy:

"Matilda! Matilda! Oh my hapless sister!"

She looked up, and saw Adolf standing before her, weeping. The tears fell thick and fast from his eyes, and his look expressed the warmest affection, the profoundest compassion.

"I am ugly; is it not so, Adolf?" she sighed forth. "You are shocked at me; you will no more love me as in days that are past?"

The knight trembled at these words; he looked at the maiden with a strange and significant expression, and replied:

"Matilda, can you entertain a doubt of my affection? Oh, then, you wrong me much. You are, indeed, changed. What illness, what sufferings have brought you so low, that the roses have thus withered on your cheek? I have wept, and have been alarmed indeed; but it is from sympathy and compassion, from the deep anguish which your hard lot has caused me. Ever, ever will I remain your brother. Matilda! I can comfort you now with joyous tidings; I can heal your sorrows with a message of gladness."

Gradually a feeling of joy and consolation stole into the maiden's heart. Adolf's voice exercised a wondrous power over her, and she replied, with cheerful animation:

"Good tidings, do you say, Adolf? Good tidings of my father? Oh speak, speak then, my friend."

With these words, she drew two chairs near her couch, and motioned to Maria and her brother to sit down upon them.

Adolf reached forth one hand to Matilda, the other to his beloved sister; and so he sat between the two maidens, as an angel of consolation, on whose words one lingered as on those of some holy hymn.

"Rejoice, Matilda, and thank God for His goodness. Your father returned to Bourges; in sadness, indeed, but in safety and in health. No one but the old chatelain and Diederik die Vos know the secret of his temporary liberation. He is already free even in his captivity; for his jailers have become his warmest friends."

"But should the evil-minded Joanna desire to avenge on him the insult which has been offered to France, who will then shield him from the executioner? You are no longer with him, my noble friend."

The Lion of Flanders

"Listen, Matilda. The guardians of the castle of Bourges are all old warriors, who, by reason of their wounds, are no longer equal to active warfare. Most of them witnessed the heroic deeds of the Lion of Flanders at Beneventum. You can not imagine with what love, with what admiration, they regard him at whose name the armies of France have so often trembled. Were Robert to seek to escape without the permission of the castellan, their master, doubtless they would prevent him. But I assure you—and I know well the noble souls of those warriors, who have grown gray beneath their coats of mail—that they would shed their last drop of blood for him whom they revere, were but a hair of his head threatened. Fear not, then; the life of your father is assured; and, but for the sorrow he felt on account of your sad fate, he would have borne his captivity in patience."

"You bring me such good tidings, my friend—your words sink so consolingly into my relieved heart—that I seem to drink in fresh life from your smile. Speak on still, if it be only that I may hear the accents of your voice."

"And yet fairer hopes has the Lion given me for you, Matilda. It may be the deliverance of your father is very near at hand; it may be that you will very soon be with him, and all your dear relations, in the beautiful Wynandael."

The Lion of Flanders

"What are you saying, Adolf? It is your friendship that prompts these words; but do not mock me with hope of a bliss that is impossible."

"Be not thus unbelieving, Matilda. Listen to the grounds of this joyful hope. You know that Charles de Valois, that noblest of Frenchmen, has drawn the bravest of the knights after him into Italy. He has not forgotten at the court of Rome that he is the guiltless cause of the captivity of your relatives. It has been a bitter thought to him that he himself, like a traitor, had delivered his friend and companion in arms, the Lion of Flanders, into the hands of his enemies; and he has been striving, in every possible way, to effect his liberation. Ambassadors have been already sent from Pope Boniface to King Philip the Fair, and have demanded of him, with urgency, the release of your father, and of all your relatives. The Holy Father is sparing no effort to restore to Flanders its rightful princes; and the court of France seems already inclined to peace. Let us embrace this consoling hope, my dear friend."

"Yes, indeed, Adolf, gladly might we surrender ourselves to these consoling thoughts; but why should we flatter ourselves with hopes so deceitful? Will not the King of France avenge his fallen soldiers? Will not De Chatillon, our most rancorous enemy, goad on his terrible niece Joanna? Think, then, Adolf, what pangs can not this bloodthirsty woman imagine, to avenge on us the bravery of the Flemings?"

"Torment not yourself; for your fears are without foundation. Probably the horrible death of his soldiers has convinced Philip the Fair that the Flemings will never bow their free necks to the yoke of the alien. His own interest will constrain him to set at liberty our country's lords; otherwise he will lose the fairest fief of his crown. You see, noble damsel, that everything is propitious to us."

"Yes, yes, Adolf; in your presence all my sorrows melt away, and disappear utterly. Your speech is so full of comfort, you awaken such sweetly-echoing tones in my heart."

They conversed thus a long time peacefully together on their fears and their hopes. When Adolf had given Matilda all the information in his power, and had filled her heart with comfort, he turned with brotherly love to his sister, and held with her a soothing discourse, which attuned them all to gladness and serenity. Matilda forgot her bygone sufferings; she breathed freely and with courage, and the veins which were spread over her cheeks like delicate network were filled with warmer blood.

Suddenly they heard a loud tumult in the street; a thousand voices rang from the roofs of the houses, and the jubilant shouts of the crowd were mingled in indistinguishable confusion; only at intervals

was the cry intelligible amid the joyous clapping
of hands: "Flanders, the Lion! hail, hail to our
Count!" Adolf and the two maidens had drawn
near to the window; they saw the countless heads
of the crowds hastening to the market-place.
Women and children swelled the procession, which
passed before the curious maidens like a billowy
sea. In another street resounded the tramp of a
multitude of horses, so that they were confirmed
in their conjecture that a troop of cavalry had entered Bruges. While they were discussing the
probable reasons of this popular commotion, a servant announced the arrival of a messenger, who
craved an audience, and who entered the room
immediately on receiving permission.

It was a youthful page, a delicate boy, whose
features bore a peculiar expression of innocence
and truthfulness: he was clothed in black and blue
silk, set off with manifold adornments. As he
drew near to the ladies, he respectfully uncovered
his head, and made lowly obeisance without
speaking a word.

"What good tidings do you bring us, dear boy?"
asked Matilda graciously. The page raised his
head, and replied with his gentle voice:

"For the most illustrious daughter of the Lion,
our Count, I bring a message from my lord and
master Guy, who has just entered the city with five
hundred horsemen. He sends his greeting to his

fair niece, Matilda de Bethune, and will in a few moments express his deep affection to her in person. This is the message, noble maiden, which I was charged to deliver to you."

And with these words he made a reverential bow, and disappeared at the door. In fulfilment of the promise which he had made to Deconinck in the wood, near the ruins of Nieuwenhove, the young Guy had arrived with the promised succors from Namur. He had taken Castle Wynandael on his way, and had put the French garrison to the sword. He had razed to the ground the Castle of Sysseele, because the castellan was a sworn Lilyard and had offered the French a refuge within its walls. The victorious entry of Guy filled the citizens of Bruges with exulting joy, and in every street resounded the cry, "Hail to our Count! Flanders! the Lion!"

When the young general with his suite had reached the Friday Market-place, the masters of the Guilds presented him with the keys of the city; and he was thus proclaimed Count of Flanders, until the liberation of Robert de Bethune, his brother. The citizens already deemed their liberty secure; for now they had a chief who could lead them forth to the fight. The horsemen were quartered among the most distinguished citizens; and so great was the zeal and the joy of the inhabitants that there was quite a struggle to seize the reins of the horses; for every one wished to receive into his house one of the Count's followers; but it is easy to imagine with what kindness and courtesy these valuable auxiliaries were welcomed.

As soon as Guy had assumed the government which Deconinck had established and secured, he hastened to the house of Nieuwland, embraced his afflicted niece, and recounted to her with joy how he had driven the aliens from their beloved Wynandael. A costly banquet awaited them, prepared by Maria in honor of her brother's return. They drank the wine of joy for the liberation of the enslaved Flemings, and consecrated a tear to the mournful memory of the poisoned Philippa.

CHAPTER II

AFTER the fearful night in which the blood of the French had flowed in such abundant streams, De Chatillon, John van Gistel, and the few others who had escaped death, were received within the walls of Courtrai. In the city they found a numerous garrison, trusting in peaceful security to the strength of the castle; for on this place the French counted most confidently, as its fortifications were really unassailable. De Chatillon, a prey to hopeless despair on account of his defeat, was burning with the desire of vengeance. He hastily drew some small companies of mercenaries from the other cities to Courtrai, in order still further to protect it in the event of an attack, and he entrusted the command of these troops to the castellan Van Lens, a bastard Fleming. Using the utmost despatch, he visited the other frontier cities, placed within them the troops that yet remained to him in Picardy, gave the command of Lisle to the chancellor, Pierre Flotte, and hastened to France, to the court of Philip at Paris, where the tidings of the defeat of his army had already preceded him.

The Lion of Flanders

Philip the Fair received the governor-general of Flanders with marked displeasure, and reproached him angrily with the tyrannical conduct which had been the cause of the disaster. De Chatillon would have undoubtedly fallen into disgrace, had not Queen Joanna, who, as we know, hated the Flemings and exulted in their oppression, found means to exculpate her uncle so dexterously that Philip at length began to believe that he deserved thanks rather than reproofs. And thus the whole wrath of the king was again turned back on the Flemings, and he swore that he would exact from them a dire revenge.

An army of twenty thousand men had been already assembled at Paris, in order to deliver the kingdom of Majorca from the hand of the infidel; and these were the troops of whose gathering Robert de Bethune had spoken to the lords of Flanders. They might easily have marched this host upon Flanders; but Philip would run no risk of defeat, and resolved therefore to postpone his vengeance a short time in order to collect more soldiers.

A proclamation was borne throughout France by swift messengers; the great vassals of the kingdom were informed how the Flemings had put to death seven thousand Frenchmen; and that the king summoned them to Paris with all the troops at their command, and with the utmost speed, in order to avenge the insult. In those times warfare and feats of arms were the sole occupation of the nobles, and they exulted at the very mention of battle; so we need not wonder that this appeal met an immediate and hearty response. From every quarter, from every castle of mighty France, poured the great feudatories of the crown with their vassals; and in a very short time the French army counted more than fifty thousand men.

After the Lion of Flanders and Charles de Valois, Robert d'Artois was the ablest warrior that Europe boasted at that time; and indeed his great and varied experience, gained in numerous expeditions, gave him, in some respects, an advantage over these two commanders. For eight whole years he had never laid aside his armor; his hair had literally grown gray beneath the helmet. The unrelenting hatred with which he regarded the Flemings, who had slain his only son at Furnes, determined the queen to give him the chief command of the whole army; and in truth no one was better qualified for this honorable post than Robert d'Artois.

Want of money, and the daily arrival of the more distant vassals of the crown, retarded for some time the departure of the host. The excessive ardor and precipitation with which the French nobles usually entered on their expeditions had so often proved prejudicial to them, and they had learnt at such heavy cost that prudence and foresight are important elements of strength, that they resolved on this occasion to take every precaution, and proceed with the greatest deliberation.

The fiery queen of Navarre sent for Robert d'Artois, and urged him to chastise the Flemings with the utmost cruelty. She enjoined on him, for instance, "to rip up all the Flemish swine, and to spit their whelps on the point of the sword, and to strike every Flemish dog dead." The swine and the whelps were the women and children of Flanders; and the dogs were those heroes who, sword in hand, were defending their fatherland The faithful chronicles have preserved for us these shameless words of a queen and a woman, as a token of Joanna's ferocious spirit.

In the meantime, the Flemings had greatly increased their army. The illustrious Master John Borluut had excited the citizens of Ghent to rise and drive out of their city the French garrison; and seven hundred were slain in this insurrection. Oudenarde and several other cities effected their freedom in like manner; so that the enemy retained possession only of a few fortified places, in which the flying Frenchmen found refuge. William van Gulick, the priest, came from Germany to Bruges with a numerous troop of archers, and as soon as Master John van Renesse had assembled four hundred Zeelanders, they united their forces, and, accompanied by a crowd of volunteers, moved toward Cassel, in order to fall upon and expel the French garrison. This city was exceedingly well fortified, so that it could not be taken by surprise. William van Gulick had counted on the cooperation of the citizens; but the French kept so vigilant a guard that they could not make the slightest movement; so that Master William found himself compelled to begin a regular siege, and await the arrival of the necessary stores and battering machines.

The youthful Guy had been received with acclamations in all the most important cities of West Flanders; his presence everywhere infused courage, and inspired every man with a burning ardor to defend his fatherland. Adolf van Nieuwland had also visited the lesser towns, in order to summon together all who were capable of bearing arms.

In Courtrai there lay about three thousand French under the command of the castellan Van Lens. Instead of endeavoring to win the affections of the people by kindness, they exhausted their patience by continued acts of depredation and petty tyranny. Encouraged by the example of the other cities, the inhabitants rose suddenly against the French, and slew more than half of them; the remainder made their escape to the citadel, which they hastily fortified in the best way that they could. There they revenged themselves by shoot-

ing burning arrows into the city; so that many of
its finest buildings, especially those surrounding
the market-place and the Beguinage, became a
prey to the flames. The citizens thereupon in-
vested the citadel with their whole forces; but
they did not number sufficiently strong to be able
to expel the French. Filled with the mournful
apprehension that their city would soon be entirely
destroyed by fire, they sent messengers to Bruges
with an earnest request to the young Count Guy
for aid.

The messenger reached Guy in Bruges on the
5th of July, 1302, and made him acquainted with
the melancholy condition of the city, and its urgent
need of aid. The Count was deeply moved by the
account they gave, and determined to hasten without delay to the hapless city. As William van
Gulick had taken all the troops with him to Cassel,
Guy had no other resource than to call together
the Guildsmen. He caused all the Deans to be
immediately summoned to the upper hall of the
prince's castle, and betook himself thither with the
few knights who were about him. An hour later,
all the Deans, thirty in number, were assembled,
and awaited, with uncovered heads and in silence,
the subject to be proposed for their deliberation.
Deconinck and Breydel, as leaders of the two most
powerful Guilds, occupied the foremost place.
Count Guy sat in a rich armchair at the upper end

of the hall; near him stood Messire John van Lichterwelde and Messire van Heyne, both peers of Flanders. There were four noble families in Flanders, of which the heads were called Beers, or peers; when the race of the Count became extinct, the new prince was to be chosen from among these Beers. The other gentlemen attending the Count were: Messire van Gavem, whose father had been slain by the French at Furnes; Messire van Bornhem, a knight templar; Robert van Leeuererghem; Baldwin van Raveschoot; Ivo van Belleghem; Henry, Lord of Lonchyn, in Luxemburg; Gorwyer van Goetzenhove and Jan van Cuyck of Brabant; Peter and Louis van Lichterwelde; Peter and Louis Goethals of Ghent; and Henry van Petershem. Adolf van Nieuwland was standing on the right hand of the Count, and engaged in confidential conversation with him.

In the centre of the vacant space, between the Deans and the knights, stood the herald of Courtrai. As soon as each had taken his place, Guy commanded him to repeat his tidings in presence of the Deans; and the herald obeyed, and began:

"The good citizens of Courtrai greet you by me, noble lords, and inform you that they have driven the French from their city, and that five hundred of them have bitten the dust. But now the city is in the greatest straits. The traitor Van Lens has fallen back on the citadel, and daily discharges burning arrows upon the houses, so that the fairest portion of the city is already reduced to ashes. Messire Arnold van Oudenarde has brought them some succors, yet is the number of the enemy too great. In this their need and distress, they beseech the Count Guy in particular, and you, friendly citizens of Bruges, in general, to send them aid; and they hope that you will not delay a single day the rescue of your distressed brothers. Such is the message which the good citizens of Courtrai send to you by my mouth."

"You have heard, Deans," said Guy, "that one of our noblest cities is in peril of utter destruction, I do not think that the cry of distress from your brothers of Courtrai will fall in vain on your ears. The matter demands haste; your aid alone can deliver them from their danger; wherefore I pray you all instantly to summon your Guilds to arms. How long time do you require to prepare your comrades to set forth?"

The Dean of the Clothworkers replied: "This afternoon, most illustrious Count, four thousand Clothworkers will stand full armed on the Friday Market-place: I will lead them whithersoever you command."

"And you, Master Breydel, you will be there also?"

Breydel advanced proudly, and replied: "Your servant Breydel will place at your disposition, my

Lord Count, not less than eight thousand of his craftsmen."

A cry of astonishment ran along the circle of knights. "Eight thousand!" said they, all at once.

"Yes, truly, messires," continued the Dean of the Butchers; "eight thousand and more. All the Guilds of Bruges, except that of the Clothworkers, have elected me their captain; and God knows how I can repay this honor. This very afternoon, if you will it so, the Friday Market-place shall be filled with your trusty townsmen; and I can assure you that in my butchers you have a thousand lions in your host; the sooner the better, noble Count; our axes are beginning to rust."

"Master Breydel," said Guy, "you are a brave and a worthy vassal of my father. The land in which such men live can never long remain enslaved. I thank you for your hearty good-will."

A smile of satisfaction showed how much pleasure Breydel's words had given to the circle of knights; but the Dean turned back again, and whispered in Deconinck's ear: "I pray you, master, be not angry with me for speaking thus to the Count. You are and will ever be my superior; for without your counsel I should do but little good. My words have not caused you displeasure?"

The Dean of the Clothworkers pressed Breydel's hand in sign of friendship and perfect accord.

"Master Deconinck," inquired Guy, "have you

made known to the Guilds my former request?
Will the requisite gold be provided for me?"

"The Guilds of Bruges place all their wealth at
your disposal, noble Count," was the answer. "If
you will but send some of your servants with a
command in writing to the Guildhall, as many
marks of silver will be delivered to them as you
may require. The Guilds beseech you not to spare
them; freedom can never cost them too dear."

Just as Guy was about to acknowledge the good-
will and confidence of the citizens with words of
gratitude, the door of the hall was opened, and
every eye was fixed with astonishment on a monk,
who entered boldly and uninvited, and drew near
to the Dean. A robe of thick brown cloth was con-
fined by a girdle around his loins; a black hood
overhung his face, and so concealed his features as
to render it impossible to recognize him. He
seemed very old; for his body was bent, and a long
beard floated on his breast. With hasty and fur-
tive glances, he regarded the knights who were
present; and his keen eye seemed to pierce the
lowest depth of their hearts. Adolf van Nieuwland recognized in him the same monk who had
brought him the letter of Robert de Bethune, and
was about to greet him with a loud voice; but the
gestures of the monk were so extraordinary that
the words died away on the lips of the young man.
All who were present began to kindle with anger;

the daring looks which the unknown bent on them were such as they would not willingly endure; yet they gave no indication of their displeasure, for they saw that the riddle would soon be solved.

When the monk had well scrutinized each of those who were present, he loosed his girdle from his loins, threw his robe and his hood on the ground, and remained standing in the middle of the hall. He raised his head proudly; he was a man of about thirty years of age, tall and of noble frame; he looked round upon the knights as though he said, "Do you not recognize me?"

The answer did not come quickly enough, and he cried out: "You are astonished, messires, to find a fox under this coat; yet he has lain concealed in it for two years."

"Welcome, welcome, dear Diederik, good friend!" exclaimed the nobles all at once; "we thought you had been long since dead."

"Then you may thank God that I have risen again," continued Diederik. "No, I was not dead; our captive brother and Adolf van Nieuwland can bear testimony to that. I have been able to console all; for as an itinerant priest I had access to the prisons; and may God forgive me the vile Latin I have uttered. Yes, you may laugh, messires, but I have spoken Latin. I bring you, moreover, news from all our hapless countrymen for their relatives and friends."

The Lion of Flanders

Some of the knights wished to make more particular inquiry concerning the fate of the prisoners; but he put them aside, and continued: "For God's sake, cease these questions; I have far more important tidings to announce to you. Hear, and tremble not; for I bring you evil news. You have shaken off the yoke, and have fought and won the battle of your freedom; I grieve that I could not share this joy with you. Honor to you, brave knights and trusty citizens; honor to you that you have freed your fatherland. I assure you that if the Flemings do not wear new chains within fourteen days, not all the devils in hell will be able to rob them of their liberty; but the new chains that are preparing make me anxious and sad."

"Explain yourself more clearly, Messire Diederik," cried Guy; "explain your meaning, and do not torture us with enigmatical hints."

"Well, then, I tell you plainly that sixty-two thousand Frenchmen are encamped before Lille."

"Sixty-two thousand!" repeated the knights, gazing in alarm on one another.

"Sixty-two thousand!" echoed Breydel, rubbing his hands for joy; "what a fine flock!"

Deconinck's head sank on his breast, and he was lost in deep thought. Soon, however, he had estimated the greatness of the danger, and considered the means to avert it.

"I assure you, messires," continued Diederik

die Vos, "that they number more than thirty-two thousand horse, and at least as many foot. They plunder and burn as though they were thereby rendering an acceptable service to Heaven."

"Are these evil tidings well founded?" asked Guy anxiously; "has not he who told you this deceived you, Messire Diederik?"

"No, no, noble Count, I saw it with my own eyes; and last evening I ate my supper in the tent of the Seneschal Robert d'Artois. He swore on his honor, in my presence, that the last Fleming should die by his hand. Consider now what it behooves you to do. For myself, I shall buckle on my armor without delay; and if I stand alone against these two-and-sixty thousand accursed Frenchmen, I will not yield an inch of ground; I, at least, will no longer witness the slavery of Flanders!"

Jan Breydel could not keep himself still a moment; his feet were in perpetual motion, and he swung his arms in angry impatience. Could he but dare to speak; but reverence for the lords who stood around restrained him. Guy and the other nobles looked at one another in helpless dismay. Two-and-thirty thousand well-equipped and war-like horsemen! It was altogether impossible that they could hope to offer a successful resistance to a force like this. In the Flemish army there were only the five hundred horsemen of Namur, whom

Guy had brought with him; and what could this handful avail against the frightful number of the foe?

"What is to be done?" asked Guy. "Speak; how is our fatherland to be delivered?"

Some were of opinion that they should throw themselves into Bruges, and there await the dispersion of the French army from want of provisions. Others wished to be let loose upon the enemy, and to fall upon them that very night. Many projects were discussed, of which the greater part were rejected as dishonorable, and the remainder as impracticable.

Deconinck stood with his head still bowed in deep thought; he heard, indeed, every proposition that was made, but the attention he gave did not hinder the course of his own reflections. At last Guy addressed him, and asked what way of escape he saw from this critical position.

"Noble Count," replied Deconinck, raising his head, "were I commander-in-chief, I should begin operations thus: I should march with all speed with the Guildsmen of Bruges upon Courtrai, in order to expel thence the castellan Van Lens. That fortress would no longer be a stronghold and place of reserve for the French, and we should have a secure shelter for our women and children, as well as for ourselves; for the citadel of Courtrai is strong, while Bruges, in its present condition, could not stand a siege, but might easily be taken by storm. I would further despatch mounted messengers into all parts of Flanders to announce the nearness of the enemy, and to summon all the Clawards to Courtrai; Messires van Gulick and Renesse should also fall back on the place. In this way, I am sure, noble Count, that the Flemish army would within four days amount to thirty thousand picked men of war, and then we need have no great fear of the French."

The knights listened in eager silence; they could not help being astonished at the extraordinary man who had in a few minutes thought out so able a method of defense, and given them such appropriate counsel. Though they had long known Deconinck's high qualities, they could scarcely believe that they were the endowments of a Clothworker, a man from the class of the people.

"You have more wisdom than all of us together," cried Diederik die Vos. "Yes, yes, it is so indeed; we are far stronger than we thought. Now we turn over a new leaf; and I am inclined to think the French will have good reason to rue their journey hitherward."

"I thank God, who has inspired you with these counsels, Master Deconinck," said the youthful Count; "your good service shall not lack its fitting reward. I will act on the plan you have advised; it is most wise and most prudent. I hope, Master

Breydel, that you will not fail to supply us the men whom you have promised."

"Eight thousand, did I say, most noble Count?" replied Breydel. "Well, now I say ten thousand. No Guildsman nor apprentice shall remain in Bruges; young and old, all must forth to the fight. I will take care that the French shall not make their entry into Flanders except over our dead bodies, and their Deans, my friends, will do the same, I know right well."

"Certainly, noble lord," exclaimed the Deans with one voice; "no man will fail in his duty, for all are longing eagerly for the fight."

"Our time is too precious to be consumed in talking," said Guy. "Go now and gather the Guildsmen together with what speed you can; in two hours I shall be ready to depart, and will place myself at the head of the expedition in the Friday Market-place. Go now, I am right well pleased with your zeal and courage."

All then left the hall. Guy immediately despatched numerous messengers in all directions to the nobles who still remained loyal to their fatherland; and at the same time he sent directions to William van Gulick and John van Renesse to fall back on Courtrai.

The alarming tidings were spread in a few moments over the whole city. As the rumor diffused itself, the number of the enemy was exaggerated in a wonderful manner, and now the French host was more than one hundred thousand strong. One may imagine with what terror and grief the sorrowful intelligence struck the women and children. In every street were weeping mothers embracing their terrified daughters with loving compassion. The children began to cry because they saw their mothers weep and tremble, and without any notion of the danger that threatened them. Their agonized sobs and the expression of mortal terror on their countenances contrasted singularly with the lofty and impatient bearing of the men.

From all sides hastened the Guildsmen to the place of rendezvous; the clatter of the iron plates, with which many were covered, mingled, like a jocund song, with the wailing cries of the women and children. Whenever a party of men met in the street, they halted a moment to exchange a few words, and kindle each other's courage to the fight for victory or for death. Here and there might be seen a father at the door of his house, embracing one by one his children and their mother; then dashing the tears from his eye, and disappearing like an arrow in the direction of the Friday Market-place; and the mother would linger on the threshold of the house, gazing on the corner round which the father of her children had vanished. That farewell seemed to her a separation forever; tears rolled down from beneath her eyelids—she pressed her children to her throbbing breast, and turned back despairingly into her home.

Already the Guildsmen stood in long files in the market-place; Breydel had kept his promise; he counted among his men twelve thousand Guildsmen of all crafts. The axes of the Butchers glittered like mirrors in the sunshine, and dazzled the beholder with their broad and fiery flashings. Over the heads of the Clothworkers arose two thousand "good-days," with keen iron heads, and one division of them carried crossbows. Guy was standing in the middle of the square, surrounded by a retinue of about twenty knights; he was awaiting the return of the remaining craftsmen, who had been despatched into the city to collect wagons and horses. A Clothworker whom Deconinck had sent to the great bell-tower advanced into the market-place at this moment with the great standard of Bruges. No sooner had the Guildsmen caught sight of the Blue Lion than they raised a deafening shout of joy, and ever anew was repeated the war-cry which had given the signal of vengeance on that night of blood:

"Flanders and the Lion! all that is French is false!"

And then they brandished their weapons, as though already in presence of the foe.

When all that was necessary had been disposed

in the wagons, the bugles gave forth their shrill tones, and the men of Bruges left their city, with waving banners, by the gate of Ghent. The women were now left without any protection; their distress was greater than ever; they saw nothing before them but misery and death. In the afternoon, Matilda left the city with all her maidens and attendants; this hasty departure led many to imagine that they would find a more secure retreat in Courtrai. They hastily gathered together a few necessaries, shut up their houses, and followed in the steps of their husbands through the gate of Ghent. Numberless families ran in this manner with bleeding feet the whole distance from Bruges to Courtrai, and watered with their bitter tears the grass which skirted the way; while in Bruges reigned a stillness —as of the grave.

CHAPTER III

IT was already dark night when Guy reached Courtrai with about sixteen thousand men. The inhabitants, apprised of their approach by mounted messengers, stood in dense crowds on the walls of the city, and welcomed their rightful lords with glad and joyous acclamations, amidst the blaze of innumerable torches. As soon as the host had entered the city, and been distributed throughout its various quarters, the citizens of Courtrai brought forth every kind of food and refreshment; they placed before their weary brethren large flagons of wine to restore their exhausted strength, and kept watch over them the whole night. While they were embracing one another with transport, and expressing their affection in every possible manner, some hastened to meet the wearied women and children, and to relieve them of the burdens they carried. Not a few of these poor creatures, whose feet were torn and bleeding with their painful march, were borne to the city on the broad shoulders of the brave citizens of Courtrai; all were lodged and carefully tended, and comforted in every way. The gratitude of the men of Cour-

trai, and their extreme kindness, strengthened won-
derfully the courage of the men of Bruges; for
men's souls are ever enlarged and elevated by
frank and noble treatment.

Matilda and Maria, the sister of Adolf van
Nieuwland, with a considerable number of the
noble ladies of Bruges, had been some hours in
Courtrai before the army arrived. They had
been already received by their friends, and had
busied themselves in providing shelter and quarters for the knights and nobles, their relatives and
friends; so that on their arrival, Guy and his companions found supper already prepared for them.

Early the next morning Guy and a few of the
most distinguished inhabitants reconnoitred the
fortifications of the citadel; and found, to their
great dismay, that it was impossible to take it without a large siege-train. The walls were far too
lofty, and the overhanging towers allowed too many
arrows to be discharged on the advancing besiegers.
He saw that a bold attack might easily cost him a
thousand men; and, after mature deliberation, he
determined not to storm the citadel at once. He
gave orders for the construction of battering-rams
and movable towers, and for the collection of every
material in the city that could be available for the
assault. It was clear that this could not take place
for five days at least; but the delay was no disadvantage to the citizens of Courtrai, for since the

arrival of the Flemish troops, the French garrison had ceased to shoot burning arrows into the city; the soldiers were, indeed, seen standing with their bows at the loopholes of the battlements, but yet they did not discharge them. The Flemings could not conceive the reason of this cessation; they thought that some artifice lay concealed therein, and remained carefully on their guard. Guy had forbidden every aggression; he would attempt nothing until he had all his machines ready for storming the citadel, and could securely reckon on the victory.

The castellan Van Lens was at his wits' end; his archers had but a very slender supply of arrows left, and prudence compelled him to reserve them for the assault. His provisions, too, were so far exhausted that he could supply only half-rations to his soldiers. Still he hoped to elude the vigilance of the Flemings, and to find some opportunity to send a messenger to Lille, where the French army lay encamped.

Arnold of Oudenarde, who had a few days before brought the citizens of Courtrai a reenforcement of three hundred men, had bivouacked with his soldiers on the Gröningen Place, close to the abbey and the walls of the city. This place was especially fitted for a general encampment, and had been chosen for that purpose by Guy and his council of war. While the Carpenters' Guild was laboring at the storming-engines, the other Flemings were set to work the next morning to dig trenches. The Clothworkers and the Butchers wielded each a pickax and a spade, and set to work with great ardor; the entrenchments and siege-works arose as by enchantment; the whole army toiled with emulous zeal, and each sought to surpass his neighbor in exertion. The spades and pickaxes rose and descended like gleams of lightning, so that the eye could not follow them; and the thick clods of earth fell on the entrenchments like showers of stones thrown down on the assailants from a besieged city.

As soon as a part of the earthworks was completed, the soldiers hastened to pitch the tents. Ever and anon the workmen would leave the poles sticking in the earth and scramble away to work at the entrenchments; and then would arise a loud shout of welcome greeting, and the cry, "Flanders and the Lion!" boomed in the distance as an answering echo. And this happened, too, whenever reenforcements arrived from the other cities. The Flemish people had unjustly accused their nobles of disloyalty and cowardice: true, a large number had declared for the alien, but the loyal were far more numerous than the traitors. Fifty-and-two of the noblest knights of Flanders pined in the prisons of France; and to these prisons their love for their fatherland and for their native princes had consigned them. The rest of the true-hearted nobles who remained in Flanders deemed it a degradation to take part with the insurgent townspeople; to them the tournament and the battle-field were the only places fit for deeds of arms. The manners of the time had given them this notion; for then the distance between a knight and a citizen was as great as that between a master and a servant now. So long as the struggle was carried on within the walls of the cities, and under the command of popular leaders, they remained shut up in their castles, sighing over their country's oppression; but now that Guy had placed himself at the head of his people, as the general-in-chief appointed by their Count, they poured in from all sides with their retainers.

On the first day, early in the morning, there entered Courtrai Messires Baldwin of Papenrode, Henry of Raveschoot, Ivo of Belleghem, Solomon of Sevecote, and the lord of Maldeghem. Toward midday a cloud of dust arose over the distant trees in the direction of Moorseele, and amid the loud shouts of the men of Bruges, fifteen hundred men of Furnes entered the city, with the renowned warrior Eustachius Sporkyn at their head. They were accompanied by a multitude of knights who had joined them on their march. Among these the most distinguished were Messires John van Ayshoven, William van Daekenem, and his brother

Peter; Messire van Landeghem, Hugo van der Moere, and Simon van Caestere. John Willebaert of Thorout had also placed himself, with a small contingent of troops, under the command of Van Sporkyn. Each moment, moreover, some stray knight would enter the camp: not a few of these were from surrounding countries, and gladly came to lend their aid to the Flemings in their struggle for liberty. In this way Henry van Lonchyn of Luxemburg, Goswyn van Goetzenhove and John van Cuyck, two nobles of Brabant, were already with Guy when the troops of Furnes marched into the city. As soon as each newcomer had recruited his strength, and refreshed himself with food, he was sent into the camp, and placed under the command of Messire van Renesse.

On the second day arrived in haste the men of Ypres. Although they had their own city to care for, they could not allow Flanders to be liberated without them. Their troops were the finest and richest in equipment of all the army. They were five hundred clubmen, all arrayed in scarlet, and with magnificent feathers in their glittering morions; they wore also breastplates and knee-plates, which gleamed wondrously in the sunshine. Seven hundred others carried enormous crossbows, with bolts of steel: and their uniform was green turned up with yellow. With them came Messires John of Ypres, armor-bearer of Count John of

Namur, Diederik van Vlamertinghe, Joseph van
Hollebeke and Baldwin van Passchendale; their
leaders were Philip Baelde and Peter Belle, the
Deans of the two principal Guilds of Ypres. In
the afternoon arrived two hundred well-appointed
warriors from east and west Vrye, the villages
around Bruges.

On the third day, early in the morning, Messires
William van Gulick, the priest, and John van
Renesse returned from Cassel. Five hundred
knights, four hundred Zeelanders, and another
detachment of the men of Bruges, marched with
them into the camp.

And now from every part the knights and warriors who had been summoned had arrived. Men
of all arms were ranged under the command of
Guy. It is impossible to express the joy which
filled the hearts of the Flemings during these days;
for now they saw that their fellow-countrymen had
not degenerated, and that their fatherland still
counted loyal and valiant sons in every quarter.
Already one-and-twenty thousand men lay encamped, fit and ready for battle, under the banner
of the Black Lion; and their number was being
hourly increased by small reenforcements.

Although the French had an army of sixty-two
thousand men, of which the half was cavalry, yet
not the slightest fear found entrance into the hearts
of the Flemings. In their enthusiasm they would

cease their work, and embrace one another, exchanging words of confidence and triumph, as though there were nothing that could rob them of their victory.

Toward evening, as the laborers were returning to their tents, the cry, "Flanders and the Lion!" arose anew over the walls of Courtrai. All ran back to the entrenchments to see what the sound could mean. No sooner did their eyes range freely over the ramparts than they sent back a loud and joyous answering shout. Six hundred horsemen, all cased in steel, sprang into the trenches amid deafening acclamations. They came from Namur; and Count John, the brother of Robert de Bethune, had sent them into Flanders. The arrival of these horsemen greatly raised the spirits and increased the joy of the Flemings; for it was in cavalry that they were particularly deficient. Although they knew right well that the men of Namur could not understand one word they said, they overwhelmed them with words of greeting and welcome, and brought them wine in profusion: and when the foreign warriors saw this friendly reception, they felt themselves animated by a like spirit of affection; and they swore that they would sacrifice both blood and life for their good hosts.

Ghent alone had sent neither message nor contingent to Courtrai. It had been long known that the Lilyards were very numerous there, and that the governor was a stanch ally of the French. Nevertheless, seven hundred French mercenaries had been slain by the townsmen, and John Borluut had promised his aid. The matter was doubtful, and so the Flemings did not venture openly to accuse their brethren of Ghent of disloyalty; nevertheless, they entertained great suspicion of them, and not seldom gave free expression to their displeasure. In the evening, when the sun had already disappeared more than an hour behind the village of Moorseele, the laborers had dispersed themselves among the tents. Here and there was still heard a song, interrupted at intervals by the clapping of hands and the chink of drinking-glasses, and the concluding verse of which was caught up and enthusiastically repeated by a multitude of voices. In other tents was heard a confused murmur, which, when one listened attentively, resolved itself into an interchange of encouragements and exhortations. In the midst of the camp, at a little distance from the tents, a large fire was blazing, which illuminated a portion of the entrenchments with its ruddy glare. About ten men were appointed to keep it burning, who, from time to time, threw large branches of trees upon it; and then would be heard the voice of the captain, saying, "Gently, my men, gently; lay the branches carefully, and do not drive the sparks toward the camp."

A few steps from this fire was the tent of the

camp sentinels. It was a covering of ox-hides, the framework of which rested on eight massive beams; the four sides were open, so that it commanded the camp in all directions.

It was Jan Breydel's duty to keep watch this night with fifty of his Butchers: they sat on little wooden stools round a table under the roof, which protected them from the dew and the rain; their axes shone in their hands like weapons of glowing flame. The sentinels they had sent out were seen in the gloom, striding slowly backward and forward. A large cask of wine and some tin cans stood on the table; and although drinking was not forbidden, one could see that they drank with unusual moderation, for they raised the cans but seldom to their lips. They laughed and chatted pleasantly together, to while away the time; each telling what splendid blows he meant to discharge on the Frenchmen in the coming battle.

"Well," said Breydel, "they may say, if they will, that the Flemings are not as good men as their fathers, now that such a camp as this has been got together by volunteers alone. Let the French come on, if they like, with their two-and-sixty thousand men. The more game, the finer hunt! They say we are nothing but a pack of ill-natured hounds. We will give them reason to pray that they mayn't get thoroughly well worried; for the hounds have right good teeth."

54

The Lion of Flanders

While the Butchers were roaring with laughter at the words of their Dean, a fine old Guildsman entered, whose gray beard attested his advanced age. One of them called out to him:

"And you, Jacob, do you think you can still manage to give a good bite?"

"My teeth may not be quite so good as yours," growled the old Butcher; "but for all that, the old dog has not forgotten how to use them. I am quite ready to stake twenty bottles of wine which of us two will give most Frenchmen a bloody grave."

"Bravo!" cried the others; "and we will join in drinking them out. Let us fetch them at once."

"Ho! ho!" interposed Breydel; "can't you keep yourselves quiet? Drink to-morrow, if you please; but whoever of you drinks to-night shall be shut up in Courtrai, and shall have no share in the fight."

This threat had a wonderful effect on the Butchers: their jests died away on their lips; they did not even dare to sing a song; the old Guildsman alone ventured to speak.

"By the beard of our Dean!" said he, "rather than suffer that, I would be roasted at this fire, like Messire St. Lawrence; for I can never expect to witness such another feast."

Breydel remarked that his threat had rather damped the spirits of his companions, for which he was sorry, as he was himself inclined to merriment. Anxious to restore their cheerfulness, he raised the cask, and, filling a bumper, he held up his can, and said:

"Well, my men, why are you so silent? There, take that, and drink that you may find your tongues. I am vexed to have spoken so to you. Do I not know you well? Do I not know that the true Butchers' blood flows in your veins? Well, then, here's to you, comrades!"

An expression of satisfaction burst from the company, and they broke out into a loud cheery laugh when they found that the threat of their Dean had no serious meaning.

"Drink again!" continued Breydel, filling his can afresh; "the cask is yours, and you may drink it to the dregs. Your comrades who are on guard shall have another supplied to them. Now we see that succors are arriving from every city, and that we are so strong, we may well be merry."

"I drink to the disgrace of the men of Ghent!" cried a Guildsman. "We have good reason to know that he who puts any trust in them leans on a broken staff. But it is no matter; they may stay at home now; and so our own good city of Bruges will have gained unshared the glory of the conflict and the liberation of our fatherland."

"Are they Flemings, those men of Ghent?" said another. "Does their heart beat for freedom? Are

there any butchers left in Ghent?   Bruges forever!
You have the true blood there."

"I do not know," added Breydel, "why Count
Guy so earnestly desires their arrival.   Our camp
is not overstocked with provisions, and it is scarcely
prudent to invite more guests to the meal.   Does
the Count imagine that we shall lose the game?
One can easily see that he has been used to Namur;
he knows not the men of Bruges, or he would not
long so much for those of Ghent.   I hope they will
stay quietly at home; we shall do very well without
them; and we want no cowards among us,"

Like a genuine citizen of Bruges, Breydel bore
no love to the men of Ghent.   The two leading
cities of Flanders kept up a hereditary rivalry,
and almost enmity, with each other; not that the
one boasted braver citizens than the other, but
simply that each did his best to ruin or divert the
trade and traffic of the other.   And the same jealousy still continues.

So impossible is it to root out the feelings which
are inborn in the mass of the people that, notwithstanding their many revolutions, and the changes
of the times, this spirit has been perpetuated to our
own day.

The Butchers continued their conversation in this
strain for a long time, and many an execration was
uttered against the men of Ghent, when suddenly
a peculiar noise excited their attention: they heard

a sound of quarreling and wrestling at some little distance, as if two men were struggling together. All sprang up to see what it meant, but, before they could leave the tent, one of the Butchers, who had been on guard, entered it, dragging a man with him by main force.

"Masters," said he, pushing the stranger into the tent, "this roving minstrel I found behind the camp; he was listening at all the tents, and slinking about in the dark like a fox. I have been tracking him for some time; and I am convinced that there is some treason at the bottom of it, for look how the rascal is trembling."

The man thus dragged into the tent wore a blue cloak, and had on his head a small cap adorned with a plume; a long beard covered half of his face. In his left hand he held a small musical instrument, which had somewhat the appearance of a harp; and he made as if he would like to play some little piece to the assembled company. Yet he trembled with fright, and his face was pale as though his last hour were come. He evidently wished to avoid the eye of Jan Breydel; for he kept his head turned in the opposite direction, so that the Dean might not see his features.

"What are you doing in the camp?" exclaimed Breydel. "Why are you listening at the tents? Answer me instantly."

The minstrel answered in a language which bore

some resemblance to German; so that it was evident he came from another part of the country:

"Master, I come from Luxemburg, and have brought a message from Messire van Lonchyn. I had been told that some of my brothers were in the camp, and I came to find them out. I am overcome with shame and vexation that the sentinel should take me for a spy; but I hope that you will do me no injury."

Breydel felt his heart touched with compassion for the minstrel. Bidding the sentinel stand back, he offered a chair to the stranger, and said:

"You are surely weary with your long journey. There, my good minstrel, sit down and drink; the can is yours. Now sing us a few songs, and we will let you go in peace. Courage, man; you are among good friends."

"Excuse me, master," answered the minstrel; "I can not remain here, for Messire van Lonchyn awaits me. I am sure you would not wish to disappoint the noble knight by detaining me."

"We must have a song!" cried the Butchers. "You shall not go hence until you have sung us a song."

"Quick, then," said Breydel; "for I promise you that, if you do not sing us something, you will be kept here until the morning. If you would only have sung at once and with good-will, you would have finished ere this. Now sing, I bid and command you."

The terror of the stranger was sensibly increased by this peremptory speech. It was with difficulty that he could hold his harp; and he trembled so violenly that the strings, touched by his clothes, gave forth some confused sounds. This yet further whetted the appetite of the Butchers for a lay.

"Are you going to play or sing to us at once?" exclaimed Breydel. "I assure you that if you don't make haste you will have cause to rue it."

The minstrel, in mortal fear, proceeded to touch the strings of the harp with his trembling fingers; but he drew forth only false and discordant tones. The Butchers saw at once that he could not play at all.

"He is a spy!" cried Breydel. "Strip him and search him, to see whether he has any treasonable papers about him."

In a moment the clothes of the stranger were torn from off him; and, in spite of his piteous cries for mercy, he was kicked about from one to another, and all that he carried about him thoroughly searched.

"Here it is! here it is!" exclaimed one of the Butchers, who had thrust his hand between the doublet and the breast of the stranger; "here is the treason."

He drew out his hand, and produced a piece of

parchment, folded three or four times over, and tied with a thread of flax, from which hung a seal. The minstrel stood aghast, as though he saw his end approaching: he looked at the Dean with anxiety and terror, and muttered a few indistinct words, to which the Butchers paid no attention whatever. Jan Breydel seized the parchment; but, eagerly as he gazed on it, its contents remained unknown to him, for he could not read.

"What is it, villain?" exclaimed the Dean.

"A letter for Messire van Lonchyn," stammered the confounded minstrel, with hesitating and interrupted words.

"We shall soon see that," continued Breydel; then taking his cross-handled knife, he cut the flax which was wound around the seal. As soon as he beheld on this seal the lilies, the escutcheon of France, he sprang wrathfully up, seized the unknown one by the beard, and roared out:

"Is that a letter for Messire van Lonchyn, traitor? No! it is one to the castellan Van Lens; and you are a spy. A bitter death shall you die!"

While speaking, he tugged so violently at the beard that the ribbons by which it was fastened gave way; in an instant Breydel recognized the miscreant, and thrust him away so violently that the spy fell against one of the poles of the tent.

"Oh, Brakels! Brakels! your last hour is come!" exclaimed the astounded Dean.

The Lion of Flanders

The cries of the Butchers had attracted a crowd from the surrounding tents; and all began to demand, with loud and angry clamor, that the traitor should be delivered up to their vengeance.

Brakels fell on his knees, and with clasped hands begged for mercy; he crawled to the feet of Breydel, and implored him:

"Oh, master! have compassion on me—I will serve our fatherland so loyally—spare me! do not put me to death!"

Breydel looked down on him with rage and contempt; and, in lieu of other answer, kicked him with his foot, so that he rolled to the other end of the tent. Meanwhile, the Butchers had the greatest difficulty in restraining the crowds, who were raging around the tent, and filling the air with cries of vengeance.

"Give us the scoundrel!" was their wild cry. "Into the fire with him! throw him into the fire!"

"I care not," said Breydel, with an authoritative look at his comrades, "that your axes should be stained with the blood of this viper. Give him up to the crowd!"

Scarcely were the words out of his mouth, when a man strode forth from the crowd, and threw a cord round the neck of Brakels; then, the other end being seized by a thousand hands, he was hurled to the ground and dragged out of the tent. His shrieks of agony mingled fearfully with the cries of the infuriated crowd. They dragged him round and round the camp, and then returning to the fire, still yelling and shouting, they drew him through it again and again, until the flames had obliterated every feature of his countenance. Then on they rushed in their mad race, and vanished in the darkness with the lifeless corpse trailing behind them. Long were their cries heard on the breeze; but at length wearied, and sated with revenge, they hung the mangled body of the traitor on a pole close to the fire; then every one betook himself to his tent; and an hour later a profound silence had succeeded to this hideous uproar.

CHAPTER IV

GUY had issued orders that the whole army, under its several captains, should muster on the Gröningen Place, in front of the camp, on the following morning; he wished to pass them all in review. In obedience to these orders, the Flemings were drawn up in a square on the appointed place. They stood like the four foundation walls of some mighty edifice, each troop being composed of eight closely compacted divisions. Deconinck's four thousand Clothworkers formed the front of the right wing. The first file of his troops consisted of archers, whose heavy crossbows hung diagonally over their shoulders; while a quiver, filled with steel-pointed shafts, was suspended at their side. They bore no other defensive armor than an iron plate, which was fastened over their breasts by four straps of leather. Over the six other divisions, thousands of spears arose ten feet high into the air. This weapon, the renowned "good-day," was with reason much dreaded by the French; for with it a horse might easily be pierced through and through. No armor could withstand its formidable stroke; the knight on whom it fell was inevitably unhorsed.

The Lion of Flanders

On the same side stood also the light troops of Ypres; their advanced division was composed of five hundred men, whose apparel was red as coral. From their graceful helmets downy plumes waved low as their shoulders; massive clubs, armed with points of steel, stood with the butt-end at the feet of each soldier; while the hilt, grasped by their strong fists, rested against their loins. Small plates of iron were buckled around their arms and thighs. The other divisions of this gallant host were all clothed in green, and their unstrung bows of steel reared themselves high above their heads.

The left wing was entirely composed of the ten thousand men furnished by Breydel. On one side of it the countless axes of the Butchers flashed before the eyes of their companions in arms, so that they were obliged to turn away their heads from time to time, so keen and dazzling were the rays of the sun reflected from these mirrors of steel. The Butchers were not heavily equipped; short brown trousers, and a jerkin of the same color, formed their only clothing. Their arms were bare to the elbows, according to their custom; for they took pride in displaying their compact and brawny muscles. Many were of fair complexion, but embrowned by exposure to the sun; huge scars, records of former combats, crossed their faces like deep furrows, and these they regarded as the laurel-wreaths which attested their bravery. The fea-

(C)—3—Vol. 9

tures of Breydel formed a strong contrast to the sombre sharp-cut faces of his followers; for while the ferocious expression of most of these filled the beholder with terror, Breydel's appearance was pleasing and noble. Fine blue eyes glowed beneath his bushy eyebrows; his fair hair fell in long wavy curls over his shoulders; and a short and delicate beard lengthened still more the graceful oval of his countenance. The contour and expression of his features were most pleasing when, as at this moment, he was full of joy and content; but when excited by passion, no lion's face could surpass his countenance in hideous expressiveness: his cheeks would gather in folds and wrinkles, he would grind his teeth with fury, and his eyebrows would meet over his flashing eyes.

In the third wing were the men of Furnes, with the vassals of Arnold of Oudenarde, and Baldwin of Papenrode. The Guildsmen of Furnes had sent a thousand slingers and five hundred halberdiers; the former stood in the front rank, and were clothed entirely in leather, that they might wield their slings without impediment. About their loins was fastened a white leather girdle, which held the round pebbles with which they supplied their slings; and in their right hands they carried a leather thong, in the middle of which was a hollow depression. These were the slings—a fearful weapon—which they wielded with such fatal precision, that the heavy missiles which they discharged at the foe very seldom missed their aim. Behind these stood the halberdiers; they were sheathed in iron, and bore heavy helmets on their heads. Their weapon was a battle-ax, with a long handle; and above the steel of the ax was a thick, sharp-pointed piece of iron, with which they were accustomed to pierce both helmet and armor, so that they gained the name of helm-cleavers. The men of Oudenarde and of Papenrode, who were ranged on the same side, bore weapons of all kinds. The first two ranks, indeed, consisted entirely of archers; but the others carried spears, clubs, or broadswords. The last wing, which completed the square, comprised all the cavalry of the army (eleven hundred well-mounted men), whom Count John of Namur had sent to his brother Guy. These horsemen seemed as though they were made of steel and iron; nothing else was to be seen except the eyes of the rider flashing through the vizor, and the feet of his steed, which appeared beneath his trappings of mail. Their long broadswords rested on their mailed shoulders, and their graceful plumes fluttered behind them in the breeze.

The army was thus drawn up, in obedience to the command of their general. A deep silence reigned throughout the host; the few questions of curiosity asked by the men-at-arms were in so low a tone, that they reached no further than the ears to which they were addressed. Guy and all the other knights who had contributed no troops were still in Courtrai; and although the whole army was drawn up in position, none of them had as yet made his appearance.

Suddenly the banner of Count Guy was descried beneath the gate of the city. Messire van Renesse, who commanded the troops in the absence of the general-in-chief, gave the word:

"To arms! Close up your ranks! Heads up! Silence!"

At the first word of the noble knight Van Renesse, every man brought his weapon into its proper position; then they closed their ranks, and stood in perfect order. Scarcely was this done, when the cavalry opened its ranks to allow the general and his numerous suite to pass into the centre of the square.

In advance rode the standard-bearer with the banner of Flanders. The Black Lion on his golden field floated gracefully over the head of his horse; and he seemed to the joyous Flemings as though he were stretching out his claws as omens of victory. Immediately behind the banner came Guy and his nephew William van Gulick. The youthful general wore a magnificent suit of armor, on which the escutcheon of Flanders was skilfully embossed; from his helmet a gorgeous plume fell down over the back of his horse. The armor of William van Gulick bore only a broad red cross; from beneath his coat-of-mail his white priestly vestment fell down over the saddle. His helmet bore no plume, and his whole equipment was simple and unadorned. Immediately after these illustrious lords followed Adolf von Nieuwland. His armor was perfect in its grace and finish. Gilded studs concealed the joints of his coat-of-mail; he bore a plume of green, and his gloves were plated with silver. Over his shirt-of-mail might be discerned a green veil, the guerdon bestowed on him by the daughter of the Lion in token of her gratitude. Near him rode Matilda, on a palfrey white as driven snow. The noble maiden was still pale; but the arrival of her brother Adolf had put her sickness to flight. A sky-blue riding-habit of costly velvet, embroidered with silver lions, fell in long folds over her feet to the ground, and the silken veil which was fastened to the point of her peaked hat swept the mane of her palfrey.

Behind them followed a troop of about thirty knights and noble damsels, all adorned with costly magnificence, and with countenances as serene and joyous as though they were riding to a tournament. The procession was closed by four squires on foot; the first two bore each a rich suit of armor and a sword, while the others carried each a helmet and a shield. Amid the solemn silence of the whole army, this brilliant cavalcade reached the middle of the square, when all halted.

Guy beckoned to him his herald-at-arms, and gave him a parchment, the contents of which he was to publish to the assembled host.

"Only add to it," said he, "the warlike name of the Lion of Flanders; for that always gladdens our good folks of Bruges."

The curiosity of the soldiers was manifested by a slight movement, followed by a silence of deepest attention; they saw that some mystery lay hidden in all these forms of solemnity, for it was not for nothing that the daughters of their nobles wore their richest adornments. The herald advanced, sounded his trumpet thrice, and then proclaimed aloud:

"We, Guy of Namur, in the name of our Count and our brother, Robert de Bethune, the Lion of Flanders, to all who shall read or hear this our proclamation, greeting and peace!

"In consideration—"

He paused suddenly; a low murmur ran throughout the various divisions of the army; and while each was eagerly grasping his weapon, the archers strung their cross-brows, as though danger were at hand.

"The foe! the foe!" echoed on all sides. In the distance were seen numerous troops of men advancing; thousands of warriors were approaching in dense masses; there seemed no end of their numbers. Still were all in doubt whether it could be the enemy, for no cavalry was visible among them. Suddenly a horseman was observed to leave the unknown host, and to ride at full gallop toward the encampment. He bent so low over the neck of his horse that his features could not be distinguished, though he was already at no great distance. When he had come quite close to the astonished troops, he raised his head and shouted:

"Flanders and the Lion! Flanders and the Lion! here come the men of Ghent!" The old warrior was at once recognized; joyous acclamations answered his shout, and his name passed quickly from mouth to mouth.

"Hail, Ghent! Hail, Messire John Borluut! welcome, good brother!"

When the Flemings saw their numbers increased by this unexpected reenforcement of troops so numerous, their impetuous joy could no longer be restrained: their commanders could scarcely keep them in their ranks. They moved about in violent commotion, and seemed beside themselves with pleasure; but Messire John Borluut cried:

"Be of good courage, my friends, Flanders shall be free! I bring you five thousand well-armed and intrepid warriors."

And then answered the whole host with irrepressible enthusiasm:

"Hail! hail to the hero of Woeringen! Borluut! Borluut!"

Messire Borluut then drew near to the young Count, and would have greeted him with courtly ceremony; but Guy hastily interrupted him:

"Spare these words of ceremony, Messire John; give me your friendly right hand. I am so glad that you are come; you who have passed your days in arms, and are so rich in experience. I was beginning to be troubled at your not arriving; you have delayed long."

"Oh, yes, noble Guy," was the answer, "longer than I wished; but those dastardly Lilyards have kept me back. Would you believe, noble lord, that they had actually formed a conspiracy in Ghent to bring back the French again? They would not let us leave the town to go to the aid of our brethren; but, God be thanked! their plot did not succeed; for the people's hatred and contempt of them exceed all bounds. The men of Ghent drove their magistrates into the citadel, and demolished the gates of the city. So here I am with five thousand intrepid men, longing for the fight more eagerly than for their dinners, though they have touched nothing this day as yet."

"I thought assuredly that some great obstacle must have detained you, Messire Borluut, and I even feared that you would not come at all."

"What, noble Guy! could I stay away from

The Lion of Flanders

Courtrai? I, who have shed my blood for strangers, was I not to stand by my fatherland in its hour of need? The French shall soon know this to their cost. I feel myself quite young again; and my men, noble lord, await only the day of battle to let you see how the French shall fall before the White Lion of Ghent."

"You gladden my heart, Messire Borluut; our men are full of fury and impetuous ardor; should ve lose the fight, I can assure you very few Flemings will see their homes again."

"Lose the fight, say you? lose it, Count Guy? Never will I believe it; our men are all animated with too noble a courage; and Breydel—victory its beaming already on his very countenance. Look you, my lord; I will wager my head, that if ou would only allow Breydel to do what he likes, he and his Butchers would cut these two-and-sixty thousand to pieces just as easily as they would mow lown a field of corn. Be of good courage; God and Messire St. George will be our aid. But, I pray you excuse me, Lord Guy; there are my men —I must leave you for a moment."

The men of Ghent had now reached the Gröningen Place; they were wearied and covered with dust, for they had made a forced march under the burning sun. Their weapons were of various kinds; and among them were all the classes of troops we have already described. About forty

73

nobles rode in advance, for the most part friends of the old warrior, John Borluut; and in the midst of the host floated the banner of Ghent with its white lion. Then the men of Bruges, who felt how unjustly they had reproached their brethren of Ghent, shouted again and again:

"Welcome, brothers, welcome! Hurrah for Ghent!"

In the meantime John Borluut drew up his men in front of the left wing of the square; he wished to make a good display of them, that the men of Bruges might see that they did not yield to them in love of their common fatherland. At Guy's command he then left the camp and entered Courtrai, that he might give his men the repose and refreshment which they so much needed. As soon as the men of Ghent had withdrawn, John van Renesse advanced into the square and cried:

"To arms! Silence!"

The group in the middle of the square returned to its former position; every one held his peace at the command of Messire van Renesse, and the attention of all was fixed on the herald, who again sounded his trumpet thrice, and then proceeded to read with a loud voice:

"We, Guy of Namur, in the name of our Count and our brother, Robert de Bethune, the Lion of Flanders, to all who shall read or hear this our proclamation, greeting and peace! In consideration of

the good and loyal service rendered to the whole
country of Flanders and to ourselves, by Master
Deconinck and Master Breydel of Bruges—we,
willing to bestow on them, in presence of all our
subjects, a token of our grace and favor—willing,
moreover, especially to requite their noble-hearted
love of our fatherland in such wise as is meet and
fitting, that their loyal services may be held in everlasting remembrance; and whereas our Count and
father, Guy of Flanders, hath thereto empowered
us, we announce and declare that Peter Deconinck,
Dean of the Clothworkers, and Jan Breydel, Dean
of the Butchers, both of our good city of Bruges,
and their descendants after them for all time, shall
be, and shall be held to be, of noble blood, and enjoy
all the rights and privileges appertaining to nobles,
in our land of Flanders. And in order that they
may be enabled to support this dignity honorably,
we assign to each of them one-twentieth part of our
good city of Bruges for the maintenance of his
house."

Long ere the herald had made an end, his voice
was drowned in the joyous acclamations of the
Clothworkers and Butchers. The great favor conferred on their Deans was, as it were, the reward of
their own bravery, an honor which was reflected
upon their Guilds. Had not the loyalty and patriotism of the Deans been so well known, their elevation to the rank of nobles would undoubtedly

have been received with suspicion and displeasure, as a stratagem of the nobility. They would have said:

"These feudal lords are depriving us of the asserters of our rights, and are seducing our leaders by these manifestations of favor." In any other case the suspicion would not have been unfounded; for men, for the most part, are easily perverted and seduced by the love of honor. Hence it is not to be wondered at that the people cherished a bitter hatred against such of their brethren as allowed themselves to be thus raised in dignity; for, instead of noble-minded friends of the people, they became, for the most part, fawning and craven flatterers, and upheld the power to which they owed their elevation. They knew that with it they must stand or fall; for they saw that the people whom they had forsaken regarded them with abhorrence and contempt as deserters and apostates.

But the Guilds of Bruges reposed too lofty a confidence in Deconinck and Breydel to admit of reflections such as these at that moment. Their Deans were now noble; they had now two men who were admitted to the councils of their Count, who dared look the enemies of their rights in the face, and oppose their lawless usurpations. They felt that their influence was thus greatly increased, and testified by repeated cries the rapturous joy they felt. At last the tumult subsided, and their gestures and beaming countenances alone betrayed their gladness.

Adolf van Nieuwland advanced to the Deans, and summoned them to appear before the commander-in-chief; they obeyed, and joined the group of knights. The features of the Clothworker betokened no elation of spirit; he moved onward calmly and sedately, undisturbed by any exciting emotion; a peaceful serenity and a noble pride filled his soul. Not so the Dean of the Butchers; he had never learned to command himself—the most trivial incident, the lightest feeling which passed through his heart, expressed itself at once upon his countenance, and it was easy to see that sincerity was the chiefest of the many good qualities which he possessed. And now he tried in vain to restrain the tears which burst from his blue eyes; he stooped his head to conceal them, and thus, with beating heart, followed his friend Deconinck. All the knights and noble dames had dismounted, and given their horses into the care of their squires.

Guy then beckoned to the four esquires-at-arms to draw near, and presented to the Deans the costly suits of armor they carried; the several pieces were put on and adjusted, and the helmet, with its plume of blue, clasped on their heads. The men of Bruges regarded this ceremonial in breathless silence; their hearts were filled to overflowing with glad emotion, and each man felt that a measure of this honor was his own also. When the Deans were fully equipped, they were directed to kneel; and Guy, advancing, raised his sword over the head of Deconinck, and said:

"Be thou a true knight, Messire Deconinck; let thine honor know no stain, and grasp thy sword then only when God, thy fatherland, and thy prince shall summon thee thereto."

With these words he touched the shoulder of the Clothworker gently with his sword, according to the custom of knighthood; and then the same ceremony was gone through with Breydel.

Matilda now advanced from the group of ladies, and placed herself in front of the kneeling Deans. She took from the squires the two emblazoned shields, and attached them to the necks of the ennobled citizens. Many of the spectators remarked that she hung the shield round Breydel's neck first; and this she must have done advisedly, for in order to effect it she had to move some steps on one side.

"These coats-of-arms have been sent to you from my father," said she, turning herself rather toward Breydel. "I feel assured that you will preserve them in all honor; and I rejoice that I have been permitted to bear a part in this requital of your noble patriotism."

Breydel regarded the noble maiden with a look of profoundest gratitude—a look which was a pledge of the most ardent loyalty and devotion; he would certainly have thrown himself at her feet, had not the stately and ceremonious bearing of the surrounding knights checked his impetuosity. He remained as one petrified, without speech or motion; for he could scarcely comprehend what had happened to him.

"You are now at liberty to return to your troops, Messires," said Guy. "We hope that you will be present this evening at our council; we have need of long deliberation with you. Lead back now your troops to the camp."

Deconinck made a lowly reverence and retired, followed by Breydel; but the latter had gone but a few steps when he felt the movements of his body impeded and restrained by the weight of the armor. He turned quickly back to Guy, and said to him:

"Noble Count, I pray you grant me one favor."

"Speak, Messire Breydel, it shall surely be granted to you."

"Look you, most illustrious lord, you have this day conferred on me a signal honor; but yet you will not, of a surety, hinder me from fighting against our enemies."

The knights, astonished at these words, drew nearer to the Dean.

"What do you mean?" asked Guy.

"I mean that this armor constrains and oppresses me beyond endurance, noble Count. I can not move in this coat-of-mail, and the helmet is so heavy that I can not bend my neck; in this prison of iron I shall be slain like a calf bound hand and foot."

"The armor will defend you from the swords of the French," remarked the knight.

"Yes," cried Breydel; "but that is quite needless in my case. So long as I am free, with my ax I fear nothing. I should cut a pretty figure standing in this stiff and ridiculous fashion. No, no, Messires, I will not have it on my body; wherefore, I pray you, noble Count, allow me to remain a simple citizen until after the battle, and then I will try to make acquaintance with this cumbrous armor."

"You may do even as you list, Messire Breydel," answered Guy; "but you are, and must remain, a knight for all that."

"Well, then," cried the Dean, eagerly, "I will be the knight of the ax! Thanks, thanks, most illustrious lord."

Thereupon he left the knightly group, and hastened toward his men. They received him with noisy congratulations, and expressed their joy in reiterated shouts. Before Breydel had reached his Butchers, the armor lay piecemeal on the ground, and he retained only the emblazoned coat-of-arms which Matilda had attached to his neck.

"Albert, my friend," he cried to one of his men, "gather this armor together, and lay it up in my tent; I will not cover my body with iron while you expose your naked breasts to the foe; I will keep the Kermes Festival in my butcher's clothes. They have made me a noble, comrades; but I can not give in to this. My heart is, and will remain, a true butcher's heart, as I mean to let the French know. Come, we will return to the camp; and I will drink my wine with you as I have ever done, and I will give each of you a measure to drink to the success of the Black Lion."

The shouting recommenced on all sides; the ranks were thrown into confusion, and the soldiers were beginning to rush back to the encampment in disorder, so great was their joy at the promise of the Dean.

"Hold there, my men," interposed Breydel, "you must not march in that fashion. Let every one of you keep his rank, or we shall become very queer friends."

The other divisions were already in motion, and returned, with sounding trumpets and flying banners, to the entrenchment, while the party of knights entered the city gate and disappeared behind the walls.

In a very short time the Flemings were sitting in front of their tents discussing the elevation of their Deans. The Butchers sat on the ground in a large circle with their goblets in their hands; huge casks of wine were standing near them, and they were singing, in exulting unison, the lay of the Black Lion. In their midst, upon an empty barrel, sat the ennobled Breydel, who began each stanza after the fashion of a precentor. He drank, in repeated drafts, to his country's liberation; and endeavored, by drawing more closely the bonds of their common hopes and sympathies, to obliterate the memory of his change of rank; for he feared that his comrades might no longer regard him as their friend and boon companion as in time past.

Deconinck had shut himself in his tent to avoid the congratulations of his Clothworkers; their expressions of affection moved him too deeply, and he could with difficulty conceal his emotion. He therefore passed the whole day in solitude, while the troops abandoned themselves to feasting and rejoicings.

CHAPTER V

THE French general had pitched his camp in a broad plain at a short distance from the city of Lille, and the tents of his countless warriors covered a space of more than two miles in extent. The breastwork which surrounded the host might have led a distant spectator to imagine that he saw before him a fortified city, had not the neighing of horses, the cries of soldiers, the smoke ascending from their numerous fires, and the fluttering of a thousand flags betrayed the presence of a military camp. The part assigned to the nobles and knights was easily distinguished by the splendor and costliness of its standards and embroidered banners; and while their velvet pavilions glowed with every color of the rainbow, the rest of the camp showed only the ordinary tents of canvas, or huts of straw. It might have been matter of wonder that such an enormous host did not perish of hunger, for in those days armies seldom took stores with them; yet they were supplied in such overflowing abundance that corn was suffered to lie about in the mud, and the most valuable articles of food were everywhere trampled under foot. The French took the best means at once to supply their own wants and to deepen the hatred with which the Flemings regarded them. They scoured the country day by day in large bands, plundering and laying waste on all sides; for the furious soldiers well understood the wishes of their general, Robert d'Artois, and their way was tracked by countless deeds of violence and devastation. As a symbol of the sweeping desolation with which they threatened Flanders, they had tied small brooms to the points of their spears; and their conduct amply redeemed their pledge, for in all the southern part of the country there remained not a house, not a church, not a castle, not a monastery, scarcely a tree standing—all were ruthlessly razed and destroyed. Neither sex nor age afforded any protection against the fury of the soldiers; women and children were pitilessly butchered, and their bodies thrown out to the birds of prey.

Thus the French commenced their expedition. In the midst of their ferocious course, no fear or apprehension of defeat occurred to them, so confidently did they rely on their overwhelming numbers. Flanders was doomed to a memorable destruction; they had sworn it. On the same morning on which Guy had bestowed on Deconinck and Breydel the meed of their loyal good service, the French general had invited his most illustrious knights to a sumptuous banquet. The tent of the

The Lion of Flanders

Count d'Artois was of unusual length and breadth, and divided into many compartments; there were rooms for the knights of his suite, rooms for the squires and standard-bearers, rooms for culinary purposes, rooms for all the various personages of his train. In the middle was a spacious saloon, capable of containing a large number of knights, and used alternately for revelry and for the deliberations of the council of war. The silk with which the tent was covered was powdered with *fleurs-de-lis;* at the entrance hung the shield of the house of Artois, and outside, on a small eminence, waved the royal standard of France. The saloon was hung with rich tapestry, and rivaled a palace in magnificence.

At the upper end of the table sat Count Robert d'Artois. He was still in the flower and full vigor of life, and a scar which traversed his right cheek at once gave evidence of his bravery and imparted to his countenance a more forbidding expression. Although his face was disfigured by deep wrinkles and stained with dark spots, yet his eyes gleamed like a fire from under his dark eyelashes with manly ardor and energy. His manner was harsh, and denoted the fierce and unrelenting man of war.

Close to him, on his right hand, sat Sigis, King of Melinde; age had silvered his hair and bowed his head, yet was he eager for the combat. In that company he felt his martial ardor return, and boasted that he would yet perform glorious feats of arms. The countenance of the old man inspired respect; it bore the impress of goodness and gentleness. Certainly the good Sigis would never have taken arms against the Flemings had he known the real state of the case; but he had been persuaded, as many others had been, that they were bad Christians, and worse than Saracens, and that it was a good work in the sight of God to chastise and exterminate them.

On the left hand of the Count sat Balthasar, King of Majorca, an impetuous and daring warrior, the gaze of whose dark eyes it was scarcely possible to endure. A wild gladness lighted up his features; for he hoped now to reconquer his kingdom, which had been seized by the Moors. Near him sat De Chatillon, the late governor-general of Flanders, the man who, as the tool of Queen Joanna, was the cause of all this disturbance. His was the guilt that so many Frenchmen had been put to death in Bruges and in Ghent; and on his tyrant head lay the blood of all that were slain in this quarrel. He remembered how disgracefully he had been expelled from Bruges; he craved no petty revenge; and he sat with joy in his heart and smiles on his face, for he held it impossible that the Flemings could oppose the combined might of so many kings, princes, and counts. Next to him, and, like him, eagerly thirsting for revenge, was his brother, Guy

de St. Pol. There might be distinguished also
Thibaud, Duke of Lorraine, between Messires
John de Barlas and Renauld de Trie; he had come
to the aid of the French with six hundred horse
and two thousand archers. On the left side of the
table, next to Messire Henry de Ligny, sat Raoul
de Nesle, a brave and noble-hearted knight; on his
face were depicted displeasure and sorrow; it was
evident that the ferocious threats which the knights
were uttering against Flanders were not to his taste.
About the middle of the right side, between Louis
de Clermont and Count John d'Aumale, sat Godfrey of Brabant, who had brought the French five
hundred horse. Near him sat one whose gigantic
form might well strike the beholder with astonishment; it was the Zeelander, Hugo van Arckel; he
raised his head proudly above the surrounding
knights, and his powerful frame sufficiently indicated how terrible an adversary he must be on the
battle-field. For many years he had had no other
abode than the camp. Everywhere known and renowned for his feats of arms, he had gathered
around him a troop of eight hundred intrepid men,
well accustomed to war; and with them he roved
from place to place wherever there was fighting to
be done. Many a time had he decided a battle in
favor of the prince whom he was aiding; and he
and his men were liberally covered with wounds
and scars. War was his element and his life; peace

and repose were unendurable to him. Now he had joined the French host, because many of his old companions in arms were there; impelled only by love of fighting, he recked little for whom or in what cause he did battle.

Besides these were present, among others, Simon de Piedmont, Louis de Beaujeu, Froald, governor of Douay, Alin de Bretagne. At the further end of the table, and apart from them, was a group of knights. It was the least honorable place; and as the French would not admit them to their company, they had found themselves obliged to occupy it. And truly the French were in the right; they were contemptible beneath contempt; for while their vassals, as genuine Flemings, were asserting their country's cause, these their feudal lords were banqueting with the foe! What blindness could lead these degenerate traitors to tear, like vipers, the bosom of their mother? They were marching under a hostile banner to shed the blood of their brethren and bosom friends on the soil of their common fatherland; and for what? that the country which gave them birth might be made a land of slaves, and humbled beneath the yoke of the alien. They had time to feel that shame and contempt were their portion, and to feel at their hearts the gnawing worm. The names of these recreants have been handed down to posterity: among many others, Henry van Bautershem, Geldof van Winghene,

The Lion of Flanders

Arnold van Eyckhove, and his eldest son, Henry van Wilre, William van Redinghe, Arnold van Hofstad, William van Cranendonck, and John van Raneel, were the most conspicuous.

The knights ate off silver dishes, and drank the choicest wines from cups of gold. The goblets which were placed before Robert d'Artois and the two kings were larger and more costly than the rest; their coats-of-arms were cunningly graven upon them, and their rims shone with rare and precious gems. During the meal, a lively conversation went on among the knights on the position and prospects of the expedition; and from its tone the fearful doom of Flanders might easily be gathered.

"Most undoubtedly," answered the general to a question of De Chatillon, "they must be all exterminated. Those cursed Flemings can be tamed only by fire and sword; and why should we let such wretched boors live? Let us make a thorough end of them, Messires, that we may not again have to stain our swords with their plebeian blood."

"Right!" said John van Raneel, the Lilyard; "you say right, Messire d'Artois. We must make no terms with the seditious rascals; they are too rich, and would soon give us trouble again. Already they refuse to recognize us, who are sprung from noble blood, as their rightful lords; they seem to think that the wealth which they gain by their industry makes their blood nobler still. They have built houses in Bruges and in Ghent which surpass our castles in magnificence; and is not that an insult to us? Certainly, we will endure it no longer."

"Unless we wish to have a fresh outbreak every day," remarked William van Cranendonck, "all the craftsmen must be put to death; for the survivors will never be quiet; and therefore I am of opinion that Messire d'Artois ought not to spare one of them alive."

"And what are we to do when we have slain all our vassals?" asked the burly Hugo van Arckel with a laugh. "By my troth, we shall have to plow our land ourselves; a goodly prospect, truly!"

"Ha!" answered John van Raneel; "I have a good plan to remedy that. When Flanders shall be cleansed of this stiff-necked race, I mean to bring French peasants from Normandy, and establish them on my lands."

"And so we shall make Flanders a genuine province of France; that is a very good notion, and I will mention it to the King, that he may urge the other feudal lords to take the same course. I pledge myself that it will not be at all difficult."

"Surely not, Messire. Do you not think it a bright and excellent plan?"

"Yes, yes; and we will carry it out too; but let

us first begin by making a clean sweep of the ground."

The features of Raoul de Nesle were working with inward emotion. The conversation greatly displeased him, for his noble heart revolted against such ferocity; and he exclaimed with ardor:

"But, Messire d'Artois, I take leave to ask you— are we knights or not? and is it seemly that we should set to work after a worse fashion than Saracens? You are carrying your ferocity too far; and I assure you that we shall become a scorn and a by-word to the whole world. Let us attack and defeat the Flemings; that will be sufficient for us. Let us not call them a herd of boors; they will give us trouble enough; and then, are they not in arms under the son of their prince?"

"Constable de Nesle," cried D'Artois in anger, "I know that you are exceedingly fond of these Flemings. It is a love which does you honor, of a truth! It is your daughter, surely, who has inspired your breast with such amiable benevolence."

Adela, the daughter of Raoul de Nesle, was married to William van Dendermonde, one of the sons of the old Count of Flanders.

"Messire d'Artois," answered Raoul, "although my daughter dwells in Flanders, that does not hinder me from being as good and true a Frenchman as any one here present—my sword has given sufficient proof of that; and I shall have to demand a reckoning at your hand for the scornful words you have uttered before these knights. But what now lies nearest my heart is the honor of knighthood itself; and I tell you that you are imperiling it by your conduct."

"What mean you?" exclaimed the general; "is it not true that you wish to spare these seditious traitors? Have they not deserved to die, since they have put to death seven thousand Frenchmen without mercy?"

"Beyond a doubt they have deserved death; and therefore will I avenge on them the honor of the crown of my prince; but they shall find their death only on the battlefield, and with arms in their hands. I appeal to these knights whether they deem it fitting that we should stain our swords by doing the work of executioners on poor unarmed people while they are peacefully plowing their fields."

"He is right," exclaimed Hugo van Arckel, with loud and angry voice; "we are fighting like the very Moors. The very proposal is a disgrace to us; let us recollect, Messires, that we have to do with Christian men. Besides, Flemish blood flows in my veins, and I will not suffer my brethren to be dealt with like dogs; they offer us battle in open and fair field, and we must fight with them according to the laws of honorable warfare."

"Is it possible," replied d'Artois, "that you can

defend these base boors? Our good prince has made trial of all other means to reclaim them; but all have been in vain. Are we to allow our soldiers to be butchered, our king to be set at naught and put to shame, and then spare the lives of these dastard rebels? No, that shall never be! I know the commands which I have received, and I will both obey them and cause them to be obeyed."

"Messire d'Artois," interposed Raoul de Nesle with angry impetuosity, "I know not what commands you have received, but I declare to you that I will not obey them unless they accord with the honor of knighthood; the king himself has no right to stain my sword with dishonor. And hearken, Messires, whether I am right or not: this morning early I went out of the camp, and found everywhere the tokens of the most revolting rapine and devastation. The churches are burnt to the ground, and the altars desecrated; the dead bodies of young children and of women were lying exposed in the fields to be devoured by ravens. I ask you, is this the work of honorable warriors?"

Having uttered these words, he rose from the table, raised a portion of the hangings of the tent, and continued, pointing to the country: "Look you, Messires, turn your eyes in all directions; everywhere you behold the flames of this atrocious devastation; the sky is blackened with smoke; the whole country is in a conflagration. What does such a war as this betoken? It is worse than if the ruthless Northmen had come again, and turned the world into a den of robbers."

Robert d'Artois became livid with anger; he moved himself impatiently in his chair, and cried:

"This has lasted too long; I can no longer permit any man to speak thus in my presence. I know well enough what I have to do; Flanders must be swept clean, and it is out of my power to prevent it. This strife of words discomposes me much, and I beseech Messire the Constable to speak no more in this tone. Let him keep his sword unstained; we will all do the same; for no disgrace can redound to us from the excesses of our soldiers. Let us now end this angry dispute; and each man see that he does his duty."

Then raising his golden goblet, he cried:

"To the honor of France and the extermination of the rebels!"

Raoul de Nesle repeated, "To the honor of France," and laid a significant emphasis on the words, so that every one might see that he would not drink to the extermination of the Flemings. Hugo van Arckel placed his hand on the goblet which stood before him; but he neither raised it from the table nor spoke a word. All the others repeated the words of the general exactly, and followed his example.

The Lion of Flanders

For some little time the countenance of Hugo van Arckel had assumed a peculiar expression; disapprobation and displeasure were depicted on it. At length he looked fixedly at the general, as though he had made up his mind to brave him, and exclaimed:

"I should do myself dishonor were I now to drink to the honor of France."

At these words the face of Robert d'Artois glowed with wrath; he struck the table so violently with his goblet, that he made all the drinking-vessels ring, and shouted:

"Messire van Arckel, you shall drink to the honor of France; it is my will."

"Messire," replied Hugo with imperturbable coolness, "I drink not to the devastation of a Christian land. Long have I warred, and in many lands; yet never have I found a knight who would defile his conscience with such base atrocities."

"You shall do my behest; I will it; I bid you."

"And I will not," answered Hugo. "Hearken, Messire d'Artois, you have already said that my soldiers demanded too high pay, and that they cost you too much; well then, you shall pay them no longer, for I will no longer serve in your camp, and so our contention is at an end."

These words caused an unpleasant sensation in all the knights, and even in the general himself; for the departure of Hugo would be no light loss.

The Zeelander meanwhile drew back his chair, threw one of his gloves on the table, and exclaimed with increasing anger:

"Messires, I aver that you are all liars! I scorn you all to your faces! There lies my glove; take it up who lists, I challenge him to mortal combat."

Almost all the knights, and among them even Raoul de Nesle, snatched eagerly at the glove; but Robert d'Artois threw himself so eagerly upon it, that he seized it before the others. "I accept your challenge," said he; "come, let us go."

But at this moment the old King Sigis von Melinde arose, and waved his hand in token that he wished to speak. The great veneration with which both the combatants regarded him restrained them, and they stood still in silence to hear him. The old man spoke thus:

"Messires, let your angry passions subside a while, and give heed to my counsel. You, Count Robert, are not at this moment master of your life. Were you to fall, the army of your prince would be deprived of its leader, and consequently exposed to disorder and disorganization; you can not resolve to risk this. And now, Messire van Arckel, I ask you, have you any doubt of the bravery of Messire d'Artois?"

"No, truly," replied Van Arckel; "I acknowledge Messire Robert to be a fearless and valiant knight."

The Lion of Flanders

"Well, then," continued the king, "you hear, general, that your personal honor is not called in question; there remains to you only the honor of France to avenge. I counsel you both to postpone the combat to the day after the battle. I pray you speak, Messires, is not my counsel wise and prudent?"

"Yes, yes," answered the knights; "unless the general will grant to one of us the favor of taking up the glove in his stead."

"Silence!" cried D'Artois; "I will not hear of it."

"Messire Van Arckel, do you agree to this?"

"That is no business of mine; I have thrown down my glove, and the general has taken it up; it behooves him to fix the time when he will give it back to me."

"Be it so," said Robert d'Artois; "and if the battle do not last until sunset, I shall come in quest of you that very evening."

"You may spare yourself the trouble," answered Hugo; "I shall be at your side before you are aware of it."

This was followed by threatenings on both sides; but they proceeded no further, for Sigis interposed with the words:

"Messires, it is not fitting that we should longer discuss this matter. Let us once more fill our goblets, and forget all bitter animosity. Be seated, Messire van Arckel."

"No, no," cried Hugo; "I sit here no longer. I leave the camp immediately. Farewell, Messires, we shall see one another again on the battlefield. Meanwhile, may God have you in His holy keeping."

With these words he left the tent, and called his eight hundred men together; and in a very short time one might have heard the sound of trumpets and the clanging armor of a departing band. The same evening he reached the camp of the Flemings, and we may imagine with what joy he was received by them; for he and his men had the reputation of being invincible, and, indeed, they had deserved it.

The French knights meanwhile had resumed the interrupted banquet, and continued to drink in peace. While they were discoursing of Hugo's temerity, a herald entered the tent, and inclined himself respectfully before the knights. His clothes were covered with dust, the sweat ran from his brow, and everything indicated that he had ridden in great haste. The knights looked at him with curiosity, while he drew a parchment from beneath his armor, and said, as he gave it to the general:

"Messire, this letter will inform you that I come from Messire van Lens at Courtrai, to report to you the extreme peril we are in."

"Speak, then," cried D'Artois impatiently; "can

not Messire van Lens hold out the citadel of Courtrai against a handful of foot-soldiers?"

"Permit me to say that you deceive yourself, noble lord," replied the messenger. "The Flemings have no contemptible army in the field; it has sprung up as if by magic; they are more than thirty thousand strong, and have cavalry and an abundant supply of provisions. They are constructing tremendous engines, in order to batter the citadel and take it by storm. Our provisions and our arrows are both exhausted, and we have already begun to devour some of our least valuable horses. If your highness shall delay but a day to bring aid to Messire van Lens, every Frenchman in Courtrai will perish; for there are no longer any means of escape. Messires van Lens, De Mortenay, and De Rayecourt beseech you urgently to extricate them from this peril."

"Messires," cried Robert d'Artois, "here is a glorious opportunity; we could have wished for nothing better. The Flemings are all gathered together at Courtrai; we will fall upon them where they are, and but few of them shall escape us; the hoofs of our horses shall avenge our wrongs on this vile and despicable people. You, herald, remain in the tent; to-morrow you shall return with us to Courtrai. Yet one toast more, Messires; then go and get your troops in readiness for departure; we must break up our encampment with all haste."

The Lion of Flanders

All now left the tent to obey the command of the general, and from every part of the camp resounded the flourish of trumpets summoning the dispersed troops, the tramp of horses, and the clash of armor; a few hours later the tents were struck, and the baggage-wagons packed—all was in readiness. Here and there a number of soldiers were occupied in plunder; but in so large a camp this excited no attention. The captains placed themselves at the head of their companies, arranged the cavalry two abreast; and in that order they marched out of the entrenchments.

The first band, which left the camp with banners flying, consisted of three thousand light cavalry, all picked men, armed with huge battle-axes, and carrying long swords hanging from the pommel of their saddles. These were followed by four thousand archers on foot. They marched onward in a dense mass, protecting their faces from the rays of the sun with their large square shields. Their quivers were full of arrows, and a short sword without a scabbard hung at their girdle. They were mostly from the south of France; but many were by nation Spaniards or Lombards. John de Barles, their captain, a brave warrior, rode here and there between the ranks to encourage them and keep them in order.

The second band was under the command of Reginald de Trie, and consisted of three thousand two hundred heavy cavalry. They were mounted on horses of unusual height and strength, and carried each a broad and flashing sword on his right shoulder; armor of unpolished iron protected their bodies. Most of them were from Orleans.

Messire the Constable de Nesle led the third band. First came a troop of seven hundred noble knights, with glittering armor on their bodies, and graceful banderoles on their long spears; their plumes fell waving behind their backs as they rode, and their coats-of-arms were painted in various colors upon their armor. Their horses were covered from head to foot with iron, and more than two hundred embroidered banners fluttered over the troop. It was truly the most brilliant band of knights that could be seen, even in that age. After them came two thousand horsemen, with battle-axes on their shoulders, and long swords hanging at their saddle-bows.

At the head of the fourth band rode Messire Louis de Clermont, an experienced warrior. It was composed of three thousand six hundred horsemen, bearing spears, from the kingdom of Navarre; and it was easy to see that they were picked and choice warriors. In front of the first column rode the banner-bearer, with the great standard of Navarre.

Count Robert d'Artois, general-in-chief of the army, had taken the middle division under his especial command. All the knights who had brought with them no soldiers, or had enrolled them in other companies, were with him; and the Kings of Majorca and Melinde rode at his side. Among the others it was easy to distinguish Thibaut II, Duke of Lorraine, by the magnificence of his armor. And then there came the gorgeous banners of Messires John, Count of Tancarville, Angelin de Vimen, Ranold de Longueval, Farald de Reims, Arnold de Wexmael, Maréchal de Brabant, Robert de Montfort, and a countless number besides, who had formed themselves into a company. This band even surpassed the third in magnificence and splendor; the helms of the knights were covered either with silver or with gold, and their coats-of-mail were adorned with golden studs, by which their joints were secured. The burning rays of the sun fell on the glittering steel of their armor, and surrounded this peerless band as with a glowing fire. The swords which hung dangling at their saddle-bows fell with a sharp and iron clank on the trappings of their steeds, producing a peculiar sound, which seemed their fittest martial music. Next to these noble knights followed five thousand other horsemen, with battle-axes and swords; and this picked troop was accompanied by sixteen thousand infantry, drawn up in three divisions. The first consisted of a thousand crossbow men; their defensive armor was simply a breastplate of steel and a flat square helmet; small quivers full of iron bolts were suspended at their girdles, and long swords hung at their side. The second was composed of six thousand men with clubs, studded at the end with horrible steel points. The third was made up of "helm-cleavers" with their long axes; and all these men were from Gascony, Languedoc, and Auvergne.

Messire James de Chatillon, the governor-general, commanded the sixth band. It consisted of three thousand two hundred horse. On the banderoles of their spears they had painted burning brooms, the emblems of the purification of Flanders; and their horses were the heaviest of the whole army. Then followed the seventh and eighth bands; the former under the command of John, Count d'Aumale, the latter under Messire Ferry of Lorraine. Each was composed of two thousand seven hundred horse, men of Lorraine, Normandy, and Picardy. These were followed by Godfrey of Brabant with his own vassals, seven hundred horsemen, who formed the ninth band. The tenth and last was entrusted to Guy de St. Pol; he was charged with the protection of the rear and of the baggage. Three thousand four hundred horsemen of all arms rode in advance; then followed a multitude of foot-soldiers with bows and swords, whose number might amount to seven thousand. On every side ran men with blazing torches, in order to set fire to everything within their reach. Behind came the endless succession of baggage-wagons, with the tents and camp-furniture and stores.

The French army, divided into ten bands, and exceeding sixty thousand strong, marched slowly through the country, and took the road to Courtrai. It is hard to conceive how far this numerous host reached; the van was already far out of sight ere the rear had left the entrenchments. Thousands of banners fluttered in the breeze above the marching host, and the sun was reflected with intolerable brightness from the armor of the valiant bands. The horses neighed and champed the bit beneath their heavy burdens; from the crash of arms arose a sound like the rolling of a stormy sea upon the strand; but it was too monotonous to break the stillness of the deserted fields. Wherever the troops had passed, the sky was ruddy with flame, and obscured by dense clouds of smoke. Not a habitation escaped destruction; neither man nor beast was spared; as the chronicles of the time bear record. The following day, when the flames were spent, and the smoke dispersed, there was neither man, nor work, nor trace of man, to be seen; from Lille to Douay and Courtrai, Flanders was so fearfully devastated that the French vandals might boast with reason that they had swept it as with a besom.

The Lion of Flanders

Deep in the night the army of Messire d'Artois arrived before Courtrai. De Chatillon knew the country very well, for he had long lived in the city; and he was accordingly summoned by the general to select a suitable spot for encamping. After a short deliberation, they turned a little to the right, and pitched their tents on the Pottelberg and in the adjacent fields. Messire d'Artois, with the two kings, and a few distinguished knights, took possession of a castle called Hoog-Mosscher, close to the Pottelberg. They placed numerous sentinels on guard, and then betook themselves in peace, and without suspicion, to rest; for they were too confident in their numbers to entertain any apprehension of an attack.

And thus the French army lay within a quarter of an hour's march of the camp of the Guildsmen of Flanders; the advanced pickets could see one another slowly pacing up and down in the gloom.

The Flemings, as soon as they had intelligence of the approach of the foe, had doubled their guard, and issued orders that no man should lie down to rest unarmed.

CHAPTER VI

THE Flemish knights who occupied Courtrai were fast asleep when the tidings of the arrival of the French, passing through the city, and diffusing terror on every side, roused them from their slumbers. Guy commanded the trumpets to sound and the drums to beat; and an hour later all the soldiers lodged within the city were assembled on the walls. As there was reason to fear that the Castellan van Lens would make a sortie into the city during the battle, the men of Ypres were summoned from the camp to watch the French garrison. At the Steenpoort a numerous guard was appointed to keep the women and children within the town; for they were so terrified, that they were bent on fleeing again during the night. Inevitable death seemed to threaten them: on the one side the Castellan van Lens, with his ruthless soldiers, might fall on them at any moment; on the other they saw the small number of their countrymen opposed to the countless hosts of France, and they dared not hope for victory. And truly, but that the heroism and intrepidity of the Flemings blinded them to all thought of danger, they had done well to bethink them of a last parting prayer; for not only did the foot-soldiers in the French camp outnumber those in their own, but there were moreover the two-and-thirty thousand horsemen to be dealt with.

The Flemish commanders calculated with perfect coolness the chances of the coming battle; great as were their valor and eagerness, they could not conceal from themselves their critical position; heroism does not prevent a man from seeing the dark and threatening side of things, nor does it drive out the inborn dread of death; but it inspires a man with might to vanquish and to brave all depressing and disheartening forebodings—further than this the soul can not push its empire over the body. For themselves the Flemings had no fear; but their hearts were full of agonizing anxiety for the liberty of their fatherland—a liberty which was set upon this cast. Notwithstanding, however, the small hope which they dared to entertain, they resolved to accept battle, and rather to die as heroes on the bloody field than survive to endure a debasing slavery.

The youthful Matilda and the sister of Adolf, with many other noble ladies, were sent to the Abbey of Gröningen, where they would find a safe asylum, even in the event of the French becoming masters of Courtrai. When this and other preliminary matters had been arranged, the knights returned to the camp.

The French general, Robert d'Artois, was a brave and experienced soldier; but, like many others of his fellow-countrymen, he was too rash and self-confident. He deemed it quite unnecessary to take ordinary precautions in his proceedings against the Flemings, so certain was he that his first attack would throw them into hopeless confusion. This rash confidence was shared by all his soldiers to such extent that, while the army of Guy was preparing for battle in the twilight, the French were sleeping on as unconcernedly as though they were quartered in a friendly city. Trusting to their numberless cavalry, they thought that nothing could resist them; whereas, had they been a little less thoughtless, they would have first inspected the field of battle, and disposed their van and rear accordingly. They would then have found that the ground between the two camps was not at all fitted for the action of cavalry—but why should they exercise a superfluous caution? Was the Flemish army worth it? Robert d'Artois thought not!

The Flemings were drawn up on the Gröningen Place. Behind them, to the north, ran the Lys, a broad river, which rendered any attack on that side impossible; in front flowed the Gröningen brook, which, though now but a narrow watercourse, was then a broad stream; and its shelving marshy banks opposed an insurmountable obstacle to the French cavalry. Their right wing rested on the portion of the walls of Courtrai near St. Martin's Church, and round the left ran a tributary of the Gröningen brook, so that the Flemings were posted, as it were, on an island; and any attempt to dislodge them must needs be difficult and perilous. The space which separated them from the French army was a succession of meadows, which lay very low, and were watered by the Mosscher brook, which converted them into a kind of marsh. Thus the French cavalry were obliged to cross two brooks before they could come into action; and this was a very difficult and tedious operation, because the horses' hoofs had no hold on the moist and slippery ground, and at every step the poor animals sank up to their knees in the morass.

The French general took no account of this; he made his plans as though the field of battle were firm and hard ground, and directed the attack in a manner quite at variance with the rules of strategy. So true is it that excessive confidence renders men blind.

Toward break of day, before the sun had shown his glowing disk above the horizon, the Flemings were drawn up in order of battle on the Gröningen brook. Guy commanded the left wing in person, and he had about him all the lesser Guilds of Bruges. Eustachius Sporkyn, with the men of Furnes, occupied the centre; the second corps was commanded by John Borluut, and numbered five thousand men of Ghent; the third, composed of the Clothworkers and freemen of Bruges, was led by William van Gulick. The right wing, which extended as far as the city walls, consisted of the Butchers, with their Dean Jan Breydel, and the Zeeland men-at-arms; and it was commanded by Messire John van Renesse. The remaining Flemish knights had no definite post assigned them, but moved hither and thither, wherever they deemed their presence and aid necessary. The eleven hundred horsemen of Namur were stationed in the rear, behind the line of battle; they were not to be brought at once into action, lest they should throw the infantry into disorder.

At length the French army began to prepare for action. A thousand trumpets uttered their shrill voices, the horses neighed, and weapons rattled on all sides with a sound so ominous in the darkness that the Flemings felt a cold shiver thrill through them. What a cloud of foes was about to burst upon them! But to these valiant men this was nothing—they were going to die, that they knew: but their widowed wives and their children, what would become of them? At that solemn moment their thoughts reverted to those most dear to them.

Fathers thought bitterly of their sons, doomed to iron bondage; sons bewailed in agony their gray-headed fathers, left the helpless prey of tyranny. Within them were two contending emotions—inflexible resolution and crushing anguish; and when these meet in men's hearts in presence of a threatening danger, they combine and fuse into a transport of rage and fury. And this effect was now produced on the Flemings; their gaze was fixed and unpitying, their teeth were clenched in fierce resolve, a burning thirst made their mouths dry and parched, and their breath came thick and rapid from their panting breasts. An appalling silence reigned throughout the army; no one expressed his apprehensions or feelings to his comrade; all were plunged in thoughts of painful gloom. They were standing thus drawn up in a long line, when the sun rose above the horizon, and disclosed to them the camp of the French.

The horsemen were so numerous that their spears stood thick as ears of corn at harvest-time. The horses of the advanced columns pawed the ground impatiently, and besprinkled their glittering trappings of steel with flakes of snow-white foam. The trumpets sent their lively tones, like some festal rejoicing, to mingle with the sighing of the trees in the Neerlander wood; and the morning breeze played wantonly with the waving folds of the standards, and with the streamers attached to the spears of the cavalry. At intervals, the voice of the general was heard above this tumult of war; and the war-cry, "Noël! Noël! France! France!" arose from one company; and as it was caught up by each in quick succession, a deafening echo ran through the whole host. The French horsemen were eager, and full of courage; they pricked the sides of their war-steeds with their spurs to goad them into fiercer fury, and then caressed them and talked to them, that they might the better know their master's voice in the thick of the fight. Who shall have the honor of the first blow? was the thought that filled every mind with eager excitement. This was a great point of honor in those days. Whenever this good fortune fell to the lot of a knight in an important battle, he boasted of it all his life long, as a proof and token of his superior valor; and hence each one held his horse in readiness, and his spear in rest, to rush forward at the first word of command, or at the slightest sign from the general.

In the meadows close about the army, the far-extended lines of the French infantry might be seen winding about the fields like the folds of some hideous serpent; the greatest stillness pervaded their ranks.

When Guy observed that the attack was about to commence, he sent a thousand slingers, under the command of Solomon van Sevecote, as far as the second brook, to harass the French outposts and sentinels; then he disposed his various companies into a square, in such a manner that the eyes of all were directed toward its centre. At that point rose an altar constructed of turf, and over it waved the great banner of St. George, the patron of warriors; on its steps knelt a priest, arrayed in the vestments of his office, who proceeded to offer the Holy Sacrifice for the good success of the battle. When the Mass was ended, the priest, still standing at the altar, turned toward the army; and in a moment, inspired by one and the same sentiment, the troops sank to the ground, and received in solemn silence the benediction of the Most Holy Sacrament. The hearts of all were deeply stirred by this holy ceremony; a spirit of lofty self-devotion seemed to kindle within them, and they felt as if the voice of God called them to a martyr's death. Glowing with this holy flame, they remembered no more all that was dear to them on earth; they rose to the full stature of the heroism of their fathers; their breasts heaved more freely; the blood flowed more impetuously through their veins, and they longed for the battle, as for their deliverance from the oppressor.

And now, as all arose in deepest silence, the youthful Guy sprang from his horse, and standing in the middle of the square, addressed them thus: "Men of Flanders, remember the famous deeds of your ancestors; never did they count their foes. Their invincible courage won for us that freedom of which an alien tyrant would now despoil us. You, too, will to-day pour out your hearts' blood in defense of this sacred heritage and deposit; and if we die, let us die a free and manly people, the never-tamed sons of the Lion. Think on God, whose temples they have burnt; on your children, whom they have sworn to slay; on your terror-stricken wives; on all that you love; on all that you hold sacred—and so, should we perish, the enemy shall not glory in his victory, for more Frenchmen than Flemings shall fall on the soil of our father-land. Be wary of the horsemen; strike with your 'good-days' between the legs of the horses, and quit not your ranks. Whoso plunders a fallen enemy, whoso leaves his appointed post, strike him dead; this is my will and command. Is there a coward among you? let him die by your hands; his blood be upon my head alone!"

And then, as if impelled by a sudden and vehement inspiration, he stooped and took some mold from the ground; and placing it in his mouth, he raised his voice and cried:

"By this beloved earth, which I will bear within me to the fight, this day will I either conquer or die!"

And the whole host in like manner stooped, and swallowed each a little earth from the soil of their fatherland. This soil, so beloved, seemed to inspire their breasts with a calm concentrated rage, and a dark unrelenting yearning for revenge. A low and hollow murmur, like the rumbling of a tempest in the recesses of a cavern, was heard throughout the excited host; their cries, their oaths, became blended in one terrific mass of sounds, among which were barely distinguishable the words, "We are ready and resolved to die!"

Again and in haste the order of battle was formed, and each returned to his position in front of the Gröningen brook.

Meanwhile Robert d'Artois, accompanied by some French generals, had approached close to the Flemish army to reconnoitre it. His archers were then brought forward and opposed to Guy's slingers, and the outposts exchanged a few arrows and stones while Robert was pushing forward his cavalry. Observing that Guy had disposed his troops in line, he arranged his own in three divisions; the first, under Raoul de Nesle, was ten thousand strong; the second, which he retained under his own command, was formed of the choicest companies, and numbered fifteen thousand picked horsemen; the third, destined for the defense of the rear and of the camp, he entrusted to Guy de St. Pol. While he was thus preparing for a tremendous attack on the Flemish position, Messire John de Barlas, captain of the foreign companies, came to him, and addressed him in these words:

"For God's sake, Messire d'Artois, let me and my men be engaged in the battle; let not the flower of the French knighthood be exposed to die by the hands of this Flemish rabble, maddened as they are by rage and despair. I know their customs well; they have left their provisions and munitions in the city. Do you remain here in order of battle, and I, with my light horse, will cut them off from Courtrai, and keep them occupied with a feigned attack. The Flemings are great eaters; and if we can cut off their supplies, they will very soon be compelled by hunger to change their position, and we shall be able to attack them on more favorable ground than this; you will thus destroy all this rabble without shedding a drop of noble blood."

The Constable de Nesle, and many other knights, thought this counsel worthy of attention; but Robert, blinded by passion, would not even listen to them, and commanded John de Barlas to hold his peace.

During these preparations time had passed away; it was now seven o'clock in the morning; the French host were within two slings' cast of the Flemings. Between the French archers and the slingers lay the Mosscher brook, so that they could not come to close quarters; and very few fell on either side. Then Robert d'Artois gave Raoul de Nesle, general of the first division, the signal to begin the attack.

The horsemen sprang eagerly onward, and soon came to the Mosscher brook; but here they sank saddle-deep in the morass. One stumbled over another; the foremost were thrown from their horses, and either slain by the slingers or stifled in the swamp. The few who contrived to extricate themselves retreated at full speed, and dared not venture to expose themselves a second time so recklessly. The Flemings meanwhile stood motionless behind the second brook, looking on at the discomfiture of the enemy in silent composure.

When the Constable de Nesle saw that the passage was impracticable for cavalry, he came to Messire d'Artois, and said:

"Of a truth I tell you, Count, that we are exposing our men to great danger, by trying to force them over the brook; there is not a horse that either will or can ford it. Let us rather try to entice the enemy from their position. Believe me, you are staking all against fearful odds in this game."

But the general was too far carried away by vexation and anger to pay any attention to this wise counsel. "Constable," exclaimed he furiously, "that is advice befitting Lombards! Are you frightened at this pack of wolves, or are you of the same breed with them?"

Raoul, stung by this reproof, and by the insinuation it conveyed, burst forth in unrestrained wrath. He came up close to the general, and answered with an expression of bitter disdain:

"You throw doubt on my courage! you dare to taunt and insult me! But, I ask you, have you courage to go with me on foot and alone into the thick of the foe? I would lead you so far that you would return no more—"

Here some of the knights threw themselves between the angry generals, and endeavored by every argument to convince the seneschal that the brook was not fordable by cavalry; but he persisted in his refusal to listen to them, and ordered Raoul de Nesle to renew the charge.

The constable, beside himself with vexation, rode furiously with his troop toward the Flemish position. But at the brook all the horsemen of the front rank were thrown from their saddles; each thrust the other deeper into the morass, and more than five hundred perished in the confusion, either stifled in the mud, or slain by the stones of the Flemish slingers. Messire d'Artois now saw himself obliged to recall Raoul; but it was scarcely possible to restore order among the survivors, so utterly were they broken and dispirited.

Meanwhile Messire John de Barlas had found

a place at which the first brook could be forded, and had crossed it with two thousand cross-bow men. Having gained the open meadow, he drew up his men in a compact mass, and poured such a shower of arrows upon the Flemish slingers, that the sky was almost darkened by them, and a large number of Flemings fell dead or wounded to the ground, while the French archers continued to make a steady advance.

Messire Solomon van Sevecote himself had seized the sling of one of the fallen Guildsmen, in order to animate the survivors by his own example; but an iron bolt from a cross-bow pierced the visor of his helmet, and flung him dead to the ground. Then the Flemings, seeing their general struck down, with so large a number of their comrades, and finding their supply of stones fall short, closed their ranks, and fell back on the camp in good order. Only one slinger from Furnes remained standing in the middle of the field, as though he scorned the arrows of the Frenchmen. He stood calm and unmoved, while the arrows flew hissing over him and around him. Slowly and with deliberation he placed a heavy stone in his sling, and measured carefully the distance of the spot at which he wished to take aim. After a few preparatory whirls, he let go the end of the sling, and the stone flew whistling through the air. A cry of anguish burst from the French captain, and in a moment he lay lifeless on the ground—the stone had pierced his helmet and crushed his skull; and Messire John de Barlas lay weltering in his blood. Thus, in the first attack, perished the leaders of the first two divisions of the French army. The archers were so infuriated by this disastrous sight, that they threw away their cross-bows, grasped their swords, and impetuously pursued the slingers as far as the second brook, which ran in front of the Flemish encampment. At this moment Messire Valepaile, who was standing by the side of Robert d'Artois, seeing the advantage gained by the cross-bow men, exclaimed:

"Oh seneschal, the rascally foot-soldiers will, after all, gain the honor of the day. While they are counting the foe, what are we knights doing here? It is foul shame; we are standing still, as though we dared not fight."

"Mountjoy St. Denis!" shouted Robert. "Forward, constable! fall on them!"

At this command all the horsemen of the first division gave their horses the rein, and rushed on impetuously and in disorder; for each wished to be the first to strike the blow of honor. So eager was their onset, that they rode over the cross-bow men, and many hundreds of the hapless foot-soldiers were trampled to death beneath the hoofs of the horses, while the remainder fled in all directions over the meadow. Thus the cavalry robbed the

French of the advantage which the cross-bow men had gained, and gave the Flemish slingers time to fill up their ranks, and form again in order. Then arose from the prostrate horsemen a groan so fearful, a death-cry so general and so prolonged, that at a distance it might have been taken for the combined shoutings of a triumphant army; on they rushed, trampling down into the marsh those who had fallen, heedless of their deprecating cries. Scarcely had the shrieks of those who first sank died away on the air, when they who had trodden them under foot were in their turn overthrown and trampled down by others; and so the death-wail was continued unceasingly. The companies in the rear, thinking that the action was become general, spurred their horses on toward the brook, and thus increased the number of the victims of the seneschal's folly and imprudence.

As yet the Flemings had made no attack upon them; they stood motionless and silent, gazing with wonder and awe on the dismal tragedy enacted before them. Their generals proceeded with more skill and more prudence; other warriors would have thought this the fittest moment for a general attack, and so would perhaps have crossed the brook and fallen on the French; but Guy, and John Borluut, his chief adviser, would not relinquish the advantage which their position gave them.

At length both the brooks were filled with dead bodies of men and horses, and Raoul de Nesle had the good fortune to force a passage with about a thousand horsemen. He formed them in a close squadron, and shouted, "France! France! forward! forward!"

They charged with furious intrepidity into the centre of the Flemish troops; but the latter planted their "good-days" firmly on the ground, and received the horsemen on the points of these frightful weapons. A large number of the assailants were thrown from their horses by the shock, and quickly despatched. But Godfrey of Brabant, who had also crossed the brook with nine hundred horse, threw himself with such impetuosity on the squadron of William van Gulick, that he overthrew both this and the three first divisions, and so broke the line of the Flemings. And now began a terrible struggle; the French horsemen had thrown away their spears, and rushed on the Flemings with their long battle-swords. The latter defended themselves bravely with their clubs and halberds, and dismounted many a horseman; but still the advantage remained with Godfrey of Brabant; his men had made a clear space all around them, and there was thus a wide breach in the Flemish line. Through this opening poured all the French who had forded the brook, in order to fall on the rear of the Flemish divisions. This was

a critical and perilous maneuvre for the Flemings
—were the foe once on their front and in their
rear, they would have had no room to wield their
"good-days," and would have been reduced to defend themselves with halberds, clubs, and swords
alone; and this would have given the French an
immense advantage: for, being mounted, their
blows were better aimed, and more deadly in effect; it was easy for them to cleave the heads of
those on foot, or to strike them from their bodies.

William van Gulick fought like a lion; he stood
alone with his standard-bearer and Philip van
Hofstade, surrounded by thirty of the enemy, who
strove to capture his banner; but as yet every arm
which had been put forth to seize it had been severed by his sword. At this moment, Arthur de
Mertelet, a Norman knight, sprang over the
brook, with a considerable number of horsemen,
and dashed at full speed toward William van Gulick. Their arrival crushed the hopes of the Flemings; for the number of the foe was now too great,
and their superiority too manifest; and when the
Norman saw William's banner, he charged toward it with the speed of an arrow, and put his
lance in rest to pierce the standard-bearer. Philip
van Hofstade, perceiving his intention, dashed
through the French foot-soldiers to stay the course
of De Mertelet. The shock of the meeting of the
two knights was so impetuous, that the lance of

each pierced the heart of his antagonist; warrior and horse were in one moment bereft of motion; it seemed as though a preternatural influence had suddenly cooled their rage; one would have thought each was leaning on his spear with all his weight, in order to thrust it deeper into the body of his antagonist; but this was but for a moment; De Mertelet's horse made a slight convulsive movement, and the corpses of both fell to the ground.

Messire John van Renesse, who commanded the right wing, seeing the danger of William van Gulick, left his position, and, with Breydel and his Guildsmen, fell back behind the line of battle on the rear of the French. Nothing could resist men like the Butchers of Bruges; they exposed themselves to every weapon with naked breast, and before their death-scorning valor everything gave way. Their axes hewed the legs of the horses, or clave the skulls of their falling riders. A moment after their arrival, the ground was so cleared that scarcely twenty Frenchmen remained behind the line of battle. Among them was Godfrey of Brabant, who blushed not to fight against those who were his brethren both by birth and by language. When John van Renesse espied him, he shouted to him:

"Godfrey, Godfrey! your course is run—you shall die!"

"Apply your words to yourself," replied Godfrey, aiming at the head of Messire John a tremendous blow; but Van Renesse, with a dexterous and rapid movement of his sword from below, struck him so violently under the chin that he rolled out of his saddle to the ground. More than twenty Butchers fell immediately upon him, and he received innumerable wounds, the last of which was mortal. Meanwhile Jan Breydel and some of his men had penetrated further and further among the enemy, and had fought long enough to win the standard of Brabant; he regained his Butchers, defending his prize at every step with furious courage, and then, tearing the banner in pieces and throwing its pole scornfully from him, he exclaimed: "Shame and dishonor to the traitors!"

The men of Brabant burning to avenge this insult, rushed with redoubled rage upon the foe, and made the most extraordinary efforts to gain and to tear in pieces the banner of William van Gulick; but its bearer, John Ferrand, struggled with the strength of madness, with all who dared to approach him. Four times was he thrown to the ground, and four several times did he rise again, still grasping his banner, though covered with wounds. William van Gulick had already laid dead at his feet a large number of the French; and every fresh blow of his huge broadsword struck down a foe. At length, wearied, covered with wounds, and exhausted by loss of blood, he grew pale, and felt his strength failing him. Filled with anger and vexation he retired to the rear to refresh himself and rest a while. John de Vlamynck, his squire, loosed the the plates of his armor and stripped him of his heavy mail, that he might breathe more freely. In the absence of William, the French had regained some of the ground they had lost, and the Flemings manifested a disposition to retreat. This threw Van Gulick into an agony of despair, and induced John de Vlamynck to adopt a singular device, which bore witness in its results to the fame of his master's bravery. He hastily put on the armor of Messire William, and threw himself into the thick of the enemy with the cry: "Give way,—back,—men of France! William van Gulick is here again!" He accompanied these words with a shower of well-directed blows, and stretched a considerable number of the bewildered foe on the ground; until at length the French gave way, and thus afforded the disordered troops time to close their ranks again.

Raoul de Nesle had thrown himself with the utmost impetuosity on the five thousand citizens of Ghent under John van Borluut; but all the efforts of the courageous Frenchmen to break their line were in vain. Thrice had the men of Ghent driven him back with prodigious slaughter, and without his obtaining the slightest advantage. John Borluut thought it too rash to abandon his position in order to pursue the soldiers of Raoul, and so bethought himself of another plan. He hastily formed his three hindmost corps into two new battalions, and posted them behind the line of battle, one close in the rear, and the other further back in the meadow; he then ordered the central division to give way before the next attack of the French. When Raoul de Nesle had collected his scattered troops, and restored order among them, he made another vigorous attack upon the men of Ghent; the centre fell back immediately, and the French, thinking that they had at length broken their line, pushed on with shouts of joy: "Noël! Noël! Victory! Victory!"

They pressed forward into the opening made in the line and thought they had now turned the rear of the army; but everywhere they found walls of spears and halberds. John Borluut now quickly closed the wings of his division, and thus his five thousand men formed a compact circle, and the thousand Frenchmen were caught as in a net. Then began a fearful slaughter; for a quarter of an hour they were hacking, slashing, piercing, and trampling down one another; horses and men lay in helpless confusion on the ground, shrieking, howling, neighing—yet they heard nothing, spoke nothing; but proceeded in silence with their work of death.

Raoul de Nesle continued a long time fighting over the dead bodies of his soldiers, though covered with wounds and besprinkled with the blood of his gallant followers; his death, he saw, was inevitable. John Borluut beheld the heroic knight with profound sympathy and compassion, and cried to him:

"Surrender, Messire Raoul; I would fain not see you die!"

But Raoul was beside himself with rage and despair; he heard, indeed, the words of Borluut clearly, and an emotion of thankfulness touched his heart; but the reproach of the seneschal had filled him with such bitter vexation that he no longer desired to live. He raised his hand and made a sign to John Borluut, as if to take a last farewell of him, and then, the same moment, struck dead two of the men of Ghent. At length, a blow from a club stretched him lifeless on the corpses of his brethren in arms. Many other knights, whose horses had been slain under them, would fain have surrendered; but no one listened to them—not a solitary Frenchman escaped alive from the net.

Meanwhile the battle raged with equal fury all along the line. Here was heard a shout: "Noël! Noël! Mountjoy St. Denis!" and this was an intimation that at that point the French had gained

some advantage; and there the cry: "Flanders! the
Lion! all that is French is false! Strike home! to
the death!" rose in mighty peals heavenward—a
sign that there some body of French troops was
broken and routed.

The Gröningen brook ran with blood, and was
choked with the bodies of the slain. The mournful
wail of the dying was scarcely drowned by the
clash of arms; it was heard, low and continuous,
like the roll of distant thunder, above the noise of
the fight. Spears and clubs flew in pieces; in front
of the line the dead lay in crowded heaps. The
wounded had no chance of escape; no one thought
of rendering them any assistance; and they were
either stifled in the marsh, or trampled miserably
to death beneath the hoofs of the horses. Hugo van
Arckel meanwhile had penetrated with his eight
hundred soldiers to the very centre of the French
army, and was so surrounded by the enemy that the
Flemings had lost sight of him altogether. They
fought too valiantly and kept together too firmly
to allow the enemy to break their small but compact mass; around them lay numbers of the French,
and whoso dared to come near them expiated his
temerity by death. At length he fought his way
to the banner of Navarre, and wrenched it from
the hands of the standard-bearer. The Navarrese,
wild with rage, turned upon him, and laid many
of his followers low; but Hugo defended the cap-

tured banner so well that the French could not retake it. He had already returned very near to the Flemish camp, when Louis de Forest struck him so tremendous a blow on the left shoulder that his arm was severed, and hung supported only by the shirt-of-mail. The blood gushed in streams from the wound, and the paleness of death overspread his features; but yet his grasp of the banner was unrelaxed. Louis de Forest was slain by some Flemings, and Hugo van Arckel reached the centre of the Flemish camp, gathered his ebbing strength to utter once more the cry, "Flanders! the Lion!" but his voice failed him, his life's blood was drained, and he sank, still grasping the conquered standard, to rise no more.

On the left wing, in front of Messire Guy's division, the conflict was yet more fierce and deadly. James de Chatillon charged the Guilds of Furnes with several thousand horse, and had cut down many hundreds of them. Eustachius Sporkyn lay grievously wounded behind the line, and employed his remaining strength in cheering on his men and urging them to hold their ground; but the impetuosity of the onset was too great—they were compelled to retreat. Followed by a large number of horsemen, De Chatillon broke the line; and the fight was continued over the prostrate Sporkyn, whose sufferings were soon ended beneath the tramp of the cavalry.

The Lion of Flanders

Adolf van Nieuwland alone remained with Guy and his standard-bearer; they were now cut off from the army, and their death seemed certain. De Chatillon made most strenuous efforts to get possession of the great standard of Flanders; but, although Segher Lonke, who bore it, had been many times thrown down, De Chatillon could not succeed in his attempt: he raged around it, and urged on his men, and dealt his blows in every direction upon the three invincible Flemings. Doubtless these could not long have continued to defend themselves against such a cloud of foes; but they had previously made such good use of their weapons that they stood surrounded and protected by a rampart of slain. Mad with rage and impatience, De Chatillon snatched a long spear from the hand of one of his horsemen, and dashed at full gallop toward Guy. He would infallibly have slain the Count; for, occupied with so many enemies, he did not notice De Chatillon's approach; the spear seemed to be already piercing his neck between the helmet and the gorget, when Adolf van Nieuwland swung his sword round with the rapidity of lightning, the spear flew in pieces, and the life of his general was saved.

The same moment, and before De Chatillon had time to seize his sword again, Adolf sprang over the heap of slain, and dealt the French knight so terrible a blow on the head that his cheek, and the part of the helmet which covered it, were severed, and fell to the ground. The blood streamed from his wound; still he persisted in defending himself; but two mighty blows from Adolf's sword hurled him from his saddle under the hoofs of the horses. Some Flemings drew him out; and having carried him to the rear, hewed him in pieces, taunting him the while with his merciless ferocity.

While this conflict was pending, Arnold van Oudenarde had come to the succor of the left wing, and changed the fate of the battle. The men of Furnes, thus encouraged, returned with them; and soon the French were thrown into hopeless disorder. Men and horses fell in such numbers, and the confusion of the foe was so great, that the Flemings deemed the battle won, and from the whole line poured forth a loud and exulting shout:

"Victory! Victory! Flanders! the Lion! Whoso is French is false! strike all dead!" And over all the battle-field raged the Butchers, their arms, their bosoms, and their axes smeared with gore, their hair streaming wildly, their features rendered undiscernible by mire and blood and sweat, yet fixed in a grim expression of bitterest hatred of the French and intense enjoyment of the conflict.

While the first division of the French army was thus defeated and destroyed, the Seneschal d'Artois stood with the second division at a distance from the Flemish camp. As the front of the enemy was not extensive enough to admit of a simultaneous attack with his whole army, he had not thought it necessary to advance. He knew nothing of the fortunes of the battle, but concluded that his troops were certainly victorious; for otherwise, he thought, some of them would have retreated. In the meantime he sent Messire Louis de Clermont with four thousand Norman cavalry through the Neerlander wood, to take the left wing of the Flemings in flank. De Clermont had the good fortune to find firm ground on this side; he crossed the brook without losing a man, and fell suddenly on the division of Guy. Attacked in the rear by fresh troops, while they were scarcely able to keep De Chatillon's men in check, they found it impossible to offer any resistance. The first ranks were broken, and cut to pieces; the others were thrown into confusion, and all this part of the Flemish army gave way and retreated. The voice of the youthful Guy, conjuring them by the memory of their fatherland to stand firm, inspired them with courage enough; but this was of no avail; the violence of the attack was too great; and all that they could do, in answer to their general's appeal, was to make their retreat as slow and orderly as possible.

At this moment Guy received so violent a blow on his helmet that he fell forward on the neck of his horse, and his sword dropped from his hand.

The Lion of Flanders

In this position, stunned and giddy, he could no longer defend himself; and would certainly have perished had not Adolf come to his rescue. The young knight sprang in front of Guy, and wielded his sword so skilfully and so valiantly that the Frenchmen were effectually prevented from striking at the Count. In a short time his arm waxed weak and weary in this desperate conflict; his blows became ever slower and weaker; the countless strokes that fell on his coat of mail made him feel his whole body bruised and swollen, and he was already on the point of taking a last farewell of the world; for he seemed to see death beckoning to him in the distance. In the meantime Guy had been carried behind the line of battle, and had recovered from his swoon. He now looked with anguish on the perilous position of his deliverer; and seizing another sword, he was in a moment at his side, and fighting with renewed vigor. Many of the most valiant of the Flemings had hastened after him; and the French would have been compelled to retreat, had they not received fresh reenforcements by way of the Neerlander wood. The intrepidity of the Flemings could not avail to check the advance of the enemy. The cry, "Flanders! the Lion!" was answered by, "Noël! Noël! the victory is ours! death to the rebels!"

The Flemings wavered, broke their ranks, and were thrown into inextricable disorder. The marvelous efforts of Guy failed to prevent their retreat; for there were at least ten horsemen to one Fleming, and the horses either trampled them down or drove them back with an irresistible impetus. Half of them fled before the advancing foe; great numbers were slain, and the remainder were so scattered that they could offer no resistance to the horsemen, and were pursued to the Leye, where many of them were miserably drowned. On the banks of this river Guy rallied a few of his men; they fought with desperation, but their heroic valor was of no avail. Though each of them had slain three or four of the horsemen, the French increased continually, while their own number diminished. Soon there remained but one hope, one thought— to die with honor avenged.

CHAPTER VII

GUY beheld the destruction of his troops, and deemed the battle lost. He could have wept aloud for anguish; but there was no room for grief in his manly heart—a moody rage had taken entire possession of it. In conformity with his oath, he desired to live no longer, and spurred his horse into the very thick of the exulting enemy. Adolf van Nieuwland and Arnold van Oudenarde kept close to his side; so desperate was their onset that the foe was appalled by their feats of valor, and the horsemen fell, on all sides, as if by magic, beneath their blows. Yet the Flemings were discomfited and almost all slain: the French continued their shouts of victory; for it seemed that nothing could extricate the remnant of Guy's division from their perilous position.

And now there appeared in the direction of Oudenarde, beyond the Gaver brook, an object that gleamed brightly between the trees; it drew rapidly near, and soon two horsemen might be distinguished in full career toward the field of battle. One was evidently a noble knight, as the magnificence of his armor attested. His coat-of-mail, and all the steel that enveloped both himself and his horse, were covered with gold, and shone with wonderful brilliancy. An enormous blue plume streamed behind him in the wind, the reins of his horse were covered with silver plates, and on his breast was a red cross, surmounted by the word "Flanders" flashing in silver letters from a black ground.

No knight in the field was so gorgeously arrayed as this unknown; but what excited most attention was his unusual stature. He was at least a head above the tallest of the knights; and he was so powerfully built, in body and in limbs, that he might well have been taken for a son of the race of giants. The horse he rode was of a size and strength proportioned to those of its rider. Large flakes of foam flew from the mouth of the noble beast, and his breath rolled in two dense clouds from his expanded nostrils. The knight carried no other weapon than a huge ax of steel, which contrasted strangely with the golden splendor of his armor.

The other horseman was a monk, very meanly attired; his mail and helmet were so rusty that they seemed streaked with red; this was Brother William van Saeftinge. In his monastery at Doest he had heard that at Courtrai the Flemings were in conflict with the French; he went at once to the stable, took thence two horses, exchanged one for the rust-eaten armor he wore, and spurred the other at his utmost speed toward the battle-field. He too was extraordinarily strong and brave; a long sword gleamed in his grasp, and the flash of his dark eye showed that he knew right well how to wield it. He had just fallen in with the wondrous unknown knight; and as both were bent on the same errand, they had continued their ride together.

The Flemings turned their eyes hopefully and joyfully toward the golden knight as he advanced in the distance. They could not distinguish the word "Flanders," and so knew not whether he was friend or foe; but in this their extremity they felt a hope that God had sent them one of His saints to deliver them. And everything combined to strengthen their hopes—the gorgeous armor—the extraordinary form and stature—the glowing red cross on the breast of the unknown. Guy and Adolf, who were fighting surrounded by foes, looked at each other with beaming joy—they had recognized the golden knight. It seemed to them as though they heard the death doom of the French, so absolute was their confidence in the prowess and skill of the new warrior. They exchanged a look which said:

"Oh, happy chance! there is the Lion of Flanders!"

At length the golden knight came near; and

before one could ask whom he came to aid, he fell with such impetuosity on the horsemen, and struck such fearful blows with his ax of steel, that the bewildered foe was smitten with a panic, and overthrew one another in their eagerness to escape from the dreaded strokes. Everything fell before his crushing ax—behind him he left a clear space, like the wake of a sailing ship on the waters; and thus, carrying death before him, he reached with marvelous rapidity the bands which were driven back upon the Leye, and cried:

"Flanders! the Lion! Follow me! Follow me!"

Repeating this cry, he hurled a number of Frenchmen into the marsh, and performed such prodigies of valor and strength that the Flemings looked on him with awe as a supernatural being.

And now the courage of the Flemings revived; with shouts of joy they rushed forward, and emulated the prowess of the golden knight. The French could no longer withstand the onset of the dauntless sons of the Lion: their front ranks gave way and fled; but they came in collision with those who were behind them, and the rout became general. A frightful slaughter began along the whole length of the line. The Flemings pushed on over heaps of slain. The cry, "Noël! Noël!" was no longer heard: "Flanders! the Lion!" alone resounded triumphantly from every part of the field.

Brother William, the monk, had dismounted, and was fighting on foot. He wielded his sword like a feather, and laughed to scorn every foe who dared to assail him. One would have thought he was playing at some amusing game, so joyous was he and so full of jests. At length he descried Messire Louis de Clermont with his banner at a little distance. "Flanders! the Lion!" shouted Brother William; "the banner is mine!" He fell on the ground like one dead, and crept on his hands and knees between the horses' legs, and suddenly stood by the side of Louis de Clermont, as though he had risen out of the earth. Blows rained on him on all sides; but he defended himself so well that he received only a few trifling scratches. At first the enemy did not observe that the standard was the object of his attack; but suddenly he turned with the speed of lightning, severed the arm of the standard-bearer at a stroke, and tore the fallen banner in a thousand pieces.

The monk would certainly have been slain, but at that moment began the general rout of the French, and in a short time he found himself surrounded by Flemings, with the golden knight at their head. Guy approached him, and hastily whispered to him:

"Oh, Robert! my brother! how I thank God for sending you to our aid! You have delivered the—"

The golden knight returned no answer, but interrupted him by placing his finger on his mouth, as if to say, "Silence! it is a secret." Adolf, too, had observed the sign, and bore himself as though he did not recognize the Count of Flanders. Meanwhile the French were completing their own destruction. The Flemings pursued them closely, despatching every fallen horseman with their clubs and halberds. Horses and men were trampled down into the moist ground; the grass of the meadows was no longer visible, nor the Gröningen brook; everywhere were the ghastly corpses of the slain. The cries of the wounded and dying mingled with the exulting shouts of the Flemings, the flourish of trumpets, the clash of swords upon the coats-of-mail, and the dismal shrieks of the dying horses. The low rumbling of a volcano on the eve of an eruption may convey some faint notion of the terrors of that scene.

The town-clock of Courtrai struck nine ere the routed horsemen of De Nesle and De Chatillon reached the Seneschal d'Artois. Scarcely had the first fugitives brought him tidings of the defeat, than he resolved in his blind rage to attack the Flemings with his still numerous reserve. It was all in vain that some of the knights tried to dissuade him; followed by his men, he dashed wildly through and over the crowd of fugitives. The fury of their attack compelled Guy's army to fall back again behind the Gröningen brook; for there the carcasses of horses formed a sort of breastwork, and impeded the action of cavalry.

The French knights could not keep their footing on the slippery soil: they fell over one another, and buried one another in the morass. Messire d'Artois lost all self-command: with some intrepid knights, he sprang across the brook and fell on the ranks of the Flemings. After a brief conflict, in which many Flemings were slain, he succeeded in seizing the great banner of Flanders, and tore a large piece of it away, with the front paw of the Lion on it. A cry of rage ran through the Flemish ranks—"Strike him dead! strike him dead!" The seneschal strove with all his strength to wrench the standard from Segher Lonke; but Brother William, throwing away his sword, sprang toward the horse of Messire d'Artois, threw his sinewy arms round the general's neck, hurled him from his saddle, and both rolled together to the ground. The Butchers had now come up; and Jan Breydel, burning to avenge the insults offered by Robert d'Artois to the standard of Flanders, struck off his right arm at a blow. The hapless seneschal saw that his end was near, and asked if there were no one of noble blood at hand to whom he might with honor surrender his sword? But his words were unintelligible to the Butchers, and were lost in their wild cry of vengeance: they hacked and hewed the luckless knight until death ended his sufferings.

The Lion of Flanders

While this was going on, Brother William had hurled the Chancellor Pierre Flotte to the ground, and had raised his sword to cleave his skull in twain. The Frenchman implored mercy; but Brother William, with a scornful laugh, struck him so violently on the back of the neck that he fell dead upon his face. De Tancarville and D'Aspremont perished in like manner beneath the arm of the golden knight; Guy clove the head of Renold de Longueval with a single blow; the kings of Majorca and Melinde, and more than a hundred nobles, fell beneath the blows of the men of Ghent.

The golden knight was now fighting, on the left wing, against a large body of horsemen; at his side were his brother Guy and Adolf van Nieuwland. The latter threw himself every moment upon the enemy; and was so often in imminent danger of death that it seemed as though he had resolved to die before the eyes of the Lion of Flanders. Matilda's father sees me! thought he; and his breath came more freely, his muscles acquired new strength, and his spirit rose with a loftier contempt of death. The golden knight warned him repeatedly not to expose himself so recklessly; but these warnings sounded in Adolf's ears like the sweetest praise, and made him only more rash and daring. It was fortunate for him that a stronger arm than his own shielded his life, and that one was by his side who had vowed, in true paternal love, to protect him to the utmost of his power.

A single banner alone now remained standing in all the French host; the royal standard still waved its glittering folds, its silver lilies, and all the sparkling jewels with which the arms of France were embroidered. Guy pointed with his hand to the place where it stood, and cried to the golden knight, "Yonder stands our prize!"

They redoubled their efforts to break through the French host; but without avail, until Adolf van Nieuwland, finding a favorable spot, pierced alone the masses of the enemy, and fought his way to the great standard. What hostile hand, what envious spirit, impelled the youthful warrior thus to certain and untimely death? Had they known what hot and bitter tears were shed for him at that moment, how fervently and with how many repetitions his name came before God on the wings of a maiden's prayers, they could not have thus ruthlessly consigned him to destruction! For the royal banner was circled round by a band of noble and valiant knights, who had sworn by their troth and by their honor that they would die rather than suffer it to be taken from their keeping. And what could Adolf do against the flower of French chivalry? Words of scornful taunting greeted him, countless swords waved above his head; and, notwithstanding his marvelous intrepidity, he could no longer defend himself. Already his blood streamed from beneath his helm, and his eyes were clouded by the mists of death. Feeling that his last moment was come, he cried, "Matilda! Matilda! farewell!" and gathering up his remaining strength, he threw himself, with the energy of despair, upon the swords of his foes, forced his way through them to the standard, and wrenched it from the standard-bearer; but it was torn from him in an instant by numberless hands, his strength forsook him, he fell forward on his horse, and the whelming sea of foes closed over him.

The golden knight saw in a moment the danger of Adolf; he thought of the hopeless anguish of the wretched Matilda were her beloved to die by the hand of the enemy; and turning to his men, he cried, with a voice which rose like a thunder-clap above the crash of battle:

"Forward, men of Flanders!"

Like the raging sea, which chafes against its embankment with fury irresistible—like that sea when, under some overmastering wave, the impediment to its mad career has been swept away, and it rolls its foaming billows over the plain, tearing up the trees by their roots, and dashing whole villages to the ground—so sprang forward the herd of Flemish lions at the cry of the unknown knight.

The French were burning with too fierce a courage for the Flemings to hope to overthrow them by one impetuous onset; but the clubs and halberds fell thick and fast as hail upon them. Long and desperate was the struggle; men and horses were mingled together in indescribable confusion; but soon the French knights were so hemmed in that they could not move, and they were driven slowly from their position. The ax of the golden knight had cleared his way to the standard, and he was closely followed by Guy and Arnold van Oudenarde, with a few of the bravest Flemings. He looked anxiously in the direction of the banner for the green plume of Adolf van Nieuwland; but it was not to be seen, and he thought he perceived it further on among the Flemings. The forty chosen knights who stood ranged around the standard now rushed upon the golden knight; but he wielded his ax with such effect that not a sword touched him. His first blow crushed the head of Alin de Bretagne, his second broke the ribs of Richard de Falaise; and all around the Flemings emulated his valor. The bearer of the standard now retreated, in order to preserve it from capture; but Robert with one blow thrust aside three or four of his foes, and pursued him into the midst of a group of Frenchmen at some distance from the spot where the conflict was raging, and succeeded at length in grasping his prize. A whole troop of knights now assailed him to retake the banner; but the golden knight, placing it as a spear in its rest, dashed impetuously among his pursuers. And thus he won his way back to the Flemish army, where he held aloft the captured standard, and cried, "Flanders! the Lion! the victory is ours!"

He was answered by a universal shout of joy; and the courage and strength of the Flemings seemed to increase every moment.

Guy de St. Pol was yet posted at the Pottelberg with about ten thousand foot-soldiers and a goodly troop of cavalry. He had already packed up all the valuables in the camp; and was about to save himself by flight, when Pierre Lebrun, one of those who had been fighting near the royal standard, dashed up to him, and cried:

"What, St. Pol! can you act thus? Can you fly like a dastard, and leave unavenged the deaths of Robert d'Artois and our brethren in arms? Stay, I implore you, for the sake of the honor of France! Let us rather die than endure this shame; advance your troops, and victory may yet be ours."

But Guy de St. Pol would hear nothing of fighting; fear had taken complete possession of him, and he replied:

"Messire Lebrun, I know my duty. I will not allow the baggage to be captured; it is better I should lead back the survivors to France than that I should hurry them to certain destruction."

"And will you, then, abandon to the enemy all

who are still fighting bravely sword in hand? Surely this is a traitor's deed; and if I survive this day, I will impeach you before the king for disloyalty and cowardice."

"Prudence compels my retreat, Messire Lebrun. I shall go, whatever you may think fit to say of me hereafter; for you are now too much excited to be capable of reflecting on all the circumstances of our position. Rage has bereft you of your reason."

"And you are benumbed and paralyzed by cowardice!" retorted Pierre Lebrun. "Do as you will; to show you that I am as prudent as yourself, I shall march with my division to cover and assist the retreat."

He then took a troop of two thousand foot-soldiers, and hastened with them to the field of battle. The number of the French was now so much reduced, and there were so many gaps in their line, that the Flemings were enabled to assail them at the same time in front and in rear. The golden knight observed at once Lebrun's movement and its intention; he saw clearly that St. Pol was about to make his escape with the baggage, and he sprang to the side of Guy to inform him of this plan of the enemy. A few moments after, several Flemish bands dispersed themselves over the plain. Messire John Borluut, with the men of Ghent, hurried along the wall of the city and fell on Lebrun's flank; while the Butchers, with their Dean,

The Lion of Flanders

Jan Breydel, made a detour round the castle of Nedermosschere, and fell on the rear of the French camp.

St. Pol's soldiers had not reckoned on fighting; they were busied in packing together a crowd of precious things, when the axes of the Butchers, and death in their train, took them by surprise. St. Pol, being well mounted, made good his escape, without bestowing further thought on the fate of his troops. Soon the camp was won, and in a few moments not a Frenchman remained alive within it; while the Flemings took possession of all the gold and silver goblets, and of the countless treasures which the French had brought with them.

On the field of battle the conflict had not yet ceased; about a thousand horsemen still persisted in their defense; they had resolved to sell their lives as dear as possible. Among them were more than a hundred noble knights, who had vowed not to survive this defeat, and so fought on with a calm and despairing courage. But at length they were driven on toward the walls of the city into the bitter marsh, and their steeds sank into the treacherous banks of the Ronduite brook. The knights could no longer manage or assist their horses; so they sprang upon the ground, ranged themselves in a circle, and continued the fight with desperate energy. Many of them were, however, stifled in the bitter marsh, which soon became a lake of blood, wherein were seen heads, and arms, and legs of slain warriors mingled with helmets and broken swords, and which has preserved a memorial of this dismal tragedy in its present name, "The Bloody Marsh."

When some Lilyards, among whom were John van Gistel, and a number of the men of Brabant, saw that escape was impossible, they mingled with the Flemings and shouted:

"Flanders! the Lion! Hail, hail Flanders!"

They thought thus to elude the notice of their countrymen; but a Clothworker rushed from the throng toward John van Gistel, and struck him a blow on the head which crushed his skull to fragments, muttering the while:

"Did not my father tell you, traitor, that you would not die in your bed?"

The others were soon recognized by the make of their weapons, and hewn down or pierced without pity, as traitors and recreants.

The young Guy felt a profound pity for the remaining knights who maintained so brave and obstinate a defense, and called to them to surrender, assuring them that their lives should be spared. Convinced that neither courage nor intrepidity could avail them, they yielded and were disarmed, and given into the custody of John Borluut. The most illustrious of these noble captives was Thibaud II, subsequently Duke of Lorraine; the remainder were all of noble race, and famed as valiant knights; their number was about sixty.

And now there remained on the field not a single enemy to be vanquished; only here and there in the distance were seen a few fugitives hastening to secure a safe retreat. The Flemings, amazed that their fighting was over, and maddened with rage and excitement, rushed in crowds in pursuit of these hapless Frenchmen; near the Plague hospital at St. Mary Magdalen, they overtook a company of St. Pol's troops, and put every man to death; a little further on they found Messire William van Mooochere, the Lilyard, who had fled from the field with a few followers. Seeing himself surrounded, he fell on his knees and begged for mercy, pledging himself to serve Robert de Bethune as a loyal vassal. But no one listened to him; the axes of the Butchers ended his pleadings and his life. And thus passed the rest of the day; until within reach of the Flemings no Frenchman, nor ally or friend of Frenchmen, was any longer to be found.

CHAPTER VIII

ALTHOUGH a great part of the Flemish troops was engaged in pursuit of the flying enemy, there still remained some companies drawn up in order on the battlefield.

John Borluut gave orders to his men to keep a strict watch on the field until the following day, according to the custom of war. The division led by Borluut consisted now of three thousand men of Ghent; and in addition to these, many others had remained on the ground, either wounded or exhausted by fatigue. And now that the victory was won, and the chains of their fatherland broken, the Flemings testified their joy by repeated cries of, "Flanders and the Lion! Victory! Victory!" Their shouts were echoed back from the walls of the city by the men of Ypres and Courtrai with even greater energy. They, too, might well shout victory; for while the battle was raging on the Gröningen Place, the castellan, Van Lens, had made a sortie from the citadel, and would have reduced the city to ashes, had not the men of Ypres made so vigorous a resistance, that they drove him back into the citadel after a long conflict. The castellan found that scarcely a tenth part of his soldiers had escaped the rage of the citizens.

The captains and knights now returned to the camp, and thronged round the golden knight, to express to him their fervent gratitude; but, fearful of betraying himself, he answered not a word. Guy, who was standing at his side, turned to the knights, and said:

"Messires, the knight who has so wondrously delivered us and all the land of Flanders, is a crusader, and wishes to remain unknown. The noblest son of Flanders bears his name."

The knights were silent immediately, and every one was endeavoring to guess who this could be, who was at once so brave, so noble, and so lofty of stature. Those of them who remembered the meeting at the wood in the valley were not long in recognizing him; but remembering their pledge, they kept profound silence. Others there were who had no doubt that the unknown was the Count of Flanders himself; but the wish of the golden knight to remain unknown imposed on them also the obligation of secrecy.

After Robert had conversed a while with Guy in a low voice, he cast his eye over the surrounding group of knights; and then turning to Guy, with trouble depicted on his features, he said: "I do not see Adolf van Nieuwland; an agonizing doubt troubles me. Can it be that my young friend has fallen beneath the sword of the foe? That would indeed be to me an intolerable and an enduring grief: and my poor Matilda! how will she mourn her good brother!"

"He can not be dead, Robert; I am sure that I saw his green plume waving just now among the trees of the Neerlander wood. He must be in close pursuit of the foe; you saw with what irrepressible fury he threw himself upon the French in the battle. Fear nothing for him; God will not have allowed him to be slain."

"Oh Guy, are you speaking the truth? My heart is wrung that my hapless child can not taste the joy of this day without an alloy of bitterness. I pray you, my brother, let the men of Messire Borluut search the field, and see whether Adolf is among the slain. I will go to console my anxious Matilda; the presence of her father will be at least a momentary consolation."

He then greeted the knights courteously, and hastened to the Abbey of Gröningen. Guy gave orders to John Borluut to disperse his men over the field, and to bring the wounded and dead knights into the tents. As they began their search, they were seen suddenly to stand still, as though arrested by some sight of horror. Now that the heat and rage of the conflict had subsided, their eyes ranged over the broad plain, where lay in hideous confusion the mangled bodies of men and horses, standards and broken armor. Here and there a wounded man stretched his hands toward them with a piteous cry, and a low wailing, more dismal than the dreariest solitude, filled the air: it was the voice of the wounded, crying, "Water! water! For God's sake, water!"

The sun poured its glowing rays upon the miserable men, and tortured them with unappeasable thirst. Flocks of ravens spread their dark wings over them; their hoarse cries were blended with the moans of the wounded; they fixed their talons in the yet quivering limbs of the dying; while troops of dogs, allured by the smell of blood, had poured forth from the city to deepen the horrors of the scene.

As the men of Ghent roamed over the field, they sought those in whose bosoms were yet some pulses of life, and brought them with care into the camp. One band was employed to fetch water from the Gaver brook; and it was a piteous sight to watch the eagerness with which the wounded seized it, and with what gratitude, with what glistening eyes, they welcomed the refreshing draft.

The soldiers had received orders to bring every knight they found killed or wounded, into the camp. They had already recovered more than half of the slain, and had traversed a considerable extent of the field of battle. As they drew near the place where the strife had been most deadly, they found the dead more numerous. They were busily removing the helmet of Messire van Machelen, when they heard close at hand a low moan, which seemed to issue from the ground. They listened, but all was still again; not one of the bodies around gave the faintest token of life. Suddenly the moan was repeated; it came from a little distance, from between two prostrate horses. After many efforts, they succeeded in drawing one of the horses aside, and found the knight from whom the sound proceded. He was lying stretched out across the bodies, and drenched in the blood of many of the foe. His armor was indented and broken by the tread of horses; his right hand still convulsively grasped his sword, while in his left was a green veil. His pallid features bore the impress of approaching death, and he gazed on his deliverers with restless wandering looks. John Borluut recognized in a moment the unfortunate Adolf van Nieuwland. They loosened in haste the joints of his mail, raised his head gently, and moistened his lips with water. His failing voice murmured some unintelligible words, and his eyes closed as if his soul had at length taken its flight from his tortured body. The cool breeze and the refreshing water had overpowered him; and he lost for some moments all consciousness. When he at length opened his eyes, like one whose life was ebbing fast, he pressed Borluut's hand,

and said—so slowly, that between each word there was a long pause:

"I am dying. You see it, Messire John; my soul can not linger much longer on earth. But bewail me not; I die contented, for our fatherland is delivered—is free—"

His voice here failed him. His breath grew shorter; his head drooped; he slowly brought the green veil to his lips, and imprinted on it a last kiss. This done, he lost all consciousness, and fell apparently lifeless in the arms of John Borluut. Yet his heart continued to beat, and the warmth of his body betokened remaining life; so that the captain of Ghent did not altogether abandon hope, but conveyed the wounded knight to the camp with the tenderest care.

Matilda had taken refuge in a cell of the Abbey of Gröningen during the battle, whither she was accompanied by Adolf's sister. Her terror and anxiety were extreme; her relatives, her beloved Adolf—all were in that fearful conflict. On the issue of this contest, waged by the Flemings against so overwhelming a foe, hung the freedom of her father; this field of battle would either win again for him the throne of Flanders, or forever crumble it to dust. Were the French victorious, she knew that the death of all she loved was inevitable, and that some horrible doom awaited herself. As the war-trumpets echoed over the field, both maidens shuddered and grew pale, as if in that sound the stroke of death had descended on them. Their terror was too great to be expressed in words; they fell on their knees, buried their faces in their hands, and hot tears streamed down their cheeks. And thus they lay in fervent prayer, motionless, almost lifeless, as though sunk in heavy slumber, while from time to time a deep groan broke from their crushed hearts. As they caught the distant sounds of the fight, Maria sighed:

"O God Almighty, Lord God of Hosts, have mercy on us! Bring us help in this our hour of need, O Lord!"

And Matilda's gentle voice continued:

"O loving Jesus, Redeemer of men, shield him! Call him not to Thee, O Jesus most merciful! Holy Mother of God, pray for us! O Mother of Christ, consolation of the afflicted, pray for him!"

Then the roar of battle came nearer, and filled their hearts with fresh alarms; and their hands shook like the tender leaves of the aspen tree. Deeper sank their heads upon their breasts, their tears flowed more abundantly, and their prayers were murmured with fainter voice; for terror had paralyzed all their energies.

The strife lasted long; the appalling cry of the troops, as they fought hand to hand, resounded through the lonely cell. For long hours those low-whispered prayers went forth; and still they prayed, when the golden knight knocked at the abbey-gate. The sound of heavy footsteps caused them to turn their eyes toward the door, and they were still and motionless with sweet anticipation.

"Adolf comes again!" sighed Maria. "Oh, our prayer is heard!"

Matilda listened with greater eagerness, and replied in tones of sadness:

"No, no, it is not Adolf; his step is not so heavy. Oh Maria, it may be a herald of evil tidings!"

The door of the cell turned on its hinges, a nun opened it; and the golden knight entered. Matilda's tender frame trembled with fear; she raised her eyes doubtfully and timidly to the stranger who stood before her and opened his arms to her. It seemed to her a delusive dream; but her agitation was fleeting as the lightning which flashes and is gone; she rushed eagerly forward, and was clasped in her father's arms.

"My father!" she exclaimed; "my beloved father! do I see you again free—your chains broken? Let me press you to my heart. O God, how good Thou art! Do not turn away your face, dearest father; let me taste all my bliss."

Robert de Bethune embraced his loving daughter with unutterable joy; and when their hearts at length beat more tranquilly, he laid his helmet and gloves of steel on the low stool on which Matilda had been kneeling. Wearied by his exertions, he sank into a couch. Matilda threw her arms around him, gazing with admiration and awe on him whose face had been ever to her so full of consolation and strength—on him whose noble blood flowed in her veins, and who loved her so deeply and tenderly; and she listened with beating heart to the words which that beloved voice murmured in her ear.

"Matilda," said he, "my noble child, God has long proved us with suffering: but now our sorrows are ended; Flanders is free—is avenged. The Black Lion has torn the Lilies to pieces, and the aliens are discomfited and driven back. Dismiss every fear; the vile mercenaries of Joanna of Navarre are no more."

The maiden listened with agonized attention to the words of her father. She looked at him with a peculiar expression; she could but faintly smile. Joy had come so suddenly upon her that she seemed deprived of all power and speech. After a few moments, she observed that her father had ceased speaking, and she said:

"O my God, our fatherland is free! The French are defeated and slain; and you, my father, I possess you once more. We shall go back again to our beautiful Wynandael. Sorrow shall no more cloud your days; and I shall pass my life joyfully and happily in your arms. This is beyond hope—beyond all that I have dared to ask of God in my prayers."

"Listen attentively, my child; and be calm, I beseech you; this day I must leave you again. The noble knight who released me from my bonds has my word of honor that I would return as soon as the battle was over."

The maiden's head sank again upon her breast, and she sighed, in bitter grief:

"They will put you to a cruel death, oh my poor father!"

"Do not be so fearful, Matilda," continued Robert; "my brother Guy has taken sixty French knights of noblest blood prisoners; Philip the Fair will be told that their lives are hostages for mine; and he can not allow the brave survivors of his army to be offered up as victims to his vengeance. Flanders is now more powerful than France. So I implore you dry your tears. Rejoice, for a blessed future awaits us; I will restore Castle Wynandael again, that we may live in it as in days gone by. Then we shall again enjoy the chase, with our falcons on our wrist. Can you not imagine how merry our first hunting party will be?"

An inexpressibly sweet smile and a fervent kiss were Matilda's answer. But on a sudden a thought of pain seemed to cross her mind; for her countenance was overspread with gloom, and she bent her eyes on the ground, like one who is overcome by shame.

Robert looked at her inquiringly, and asked:

"Matilda, my child, why is your countenance so suddenly overcast with sadness?"

The maiden only half raised her eyes, and answered with a low voice:

"But—my father—you say nothing of Adolf—why did he not come with you?"

There was a slight pause before Robert replied. He discerned that, unknown to herself, a profound feeling was slumbering in Matilda's heart; therefore it was not without design he answered her thus:

"Adolf is detained by his duty, my child; fugitives are scattered over the plain, and I believe he is pursuing them. I may say to you, Matilda, that our friend Adolf is the most valiant and the most noble knight I know. Never have I seen more manliness and intrepidity. Twice he saved the life of my brother Guy; beneath the banner-royal of France the enemy fell in numbers beneath his sword; all the knights are repeating his praises, and ascribe to him a large share in the deliverance of Flanders."

While Robert was uttering these words, he kept his eye fixed on his daughter, and scrutinized every emotion that flitted across her expressive features. He read therein a mingled pride and rapture, and had no further doubt that his conjecture was well founded. Maria, the while, stood with her eyes fixed on Robert, and drank in with eager joy the praises which he bestowed so lavishly on her brother.

While Matilda was gazing on her father in a transport of bliss, there was heard suddenly a confused noise of voices in the court of the monastery. After a few moments all was again still; then the door of the cell opened, and Guy entered slowly, and with a disturbed countenance; he came near to his brother, and said:

"A great disaster has betallen us, my brother, in the loss of one who is most dear to us all; the men of Ghent found him on the field of battle, lying under a heap of slain, and they have brought him here into the monastery. His life trembles on his lips, and I think the hour of his death can not be very distant. He anxiously begs to see you once more ere he quits this world; wherefore I pray you, my brother, grant him this last favor." Then, turning to Maria, he continued: "He desires to see you also, noble maiden."

One cry of bitter anguish broke from the hearts of both maidens. Matilda fell lifeless into her father's arms; and Maria flew to the door, and rushed from the chamber in an agony of despair. Their cries brought two nuns into the cell, who took charge of the unhappy Matilda; her father stooped and kissed her, and turned to visit the dying Adolf; when the maiden, perceiving his intention, tore herself from the arms of the nuns, and clinging to her father, cried:

"Let me go with you, my father; let me see him once more! Woe, woe is me! what a sharp sword pierces my heart! My father, I shall die with him; I feel already the approach of death. I must see him: come, come speedily; he is dying! Oh, Adolf! Adolf!"

Robert gazed on his daughter with tender compassion; he could not doubt now the existence of that secret feeling which had slowly and quietly taken root in his daughter's heart. The discovery gave him no pain, caused him no displeasure; unable to comfort her with words, he pressed her to his heart. But Matilda disengaged herself from these tender bonds, and drew Robert toward the door, crying:

"Oh, my father, have pity on me! Come, that I may once more hear the voice of my good brother, that his eyes may look on me once more before he dies."

She knelt down at his feet, and continued, amid burning tears:

"I implore you, do not reject my petition; hear me; grant it, my lord and my father."

Robert would have preferred leaving his daughter in the care of the nuns; for he feared, with reason, that the sight of the dying knight would completely overwhelm her; yet he could not deny her urgent prayers; he took her, therefore, by the hand, and said:

"Be it so, my daughter; go with me, and visit the unfortunate Adolf. But, I pray you, disturb him not by your grief; think that God has this day bestowed on us a great mercy, and that He may be justly provoked to anger by your despair."

Ere these words were ended they had left the cell. Adolf had been brought into the refectory of the monastery, and laid carefully on a feather-bed upon the floor. A priest, well skilled in the healing art, had examined him with care, and found no open wound; long blue stripes indicated the blows he had received, and in many places were large bruises and contusions. He was bled; and then his body was carefully washed, and a restorative balsam applied. Through the care of the skilful priest he had recovered a measure of strength: but yet he seemed at the point of death, although his eyes were no longer so dull and lustreless. Around his bed stood many knights in deep silence, mourning for their friend. John van Renesse, Arnold van Oudenarde, and Peter Deconinck assisted the priest in his operations; William van Gulick, John Borluut, and Baldwin van Papenrode stood at the left hand of the couch, while Guy, Jan Breydel, and the other more illustrious knights, gazed on the wounded man with their heads bowed low in sorrow and in sympathy.

Maria was kneeling weeping near her brother; she had seized his hand, and was bedewing it with her tears, while Adolf bent on her an unsteady and almost vacant look. As Robert and his daughter entered the refectory, the knights were all struck with wonder and emotion. He who had come in their hour of need, their mysterious deliverer, was the Lion of Flanders, their Count! They all bowed before him with profound reverence, and said:

"Honor to the Lion, our Lord!"

Robert left his daughter's hand, raised Messires John Borluut and Van Renesse from the ground, and kissed both of them on the cheek; he then beckoned to the other knights to rise, and addressed them thus:

"My true and loyal vassals, my friends, you have shown me to-day how mighty is a nation of heroes! I wear my coronet now with a loftier pride than that with which Philip the Fair wears the crown of France; for of you I may well boast and glory."

He then approached Adolf, took his hand, and looked at him for some time in silence; a tear glistened awhile beneath each eyelid of the Lion, and at length dropped—a pearl of price—upon the ground. Matilda was kneeling at the head of Adolf's couch; she had taken her green veil from his hand; and her tears fell hot and fast upon this token of her affection, and of his self-sacrifice and devotedness. She spoke not a word; she did not even steal a look at Adolf; but covered her face with her hands, and wept bitterly.

The priest, too, stood motionless, his eyes steadily fastened on the wounded knight. He marked some wonderful change passing over his features; something which, increasing every moment, spoke of returning life and vigor. And in truth his eyes had lost their fixed and glassy expression, and his countenance no longer bore the signs of approaching death. Soon he raised his eyes to Robert, with a look of intense love and devotion; and said slowly, and with a voice broken by suffering and weakness:

"Oh, my lord and Count! your presence is to me a sweet consolation. Now I can die in peace— Our fatherland is free! You will occupy the Lion's throne in peaceful and happy days— Gladly do I now quit this earth, now that the future promises so much happiness to you and to your noble daughter. Oh, believe me, in this my hour of death, your mischances were more grievous to me, your unworthy servant, than to yourself. Often have I, in the still night, moistened my bed with my tears, as I thought of the mournful lot of the noble Matilda, and of your captivity—" Then turning his head slightly toward Matilda, he made her tears flow yet more abundantly, as he said:

"Weep not, noble maiden; I merit not this tender compassion. There is another life than this! There it is my hope and trust I shall see my good sister again. Remain on earth, the stay and solace of your father's old age; and sometimes in your prayers think of your brother, who must quit you—"

Suddenly he stopped, and looked around him in astonishment.

"Merciful God!" cried he, turning an inquiring look on the priest, "what means this? I feel a renewed vigor; my blood flows more freely in my veins!"

Matilda arose at these words, and gazed at him in painful expectation. All looked anxiously and inquiringly at the priest, who had been attentively watching Adolf during this scene, and noting his most fleeting expression and emotion. He took Adolf's hand and felt his pulse, while all the by-standers followed his every movement with eager curiosity; and at length they read in the good priest's countenance that he had not abandoned all hope of restoring the wounded knight. The skilful leech opened the eyelids of his patient in silence, and attentively examined his eyes; he opened his mouth, and passed his hand over his uncovered breast; and then turning to the knights around the couch, he said, in a tone of decided conviction:

"I can now assure you, Messires, that the fever

which threatened the life of the youthful knight has subsided: he will not die."

A sensible tremor passed over all present, and one might have thought the priest had uttered a doom of death; but soon this convulsive thrill was succeeded by a bounding joy, which broke forth in words and gestures.

Maria had answered the assurance of the priest with a piercing cry, and clasped her brother to her breast; while Matilda fell on her knees, raised her hands toward Heaven, and cried with a loud voice:

"I thank Thee, O God all-merciful, full of compassion, that Thou hast heard the prayers of Thine unworthy handmaiden!"

And after this brief thanksgiving she sprang up, and threw herself, tremulous with joy, into her father's arms.

"He will live! he will not die!" she exclaimed, in a transport of gladness. "Oh, now I am happy!" and she rested a moment exhausted on Robert's breast. But soon she turned again eagerly back to Adolf, and exchanged words of joy and gratitude with him.

What appeared a miracle to all present was but a natural result of Adolf's condition. He had received no open nor deep wound, but many bruises; the pain which these occasioned him had induced a violent fever, which threatened his life; but the presence of Matilda seemed to have brought the malady to a crisis, and, by imparting fresh energy to his soul, gave him strength to battle with it, and, as it were, to cast it off; and thus did she appear as an angel of life to rescue him from the grave, which already yawned to receive him.

Robert de Bethune allowed his daughter, who was beside herself with joy, to remain kneeling by Adolf's side; and, advancing toward the knights, he addressed them in these words:

"You, noble sons of Flanders, have this day won a victory, the memory whereof shall live among your children's children as a record of your lofty prowess; you have shown the whole world how dearly the alien has expiated his temerity in setting his foot on the soil of the Lion. The love of your fatherland has exalted you into heroes; and your arms, nerved by a most righteous vengeance, have laid the tyrant low. Freedom is a precious thing in the esteem of those who have sealed it with their heart's blood. Henceforth no prince of the South shall enslave us more; you would all rather die a thousand deaths than allow the alien to sing over you a song of triumph. Now this fear exists no longer. Flanders is this day exalted high above all other lands; and this glory she owes to you, most noble knights! And now our will is, that rest and peace should recompense the loyalty of our subjects; our highest joy will be that all should greet us by the name of father, so far as our loving care and unsleeping vigilance can render us worthy of this title. Nevertheless, should the French dare to return, again would we be the Lion of Flanders, and again should our battle-ax lead you on to the conflict. And now let our victory be unstained by further violence; above all, pursue not the Lilyards; it behooveth us to protect even their rights. For the present I must leave you; until my return, I pray you obey my brother Guy as your liege lord and count."

"What! speak you of leaving?" cried the skeptical John Borluut; "you are surely not going back to France! They will avenge their defeat on you, noble count."

"Messires," said Robert, "let me ask you, who is there among you who would, from fear of death, break his word of honor and stain his knighthood's loyalty?"

All at once hung their heads, and uttered not a word. They saw with sorrow that they dared not oppose their count's return. He continued:

"Messire Deconinck, your lofty wisdom has been of essential service to us, and we hope to task it still further; you are now a member of our council, and I require you to live with us in our castle. Messire Breydel, your valor and fidelity merit a great reward; I appoint you commander-in-chief of all your fellow-citizens who may be able to assist us in time of war; I know how well this office beseems you. Moreover, you henceforth belong to our court, and will dwell there whenever it pleases you. And you, Adolf—you, my friend, deserve a yet richer recompense. We have all been witnesses of your prowess; you have approved yourself worthy of the noble name of your forefathers. I have not forgotten your self-devotion; I know with what care, with what love, you have protected and consoled my unhappy child; I know the pure, the profound feeling that has taken root and sprung up, unconsciously to yourselves, in the hearts of you both; and shall I allow you to outstrip me in noble generosity? Let the illustrious blood of the Counts of Flanders mingle its stream with that of the noble lords of Nieuwland, and let the Black Lion add its glories to your shield. I give you my beloved child, my Matilda, to wife."

From Matilda's heart burst one only word—the name of Adolf. Trembling violently, she seized his hand, and looked steadfastly in his eyes; then she wept precious tears, tears of joy, joy impetuous and overwhelming. The youthful knight uttered not a word; his bliss was too great, too profound, too sacred to be expressed in words. He raised his eyes, beaming with love, on Matilda; then turned them, full of gratitude, to Robert; and then upward in adoration to God.

For some little time a noise had been heard in the courtyard of the monastery; and it seemed as though a large crowd of people were gathered there. The tumult waxed greater and greater, and at intervals was heard a mighty shout of joy. A nun brought the tidings that a great multitude stood at the abbey gate, and demanded, with repeated cries, to see the golden knight. As the door of the hall was opened, Robert caught distinctly the cry:

"Flanders! the Lion! hail to our deliverer! hail! hail!"

Robert turned to the nun, and said:

"Tell them that the golden knight, whom they demand to see, will appear among them in a few moments."

Then he approached the sick knight, seized his yet feeble hand, and said:

"Adolf van Nieuwland, my beloved Matilda will be your wife. May the blessing of the Almighty rest upon your heads, and give to your children the valor of their father and the virtues of their mother! You have merited yet more than this; but I have no more precious gift to bestow on you than the child who might have been the solace and the stay of my declining age."

While words of heartfelt gratitude flowed from Adolf's lips, Robert hastily approached Guy, and said:

"My dear brother, it is my wish that the marriage should take place as soon as possible, with all fitting magnificence, and with the customary religious ceremonies. Messires, I am about to leave you, with a hope that I shall soon return to you, free and unshackled, to labor for the happiness of my faithful subjects."

After these words, he again drew near to Adolf, and kissed him on the cheek:

"Farewell, my son," he said.

And pressing Matilda to his heart:

"Farewell, my darling Matilda. Weep no more for me; I am happy now that our fatherland is avenged; and I shall soon return again."

He then embraced his brother Guy, William van Gulick, and some other knights, his especial friends. He pressed with deep emotion the hands of all the others, and exclaimed as he took his departure:

"Farewell, farewell all, noble sons of Flanders, my true brothers-in-arms!"

In the courtyard he mounted his horse and resumed his armor; then he lowered his vizor, and rode through the gateway. A countless multitude was there assembled; and as soon as they caught sight of the golden knight, they drew back on both sides to make way for him, and greeted him with exulting acclamations.

"Hail to the golden knight! victory! victory! Hail to our deliverer!"

They clapped their hands, they gathered the

earth he trod, and kept it as a sacred relic; for in their simplicity they believed that St. George, who had been invoked during the battle in every church of Courtrai, had come to their aid in this majestic form. The slow measured tread of the knight, and his deep silence, confirmed them in their belief; and many fell on their knees as he passed by them. They followed him for more than a league into the country, and it seemed as if their gaze of veneration could never be satiated; for the longer they gazed, the more wonderful did the golden knight appear in their eyes. Their fancy lent him the form and features wherewith the saints are wont to be depicted; one sign from Robert would have laid them in the dust prostrate and adoring.

At length he gave his horse the spur, and vanished like an arrow into the wood. The people strove long to catch the gleam of his golden armor between the trees—but in vain; his charger had borne him far beyond the range of their vision; and then they looked sadly on each other and said with a sigh:

"He has gone back to heaven again!"

CHAPTER IX

OF the sixty thousand men whom Philip the Fair had sent to lay waste Flanders, only seven thousand succeeded in returning to France. Guy de St. Pol had gathered five thousand men at Lille, and hoped to march them safely to France: but a division of the Flemish army fell on them, and after an obstinate conflict nearly all who had fled from Courtrai were overcome and slain. The "excellente Chronike" tells us:

"And the number of those who fled and escaped may have been in all about three thousand men, sole remains of the enormous host which had gone forth to plunder and lay waste Flanders: and these had a tale to tell at home which was far from being edifying or joyous."

All the most illustrious nobles and bravest knights were slain at Courtrai. There was scarcely a castle of France where there was not wailing and lamentation for the death of a husband, a father, or a brother. The Flemish generals took care that the fallen kings and knights should receive honorable burial in the abbey of Gröningen, as appears from an ancient painting still to be seen in St. Michael's Church at Courtrai. There is also in the Museum of Messire Goethals-Vercruyssen at Courtrai a stone which once lay on the grave of King Sigis; it bears his arms, and the following inscription:

"In the year of our Lord MCCCII, on St. Benedict's day, was fought the battle of Courtrai. Under this stone lies buried King Sigis. Pray God for his soul! Amen."

Besides the vessels of gold, costly stuffs, and rich armor, there were found on the battle-field more than *seven hundred golden spurs*, which knights alone had the privilege of wearing; these were suspended with the captured banners from the vault of our Lady's church at Courtrai, and thence this battle acquired the name of *"The Battle of the Golden Spurs."* Several thousand horses also fell into the hands of the Flemings, who used them with great effect in subsequent battles. In front of the gate of Courtrai which opens toward Ghent, in the centre of the battle-field, there was in the year 1831 a chapel of our Lady of Gröningen; on its altar were to be deciphered the names of the French knights who had fallen in the fight, and one of the genuine old spurs of gold was still suspended from the vault. In Courtrai the anniversary of the battle was kept as a day of public rejoicing, and its memory still lingers in a Kermes, which is called the Vergaderdagen, or day of gathering. Every year in the month of July, the poor of Courtrai go from house to house begging for old clothes, which they sell in commemoration of the sale of the rich booty of 1302. Then, accompanied by a player on the violin, they betake themselves to the Pottelberg, the old camp of the French, and drink and dance until evening.

When tidings of this terrible defeat reached France, the whole court was filled with consternation and grief. Philip burst into a furious passion with Joanna of Navarre, whose evil counsels were the cause of all these disasters, and of all their consequences; and his reproaches may be read in some quaint contemporary verses by Lodwyk van Vilthem. The historians of France, indeed, have described Joanna in much brighter colors; but it is an amiable peculiarity of their national character to handle very indulgently the vices of their monarchs, at least of their *dead* monarchs; and it is an undoubted truth that the Flemish chronicles give a far more trustworthy description of the odious disposition of Queen Joanna.

The magistrates of Ghent, who were all Lilyards, and thought that King Philip would send a fresh expedition into Flanders with all haste, closed their gates, intending to hold out their city as long as possible for France. But they met their punishment at the hands of the men of Ghent themselves. The people rushed to arms, the magistrates and every other Lilyard were put to death, and Guy received the keys of the city, and with them a pledge of everlasting fidelity, from the hands of the principal citizens.

Meanwhile Count John of Namur, brother of Robert de Bethune, returned to Flanders and assumed the government; he collected in haste a new and far larger army, to resist any further attempt on the part of the French, and restored order everywhere. Without allowing his troops any repose, he marched to Lille, where some disturbances had broken out; thence he proceeded to Douay, which he captured, taking the garrison prisoners; and Cassel yielded after a very brief resistance. After taking some other garrisons of lesser note he was obliged to return; for not an enemy remained on the soil of Flanders; and as he deemed a small band of picked soldiers sufficient for all purposes of defense, he disbanded his army.

The land was still and at rest; trade and commerce flourished with renewed vigor; the wasted fields were sown with better hope of a bounteous harvest, and it seemed as though Flanders had acquired new life and new strength. Men thought with reason that the lesson France had received was sufficient. Philip the Fair himself had, in fact, little desire to renew the strife; but the reproaches which burst from all France, the lamentations of the knights whose brothers had fallen at Courtrai, and, above all, the instigations of Joanna, who thirsted for revenge, compelled him at length to declare war. He collected a force of eighty thousand men, among whom were twenty thousand cavalry; but it was far inferior to the former army, inasmuch as it consisted chiefly of mercenaries, or of recruits levied by force. The command was entrusted to Louis, King of Navarre; he was instructed, before venturing on a general action, to take Douay and other French frontier towns from the Flemings; and with this commission, he pitched his camp in a plain near Vitry, a few miles from Douay.

No sooner did the Flemings hear that a fresh army was being assembled in France than the cry "To arms!" resounded through the length and breadth of the land. Never was so universal and so intense an enthusiasm known; from every village the inhabitants poured forth with weapons of all kinds; on they came, singing and shouting in such numbers that John of Namur was obliged to send many of them back to their abodes, fearing that it would be impossible to provide for so enormous a host. Those who had formerly been Lilyards longed now to wipe out the stain, and implored, with tears in their eyes, to be allowed a part in the conflict; and this was readily granted them. Besides John of Namur, most of the knights who had shared the glories of Courtrai repaired to the army. Guy, William van Gulick, John van Renesse, John Borluut, Peter Deconinck, Jan Breydel, and many others, were among them. Adolf van Nieuwland had not yet recovered from his wounds, and could not therefore accompany them.

The Flemings marched against the enemy in two divisions, and at first took up a position about three leagues from the French camp; but they soon advanced to the Scarpe, a small river near Flines. The Flemings daily challenged the French; but as the generals on both sides wished to avoid an action, day after day passed on without any result. The cause of this pacific attitude was, that John of Namur had sent ambassadors to France to treat with the king for the liberation of the old Count and of Robert, and to conclude, if possible, a treaty of peace. But the French court could not agree on the terms to be proposed or accepted, and the answer was unfavorable.

The Flemings meanwhile began to murmur, and longed to fall on the French, in spite of the prohibition of their general; and the discontent became at last so alarming, that John of Namur was compelled to cross the Scarpe and attack the enemy. A bridge of five boats was thrown across the stream, and the Flemish army passed over, singing and shouting with joy that they were at length going to fight; but an ambiguous message from France kept them still for some days longer on the further side of the river. At length the army would be no longer restrained, and the murmurs threatened to become serious. Everything was ready for the attack, and the army was put in motion; when the French, not daring to meet it, hastily broke up their camp, and retreated in confusion. The Flemings put themselves in pursuit, and slew a great number of them; they possessed themselves beside of the castle of Harne, where the King of Navarre had taken up his quarters. Their stores, tents, and everything the French army had brought with them, fell into the hands of the Flemings; and after a few insignificant skirmishes, the French were driven back into France overwhelmed with disgrace.

When the Flemish generals saw that no enemy remained in the open field, they disbanded a part of their force, and retained only as many soldiers as were necessary to keep the French frontier garrisons in check, and to prevent their plundering expeditions.

For a long time there were occasional battles and enterprises of lesser importance and of various success. At length Philip collected a third army to avenge the defeat of Courtrai. The command was given to Walter de Chatillon, and he was instructed, on his arrival in Flanders, to take with him all the troops in garrison on the frontier, which would make his army far more than one hundred thousand strong.

Philip, one of the sons of the old Count of Flanders, had inherited the territories of Tyetta and Loretto in Italy. As soon as he heard of the French levy, he hastened to Flanders with his troops, and was appointed by his brothers to the chief command of the army. He assembled about fifty thousand men, and marched on St. Omer to await the French assault.

The two armies soon met; for two days there were only some lesser actions, in one of which, however, Peter de Coutrenel, one of the French generals, fell, with his sons and many of his soldiers. Walter dared not stake all on a decisive battle; in the night he decamped, and marched on Utrecht; and this so quietly, that the Flemings knew nothing of his departure, until they opened their eyes with astonishment in the morning on a vacant encampment. Philip then took by storm several French towns, and the army returned laden with spoil.

The King of France saw at length that it was impossible to subjugate Flanders by force of arms, and sent Amadeus of Savoy to Philip with proposals of peace. The children of the captive Count were eager for the liberation of their father and brother, and inclined gladly to peace; they therefore smoothed all difficulties, and a truce was proclaimed, which was to last until a treaty of peace should be signed by both parties. This was framed at the French court, and contained many articles much to the disadvantage of the Flemings; but Philip the Fair hoped to obtain its acceptance by cunning. He liberated the old Count of Flanders, and allowed him to depart, on his word of honor that he would return to his prison in the following May, if he did not obtain the recognition of the treaty in all its articles.

Count Guy was received in Flanders with the utmost rejoicing, and returned to Wynandael. But when he read the treaty to the assembled states, it was rejected; and the old Count saw himself obliged to return, like another Regulus, to France in the following April. During the truce, Philip the Fair had made every exertion to collect a mighty army. Mercenaries were everywhere enlisted, and heavy taxes imposed to meet the expenses of the war. The king himself marched with the army to the Flemish frontier toward the end of June. Besides the land forces, a large fleet, commanded by Renier Grimaldi of Genoa, sailed along the coast of Flanders, to attack the young Guy and John van Renesse in Zeeland.

Philip of Flanders had meanwhile sent forth his proclamation through the land, and gathered a valiant army around his standard; and with these he marched to give battle to the enemy. On the first day there was a partial engagement, in which one of the French generals was slain, with many of his men. The next day the Flemings stood drawn up eager for the fight, and prepared for an impetous attack; but the French were again panic-stricken, and fled to Utrecht, leaving their camp a prey to the Flemings. Then Philip a second time stormed Bassé, and burnt the suburbs of the city of Lens.

The king next resolved to attack Flanders on the side of Henegauw, and marched toward Doornyk; but the very first day the Flemings had overtaken him. He was the less willing to accept battle, that he had received no tidings of his fleet; and in order to avoid an engagement, he broke up his camp in the night, and fled from place to place, closely pursued by the Flemings.

The action between the two fleets was fought on the 10th of August, 1304; it lasted two whole days from morning to night. The first day the Flemings had the advantage, and would certainly have gained a total victory, had not some of their ships been driven on a sand-bank in the night. This gave the French a great superiority of force, so that they gained the battle with little difficulty, burnt all the ships, and even took the young Guy prisoner. John van Renesse, the valiant Zeelander, who was in garrison at Utrecht, wishing to leave the city, attempted to cross the river in a small barge. The barge was unhappily overladen; it sank in the middle of the stream, and the noble warrior was drowned.

When the news of the happy issue of the sea-fight reached the French camp, it was posted near Lille, on the Peuvelberg. Advantageous as the position was, Philip quitted it; and it was immediately taken possession of by the Flemings. The latter would no longer delay the action; the generals found it impossible to restrain their ardor, and so they drew them up in order for an attack. Philip the Fair no sooner saw this, than he sent a herald with conditions of peace; but the Flemings would not hear of peace, and struck the herald dead. They then fell with wild shouts, on the French army, which fled in astonishment and terror. The Flemings fought with even more intense bitterness of hatred than at Courtrai, and their commanding position helped them much. Philip of Flanders and William van Gulick pierced through the enemies' ranks, and reached the king himself, who was for a moment in extreme peril. His bodyguards were struck down at his side; and he would certainly have been taken, had not those who stood by removed his mantle and other insignia of royalty. He was thus enabled to escape unnoticed, with only a slight wound inflicted by an arrow.

The Flemings gained a complete victory; the oriflamme itself was seized and torn in

pieces. This battle was fought on the 15th of
August, 1304.

William van Gulick the priest lost his life in
this action. The Flemings were busy until evening pillaging the king's tent, and amassing incred-
ible spoil. They then returned to the Peuvelberg
to refresh themselves; and finding nothing there,
marched on to Lille. The day after they resumed
their march homeward.

Fourteen days after this, Philip the Fair came
again with a large army, and laid siege to Lille.
The citizens closed their shops, and seized their
weapons; and Philip of Flanders collected the
men of Courtrai, and marched them to Lille in a
few days. When the king saw their numbers, he
exclaimed:

"Methinks Flanders must spawn or rain soldiers."

He risked no further defeat; but, after some at-
tempts at evasion, proposed a peace, and meanwhile proclaimed a truce. It was long before
both sides could agree upon the terms of the treaty.
While it was pending, the old Count died in prison
at Compiègne, and was soon followed by Joanna
of Navarre.

Not long after the peace was concluded, and
the treaty signed by Philip the Fair and Philip of
Flanders, Robert de Bethune, with his two brothers
William and Guy, and all the captive knights,

were set at liberty, and returned to Flanders. The people, however, were not content with the articles of the treaty, and called it the "Treaty of Unrighteousness"; but their dissatisfaction had no further consequence at the time.

Robert de Bethune was received on his return to Flanders with surpassing magnificence, and publicly recognized as Count. He lived seventeen years after his liberation, upheld the honor and the renown of Flanders, and fell asleep in the Lord on the 18th of September, 1322.

THE END

FATE

LIFE OF COUPERUS

FROM Louis Marie Anne Couperus, now aged but forty-three, his masterpiece is yet to be expected. This is the opinion of several critics, among them Edmund Gosse, who, like his colleagues, thinks very highly of "Fate." The publication of this, his first novel, drew down upon Couperus the displeasure of Holland's religious papers; one of them alleged that the book in question was responsible for a young man's suicide, while others clamored for the institution of a national Index Expurgatorius, so that all such pernicious literature might be safely disposed of. "Eline Vere," a much longer story, was published a year later, namely, in 1892, and "Ecstasy" was brought out about the same time. In 1894 appeared "Majesty," which through its serial publication in the principal Dutch review, "De Nieuwe Gids," substantially improved the fortunes of that magazine. Curiously enough, the well-known French author Jules Lemaître coincidently wrote a novel on a similar theme, naming it "Kings." "Majesty" was followed by a double sequel, "Universal Peace" and "Primo Cartello," and in 1901 "Little Aims" was put into print.

Couperus's first literary endeavors did not, however, take the form of prose. His virgin volume, so to speak, was a collection of poems entitled "Orchids," presented to the Dutch public when the author was twenty-four years old. The fervent tone and glowing Oriental imagery of these verses one may partly attribute to the young man's early residence in the East Indies, at Batavia, where his father occupied an official post under the Dutch Government. It is said that the author of "Fate," who was born at The Hague on the 10th of June, 1863, is of Scottish ancestry, his surname being really a Latinized form of "Cowper."

FATE

CHAPTER I

His hands in his pockets, and the collar of his fur coat turned up, Frank was making his way one evening, through squalls of snow, along the deserted length of Adelaide Road. As he approached the villa where he lived—White-Rose Cottage, it was called—sunk, buried, wrapped in white snow, like a nest in cotton wool, he was aware of some one coming to meet him from Primrose Hill. He looked steadily in the man's face, since he evidently intended to address him, doubting as to what his purpose might be this lonely, snowy night, and he was greatly surprised when he heard said in Dutch:

"Pardon the intrusion. Are you not Mr. Westhove?"

"Yes," replied Frank Westhove. "Who are you? What do you want?"

"I am Robert van Maeren. You may perhaps remember—"

"What! you, Bertie?" cried Frank. "How came you here in London?"

Fate

And in his amazement there rose up before him, through the driving snow, a vision of his youth; a pleasing picture of boyish friendship, of something young and warm.

"Not altogether by chance," said the other, whose voice had taken a somewhat more confident tone at the sound of the familiar "Bertie." "I knew that you lived here, and I have been to your door three times; but you had not come in. Your maid said that you were expected at home this evening, so I made so bold as to wait here for you." And again his voice lost its firmness and assumed the imploring accent of a beggar.

"Is your business so urgent, then?" asked Frank in surprise.

"Yes. I want—perhaps you could help me. I know no one here—"

"Where are you living?"

"Nowhere. I only arrived here early this morning, and I have—I have no money."

He was shivering from standing in the cold during this short dialogue, and seemed to shrink into himself, almost fawning, like a cowed dog.

"Come in with me," said Frank, greatly astonished, but full of sympathy and of the affectionate reminiscences of his boyhood. "Come and spend the night with me."

"Oh, gladly!" was the reply, eager and tremulous, as if he feared that the heaven-inspired words might be retracted.

They went together a few steps further; then Frank took a key out of his pocket, the key of White-Rose Cottage. He opened the door; a hexagonal Moorish lantern was burning low, and shed a soft light in the hall.

"Go in," said Frank. And he locked the door and bolted it behind them. It was half-past twelve.

The maid had not yet gone to bed.

"That gentleman called here a little while ago, two or three times," she murmured, with a look of suspicion at Bertie. "And I have seen him hanging about all the evening, as if he was on the watch. I was frightened, do you know; it is so lonely in these parts."

Frank shook his head reassuringly.

"Make the fire up as quickly as possible, Annie. Is your husband still up?"

"The fire, sir?"

"Yes. Bertie, will you have something to eat?"

"Gladly, if it gives you no trouble," replied Bertie in English, for the benefit of the maid, and he looked with an insinuating expression to meet the surprised, cold blue eyes of the neat, brisk young woman. His voice was persuasive and low; he tried to take as little room as possible in the small hall; and to avoid her gaze, he seemed to shrink, to efface himself in a corner where the shadow fell.

Frank led the way into a large back room, cold and dark when they entered, but soon lighted up, and before long genially warmed by the huge fire which blazed up in the grate. Annie laid the table.

"Supper for one, sir?"

"Lay for two; I will eat something," said Frank, thinking that Bertie would feel more at his ease.

At his friend's invitation the visitor had seated himself in a large armchair by the fire, and there he sat, bolt upright, without speaking, feeling shy before the woman, who came and went. And now, in the light, Frank could see the poverty of his appearance; his thin, shabby coat, shining with grease and bereft of buttons; his worn, fringed trousers; his dirty comforter, hiding a lack of underlinen; his ripped and slipshod shoes. In his confusion and awkwardness he still held his battered hat. This garb accorded ill with the aristocratic elegance of his figure; the thin, pale, chiseled features, full of distinction in spite of the unkempt light hair and unshaven stubble of beard. It was like a masquerade of rank and culture in the rags of misery, beseeming it as ill as an unsuitable part in a play. And the actor sat motionless, staring into the fire, ill at ease in the atmosphere of luxury which surrounded him in this room, evidently the home of a young man of fortune, who had no yearnings for domestic society. The curtains and carpets were of handsome quality, so were the furniture and ornaments, but arranged without any reference to comfort; the chairs and tables against the wall, stiff and orderly, and shining with polish. But it did not make this impression on Bertie, for a sense of the blessedness of warmth and shelter possessed him wholly; of peace and reprieve, as calm as a lake and as delightful as an oasis—a smiling prospect after the snow and cold of the last few hours. And when he saw that Frank was gazing at him in visible wonder at his motionless attitude by the glorious fire, where the dancing flames flew up like yellow dragons' tongues, at last he smiled, and said with humble gratitude in the tone of a beggar:

"Thank you very much—this is good—"

Annie had not much to set before them: the remains from the larder of a young fellow who lives chiefly away from home—a bit of cold beefsteak and salad, some biscuits and jam; but it bore some resemblance to a supper, and Bertie did it full honor, eating and drinking with systematic deliberateness, hardly conscious of what; and imbibing hot grog without confessing the hunger which had nipped his very vitals. At length Frank tried to make him speak, drew him into talk, and into telling him what had reduced him to such misery. Bertie told his tale in a fragmentary fashion, very abjectly, every word sounding like a petition:

Disputes with his father about his mother's fortune—a trifle of a few thousand gulden quickly spent; vicissitudes in America, where he had been by turns a farm-servant, a waiter in a hotel, and a *super* on the stage; his return to Europe on board a liner, working out his passage in every variety of service; his first day in London—without a cent. He remembered Westhove's address from letters bearing date of some years back, and had at once made his way to White-Rose Cottage, only fearing that meanwhile Frank might have moved half a dozen times, and left no traces—

Oh! his anxiety that night, waiting in the cold wind, while it grew darker and darker; the gloom, with no relief but the ghostly whiteness of the deathly silent snow! And now, the warmth, the shelter, and food! And again he thanked his friend, cowering, shriveled, in his threadbare clothes.

"Thank you, thank you—"

Annie, sulky over so much trouble at this hour of the night, and for such a vagabond brought in from the street, had nevertheless prepared a bedroom. And Frank led him upstairs, shocked by his exhausted appearance and ashy paleness. He patted him on the shoulder, promising to help him; but now he must go to bed—to-morrow they would see what could be done.

When Bertie found himself alone he looked about him. The room was very comfortable; the bed ample, soft, and warm. He felt himself squalid and dirty, amid such surroundings of luxury; and by a natural instinct of decency and cleanliness, though his teeth were chattering with cold, he first carefully and elaborately washed himself—lathering, rubbing, brushing—till his whole body was rosy and glowing, and smelling of soapsuds. He looked in the glass, and only regretted that he had no razors; he would have shaved. At last, having slipped on a nightshirt which lay ready for use, he crept in between the blankets. He did not immediately fall asleep, reveling in the comfort, in his own purification, in the whiteness of the sheets, the warmth of the quilt; in the gleam of the nightlight even, which showed discreetly through a green shade. A smile came into his eyes and parted his lips—and he was asleep; without a thought of the morrow. Happy in the respite of to-day, and the warmth of the bed, his mind almost vacant, indeed, but for the single recurring thought that Frank was really a good fellow!

CHAPTER II

NEXT morning there was a hard frost; the snow glittered like crystals. They had breakfasted, and Bertie was relating his disasters in America. He had been trimmed and shaved by Frank's barber, and he was wearing Frank's clothes, which were "a world too wide" for him, and a pair of slippers in which his feet were lost. He already felt more at home and began to bask, like a cat which has found a warm spot of sunshine. He lounged at his ease in the armchair, smoking comfortably, and was on the old familiar terms with Frank. His voice was soft and mellow, with a ring of full content, like an alloy of gold. Westhove was interested, and let him tell his story in his own way; and he did so very simply, without making any secret of his poverty; but everything had happened inevitably, and could not have turned out otherwise. He was no favorite of fortune, that was all. But he was tough; many another would not have pulled through as he had.

Frank looked at him in astonishment; he was so frail, so pale, so delicate, almost devoid of all manly development; he was lost in the grotesque amplitude of Frank's coat and trousers—a mere stripling as compared with his own stalwart, angular frame! And he had gone through days of hunger, nights without a shelter, a depth of poverty which to Frank—well fed and ruddy with vigorous health—seemed unendurable; and he spoke of it so coolly, almost jestingly; without complaining, only looking with regretful pity at his hands, which were thin, and blue with the biting cold, and chapped and raw about the knuckles. At the moment the state of his hands seemed to be the only thing that troubled him. A very happy nature, thought Frank, while he laughed at him for his concern about his hands.

But Bertie himself was shocked at his own heedlessness, for he suddenly exclaimed:

"But what am I to do—what am I to do?"

He gazed into vacancy, helpless and desperate, wringing his hands. Frank laughed him out of his despair, poured him out a glass of sherry, and told him that for the present he must stay where he was, to recover. He himself would be heartily glad of Bertie's company for a few weeks; he was a little sick of his wealthy bachelor life; he belonged to a circle of idlers, who went out a great deal, and spent a great deal, and he was tired of it all—dinners and balls in the world, and suppers and orgies in the half-world. It was always the same thing; a life like a *Montagne Russe,* down

and then up again, down and then up again, without a moment for thought; an existence made for
you, in the position you made for yourself. At
the moment he had but one anxiety; Bertie himself. Frank would help him, after a few weeks'
rest, to find an appointment, or some employment;
but, above all, he was not to worry himself for
the present. Westhove was glad to have his old
friend under his roof. Memories rose up before
him like dissolving views, pale-hued and swift,
but appealing to his sympathy—memories of his
school-days, of boyish mischief, zigzag excursions,
picnics among the sand-hills near The Hague—
did Bertie remember? Frank could see him still,
the slight, fragile lad, bullied by louts, protected
by himself—Frank—whose fists were always ready
to hit out, right and left, in defense of his friend.
And, later on, their student days in Delft; Bertie's
sudden disappearance without leaving a trace,
even for Frank; then a few letters at rare intervals, and then years of silence. Oh! he was glad
indeed to see his friend at his side once more; he
had always had a great love for Bertie, just because Bertie was so wholly unlike himself, with
something of the cat about him—loving to be
petted and made much of, but now and then irresistibly prompted to flee over roofs and gutters, to
get miry and dirty, and return at last to warm and
clean himself on the hearth. Frank loved his

friend as a twin-brother quite different from himself, imposed upon by Bertie's supercilious and delicately egoistic fascination—a catlike creature altogether.

Bertie found it a great luxury to stay indoors the whole of that day, sitting by the fire, which he kept blazing by feeding it with logs. Frank had some capital port, and they sat after lunch sipping it, dreaming or talking; Bertie telling a hundred tales of his adventures in America, of his farmer master, of his hotel, and the theatre where he had acted; and one anecdote led to another, all garnished with a touch of singular romance. Frank presently wanted a little fresh air, and said he would go to his club; but Bertie remained where he was; he could not go about in rags, and he could not appear anywhere with Frank in the clothes he had on. Frank was to return to dinner at eight o'clock. And then suddenly, as if it had come to him like a lightning flash, Bertie said:

"Say nothing about me, pray, to any of your friends. They need not be told that you know such a bad lot as I am. Promise me."

Frank promised, laughing; and, holding out his hand, the "bad lot" added:

"How can I ever repay you? What a happy thing for me that I should have met you! You are the most generous fellow I ever knew!"

Frank escaped from this volley of gratitude, and

Fate

Bertie remained alone in front of the hearth, toasting all over in the blaze, or stretching his legs, with his feet on the shining bars. He poured himself out another glass of port, and made himself think of nothing, reveling in the enjoyment of idleness, while he seriously examined his damaged hands, wondering how best to ensure their rapid recovery.

CHAPTER III

BERTIE had been a month at White-Rose Cottage, and was now hardly recognizable in the young man who sat by Frank's side in a victoria, in an irreproachable fur-lined coat, a fashionable tall hat; both the men wrapped about the knees in a handsome plaid. He now mixed quite at his ease with Frank's other acquaintances, carefully dressed, agreeable, and entertaining, and lisping English with an affected accent, which he thought elegant. He dined with Frank every day at the club, to which he was introduced; criticized game and wines with the most blasé air in the world, and smoked Havanas at two shillings apiece as if they were mere straw. Frank had in his inmost soul the greatest belief in him, and watched him with a smile of secret satisfaction, as he calmly went his own way chatting with men of the world, without ever for a moment feeling shy; and Frank thought the comedy altogether so amusing that he introduced his friend wherever he went.

Winter yielded to a foggy spring; the London season was upon them, and Bertie seemed to find great pleasure in assisting at afternoon teas, and evenings at home; in sitting at a grand dinner between two pairs of fine shoulders, and flirting with each in turn, never dazzled by the glitter of jewels, nor bewildered by the sparkle of champagne; in leaning with languid grace in the stalls or dress circle, his chiseled features full of distinction and lordly repose, a fragrant white flower gleaming in his button-hole, and his opera-glass dangling between his snow-white fingers, as though not one of the ladies was worthy of his inspection. Frank, for lack of occupation, as a man who takes his pleasure where he finds it, had pushed Bertie forward in the world, not merely to help him, but also for the fun of it—a silly amusement, to make a fool of society! Bertie himself had many scruples, and kept note in a pocketbook of everything Frank spent upon him—when times were better he would repay him all—and in a fortnight it had mounted up to a total of some hundred pounds.

Even at home Frank found him amusing. Bertie, who had contrived, by a few kind words, to win the good graces of Annie and her husband, Westhove's valet and butler, turned all the furniture about in whimsical disorder, bought statuettes, palms, and Oriental stuffs, and changed the unsociable aspect of the room into one of artistic comfort, which invited to indolence; a subdued light, wide divans, the atmosphere of an alcove redolent of Egyptian pastils and fine cigarettes, in which thought floated into dreams, and the half-closed eyes rested on the nude figures of bronze nymphs seen through the greenery of plants. Here, in the evening, high festivals were held; orgies with a few chosen friends, and select fair ones; two ladies from a skating-rink, and a figurante from a theatre, who smoked cigarettes with their vermilion lips and drank to Bertie's health. Frank laughed to his heart's content to see Bertie, a contemner of the fair sex, quite insensible to the three charmers; making game of them, teasing them, setting them by the ears till they were almost ready to claw each other, and, to conclude the matter, pouring floods of champagne down their *décolletés* throats.

No; Frank had never been so well amused during all his long residence in London, where he had settled as an engineer in order to give —as he said—a cosmopolitan character to his knowledge of the world.

He was thoroughly good-hearted, and too highly prosperous to be a deep thinker. He had tasted of every pleasure, and had no high opinion of life, which was after all but a farce, lasting, according to statistics, on an average six-and-thirty years. He made small pretense of any philosophical views of existence, beyond a determined avoidance of everything that was not amusing. Now Bertie was very amusing, not only in his fun with women, the cruel sport of a panther; but especially in the farcical part he played in Frank's world, where he figured as a man of fashion—he, a vagabond, who only a month since had stood shivering in rags on the pavement. It was a constant secret delight to his friend, who gave Bertie *carte blanche* to enable him to keep it up; a *carte blanche* which was amply honored, bringing in heavy tailors' bills—for Bertie dressed with refined vanity, bought ties by the dozen, adopted every fancy that came into fashion, and scented himself with all the waters of Rimmel. It was as though he were fain to plunge into every extravagant refinement of an exquisite, after having been a squalid scarecrow. And although at first he kept faithful record of his outlay, he soon forgot first one item and then another, till at last he forgot all.

Thus weeks slipped by, and Frank never thought of troubling himself to inquire among his influential acquaintances for employment for his companion. Their life as wealthy idlers filled their minds entirely; Frank's at any rate, for Bertie had brought a new charm into it.

But suddenly a strange thing happened. One day Bertie went out in the morning alone, and did not come in to lunch. After luncheon, at the club, no Bertie, nor yet at dinner. He did not come home in the evening; he had left no clue. Frank, extremely uneasy, sat up half the night—

no one. Two days went by—still no one. Frank inquired right and left, and at last gave information to the police.

At last one morning, before Frank was up, Bertie appeared at his bedside with an apologetic smile; Frank must not be angry with him; he surely had not been alarmed? You see such a monotonously genteel life had suddenly been too much for him. Always these elegant ladies, with trains and diamonds; always clubs full of lords and baronets; and skating-rinks—the pink of finery! Always a chimney-pot hat, and every evening full dress, with the regulation button-holer. It was intolerable! He could endure it no longer; it had been too much for him

"But where did you hide yourself?" asked Frank, in utter amazement.

"Oh, here and there, among old acquaintances, I have not been out of London."

"And you did not know a soul here?"

"Oh, well, no fashionable folk, like your friends, but a scapegrace or two. You are not vexed with me?"

Frank had sat up in bed to talk to him. He saw that he looked pale, weary, and unkempt. His trousers were deeply bordered with mud; his hat crushed; there was a three-cornered rent in his greatcoat. And he stood there in evident confusion, like a boy, with his doubting, coaxing smile.

"Come, do not be cross with me; take me into favor once more."

This was too much for Frank. Provoked beyond measure, he exclaimed:

"But, Bertie, what a cad you look! And where on earth have you been?" he asked again.

"Oh, here and there."

And he could get no more out of him. Bertie would only say that he had wanted to disappear; and now he was tired—he would go to bed. He slept till three in the afternoon. Frank laughed over it all day, and Bertie went into fits when he heard of the police. At dinner, at the club, he related, with a melancholy face, that he had been out of town for a few days, attending a funeral. Frank had failed to receive a note through the carelessness of a servant.

"But where in the world have you really been?" whispered Frank for the third time, infinitely amused and inquisitive.

"Here and there, I tell you—first in one place, and then in another," answered Bertie, with the most innocent face in the world; and, dapper as ever, he delicately lifted an oyster, his little finger in the air, and swallowed down his half dozen without another word on the subject.

Fate

CHAPTER IV

THE season passed away, but Bertie remained. Sometimes, indeed, he talked of going to Holland; he had an uncle, a stockbroker, in Amsterdam. Possibly that uncle— But Westhove would not hear of it; and, when his friend's conscience pricked him for sponging on him, he talked him down. What did it matter? If Bertie had been the rich man, and he the pauper, Bertie would have done the same by him. They were friends.

A true appreciation of the case began to dawn on him in the now firmly established habits of their life. Frank's moral sense whispered drowsily in the ease of their luxurious existence. Now and then, indeed, he had something like a vague suspicion that he was not rich enough for two; that he had spent more in the last few months than in any former season. But he was too heedless to dwell long on such unpleasant doubts. He was lulled to sleep by Bertie as if by opium or morphia. Bertie had become indispensable to him: he consulted his friend on every point, and allowed himself to be led by him on every occasion, completely subjugated by the ascendency held over him by the fragile little man, with his velvet paws, as though he had him under a yoke. Every now and then—erelong at frequent intervals of about a fortnight—Bertie disappeared, stayed away four or five days, and came back one fine morning, with his insinuating smile, exhausted, pale, and tired out. These were, perhaps, some secret excesses of dissipation—mysterious adventure-hunting in the sordid purlieus of the lowest neighborhoods—of which Frank never heard nor understood the truth; a depth of depravity into which Frank seemed too precise and dainty to be initiated; sins in which he was to have no part, and which Bertie, in his refinement of selfishness, kept for himself as an occasional treat.

Then Frank's hours were passed in disgust of life; he missed the unwholesome stimulant of his existence; in his solitude he sank into gray melancholy and sadness, verging on despair. He stayed at home all day, incapable of any exertion, sulking in his lonely house, where everything—the draping of the handsome curtains, the bronze nudity of the statues, the careless disarray of the cushions on the divan—had still, as it were, an odor of Bertie, which haunted him with regret. On such days as these he was conscious of the futility of his existence, the odious insignificance of his sinewless, empty life: useless, aimless, null!

Fate

Sadly sweet memories would come over him; reminiscences of his parental home, shining through the magic glass of retrospect like bright, still pools of tender domestic harmony, in which the figures of his father and mother stood forth grand and noble, glorified by childlike affection. He longed for some unspeakable ideal, something pure and chaste, some high aim in life. He would shake off this torpor of the soul; he would send away Bertie—

But Bertie came back, and Bertie held him tightly once more in his silken bonds, and he saw more clearly every day that he could not live without Bertie. And then, catching sight of himself in a mirror—tall and brawny and strong, the healthy blood tinging his clear complexion—he could not forbear smiling at the foolish visions of his solitude, which struck him now as diseased imaginings, quite out of keeping with his robust vigor. Life was but a farce, and the better part was to play it out as a farce, in mere sensual enjoyment. Nothing else was worth the pains— And yet sometimes at night, when his big body lay tired out after some riotous evening, a gnawing dissatisfaction would come over him, not to be conquered by this light-hearted philosophy, and even Bertie himself would lecture him. Why did not Frank seek some employment—some sphere of action? Why did not he travel for awhile?

Fate

"Why not go to Norway?" asked Bertie one day, for the sake of saying something.

London was beginning to be intolerable to Bertie; and as the notion of traveling smiled on Frank, both for a change and for economy—since they could live more cheaply abroad than in the whirl of fashionable London—he thought it over, and came to a decision to leave White-Rose Cottage for an indefinite period to the care of Annie and her husband, and spend a few weeks in Norway. Bertie should go with him.

Fate

CHAPTER V

AFTER luncheon at the *table d'hôte* of the Britannia Hotel at Trondhjem, the friends made their way along the broad, quiet streets with their low, wooden houses, and they had left the town, going in the direction of the Gjeitfjeld, when they overtook, in the village of Ihlen, an elderly gentleman with a young girl, evidently bent on the same excursion. The pair had sat a few places off at the *table d'hôte*, and as this much acquaintance justified a recognition in so lonely a spot, Westhove and his friend lifted their hats. The old gentleman immediately asked, in English, whether they knew the road to the Gjeitfjeld: he and his daughter— who, during the colloquy, never looked up from her "Baedeker"—could not agree on the subject. This difference of opinion led to a conversation: the two young men begged to be allowed to join them, Frank being of opinion that "Baedeker" was right.

"Papa will never believe in 'Baedeker!'" said the young lady with a quiet smile, as she closed the red volume she had been consulting. "Nor

215

will he ever trust me when I tell him I will guide him safely."

"Are you always so sure of knowing your way?" said Frank, laughing.

"Always!" she saucily declared, with a gay laugh.

Bertie inquired how long a walk it was, and what was to be seen at the end of it; Frank's everlasting walks were a weariness and a bore. During his residence with his friend he had so spoiled himself, in order to forget his former wretchedness, that he now knew no greater pleasure than that of lying on a bench with a cigar, or a glass of port, and, above all, would avoid every exertion. But now, abroad—when a man is traveling—he can not forever sit dozing in his hotel. Besides, he was quite stiff with riding in a cariole; all this useless rushing about was really monstrous folly, and White-Rose Cottage was not such a bad place. Frank, on the contrary, thoroughly enjoyed the clear, invigorating air of this brilliant summer day, and he drank in the sunshine as though it were fine wine cooled by a fresh mountain breeze; his step was elastic and his voice had a contented ring.

"Are you an Englishman?" asked the gentleman.

Westhove explained that they were Dutch, that they lived in London; and his tone had the frank briskness which a man instinctively adopts to fellow-travelers, as sharing his lot for the moment, when the weather is fine and the landscape pleasing. Their sympathy being thus aroused by their admiration of Norwegian scenery, they walked on side by side, the elder man stepping out bravely, the young lady very erect, with her fine figure molded in a simple, close-fitting blue cloth dress, to which a cape with several folds—something like an elegant type of coachman's cape—lent a dash of smartness. She wore a sort of jockey-cap, with a mannish air, on her thick twists of ruddy-gold hair.

Bertie alone could not understand how all this could be called pleasure; but he made no complaint. He spoke little, not thinking it necessary to make himself agreeable to people whom he might probably never set eyes on again after the morrow. So he just kept up with them, wondering at Frank, who had at once plunged into eager conversation with the young lady, but perceiving on a sudden that his own politeness and tact were a mere superficial varnish as compared with Frank's instinctive good breeding. At that moment, for the first time, notwithstanding his better features and natty traveling costume, he felt himself so far Frank's inferior that a surge of fury resembling hate thrilled through him. He could not bear this sense of inferiority, so he approached the old gentleman, and, walking by his side, forced himself to a show of respectful amiability. As they followed the windings of the upward and diminishing path they by degrees lagged behind Frank and his companion, and thus climbed the hill two and two.

"So you live in London. What is your name?" asked the young lady, with calm curiosity.

"Frank Westhove."

"My name is Eva Rhodes; my father is Sir Archibald Rhodes, of Rhodes Grove. And your friend?"

"His name is Robert van Maeren."

"I like the sound of your name best. I believe I can say it like English. Tell it me again."

He repeated his name, and she said it after him with her English accent. It was very funny, and they laughed over it—"Fraank. Fraank Westhoove."

And then they looked back.

"Papa, are you tired?" cried Eva. The old man was toiling up the height with his broad shoulders bent; his face was red under his traveling cap, which he had pushed to the back of his head, and he was blowing like a Triton. Bertie tried to smile pleasantly, though he was inwardly raging in high dudgeon over this senseless clamber. They had half an hour more of it, however, before the narrow track, which zigzagged up the hill-side like a gray arabesque, came to an end, and they sat down to rest on a block of stone.

Eva was enchanted. Far below lay Trondhjem with its modern houses, encircled by the steely waters of the Nid and its fjord, a magic mirror on which floated the white mass of the fortress of Munkenholm. The mountains rising on all sides were blue; nearest to them the bloomy, purple blue of the grape; then the deep sheeny blue of velvet; farther off the transparent, crystalline blue of the sapphire, and in the distance the tender sky-blue of the turquoise. The water was blue, like blue silver; the very air was blue as pearls are or mother-of-pearls. The equable sunlight fell on everything, without glare and without shadow, from exactly overhead.

"It is almost like Italy!" exclaimed Eva. "And this is Norway! I had always pictured Norway to myself as being all like Romsdal, wild and barren, with rocky peaks like the Romsdalhorn and the Trolltinder, and with raging cascades like the Sletta fos; but this is quite lovely, and so softly blue! I should like to build a house here and live in it, and I would call it Eva's Bower, and keep a whole flock of white doves; they would look so pretty flying in the blue air."

"Dear child!" laughed Sir Archibald. "It looks very different in winter, I suspect."

"No doubt different, but still lovely. In winter

I should love the fury of raging winds, and the roar of the waves of the fjord below my house, and gray mists would hang over the hills! I can see it all!"

"Why, you would be frozen," argued the father, gravely.

"Oh, no; and I should sit at my turret window, dreaming over Dante or Spenser. Do you love Dante and Spenser?"

The question was addressed to Frank, who had listened somewhat puzzled to Eva's raptures, and was now a little startled; for, you see, though he knew Dante by name, he had never even heard of the poet Spenser; only of Herbert Spencer.

"What, do you not know the Faery Queen, Una, and the Red-cross Knight, and Britomart? How very strange!"

"Dear child, what a little fanatic you are over those silly allegories!" said papa.

"But they are glorious, papa!" Eva insisted. "Besides, I love allegory above all things, and admire no other kind of poetry."

"The style is so affected! You are drowned in symbolism!"

"It is the keynote of the Renaissance," Eva protested. "In the time of Elizabeth all the Court talked in that high-flown style. And Edmund Spenser's images are splendid; they sparkle like jewels!"

Bertie thought this discourse much too learned, but he kept his opinion to himself, and made some remark about Dante's "Inferno." They were by this time rested and went on again up the hill.

"My daughter is half an 'Esthetic,'" said the old gentleman, laughing. And Eva laughed too.

"Nay. That is not the truth, papa. Do not believe him, Mr.—Mr. Westhove. Do you know what makes papa say so? A few years ago, when I had but just left school, I and a few girls I knew were perfectly idiotic for a while. We tousled our hair into mops, dressed in floppy garments of damask and brocade with enormous sleeves, and held meetings among ourselves to talk nonsense about art. We sat in attitudes, holding a sunflower or a peacock's feather, and were perfectly ridiculous. That is why papa still says such things. I am not so silly now. But I am still very fond of reading; and is that so very esthetic?"

Frank looked smilingly into her honest, clear, gray eyes, and her ringing, decided voice had an apologetic tone, as if she were asking pardon for her little display of learning. He understood that there was nothing of the blue-stocking in this girl, as might have seemed from her sententious jest before, and he was quite vexed with himself for having been compelled to confess that he knew nothing of the poet Spenser. How stupid she must think him!

Fate

But it was a moment when the beauties of the scenery had so bewitched them that they moved, as it were, in a magic circle of sympathy, in which some unknown law overruled their natural impulses, something electrically swift and ethereally subtle.

As they climbed the meandering mountain track, or made short cuts through the low brushwood, where the leaves glistened in the sun like polished green needles, and as he breathed that pure, intoxicating air, Frank felt as though he had known her quite a long time, as if it were years since he had first seen her at the *table d'hôte* at Trondhjem. And Sir Archibald and Bertie, lingering behind, were far off—miles away—mere remembered images. Eva's voice joined with his own in harmonious union, as though their fragmentary talk of art and poetry were a duet which they both knew how to sing, although Frank candidly confessed that he had read but little, and that what he had read he scarcely remembered. She playfully scolded him, and her sweet clear tones now and then startled a bird, which flew piping out of the shrubs. He felt within him a revival of strength—a new birth; and would fain have spread his arms to embrace —the air!

CHAPTER VI

THAT evening, on their return from their walk, after dinner, over a cup of coffee, they discussed their further projects.

"We are going to Molde," said Sir Archibald.

"And so are we!" Frank exclaimed.

The old gentleman at once expressed a wish that the friends would continue to give him and his daughter the pleasure of their society. Frank had taken a great fancy to him, and Bertie thought him courteous, and good company; Bertie had talked a good deal about America, but he had not told the whole history of his farming experiences in the far West; he had indeed idealized it a little by speaking of "my farm." And Frank did not contradict him.

By the end of two days spent at Trondhjem they were the best of friends; with that confidential intimacy which, on a tour, when etiquette is out of court, sometimes arises from mere contact, without any knowledge of character on either side, simply from sympathy in trifles and mutual attraction, a superficial sentiment of transient admiration which occupies the traveler's leisure. The day on the sea by steamboat to Molde was like a party of pleasure, in spite of the rain which drove them below; and in the cabin, over a bottle of champagne, Miss Eva and the three men played a rubber of whist. But afterward, in a gleam of pale sunshine, there was an endless walk to and fro on the wet deck. The low rocky shore glided slowly past on the larboard side; the hills, varying in outline—now close together, and again showing a gap—covered with brown moss down by the water, and gray above with patches of pale rose or dull purple light. At Christiansand they were far from land, and the waters, now rougher, were crimson in the glory of the sinking sun, fast approaching the horizon. Every wave had a crest of flame-colored foam, as though the ocean were on fire. Frank and Eva, meanwhile, pacing up and down, laughed at each other's faces, reddened like a couple of peonies, or like two maskers rouged by the glow of the sun to the semblance of clowns.

They reached Molde late at night, too late to see its lovely fjord. But next morning, there it lay before them, a long, narrow inlet, encircled by mountains capped with snow; a poem, a song of mountains; pure, lofty, beautiful, severe, solemn, without one jarring note. The sky above them was calmly gray, like brooding melancholy, and the peace that reigned sounded like a passionless *andante*.

Next day, when Sir Archibald proposed a walk up Moldehoï, Bertie declared that he was tired, and did not feel well, and begged to be left at home. In point of fact, he thought that the weather did not look promising; heavy clouds were gathering about the chain of hill-tops which shut in the fjord, like a sweeping drapery of rain, threatening erelong to fall and wrap everything in their gloomy folds. Eva, however, would not be checked by bad weather: when people were traveling they must not be afraid of a wotting. So the three set out; and Bertie, in his patent slippers, remained in the drawing-room of the Grand Hotel, with a book and a half-pint bottle.

The road was muddy, but they stepped out valiantly in their waterproofs and stout boots. The rain which hung threateningly above their heads did not daunt them, but gave a touch of romantic adventure to the expedition, as though it threatened to submerge them in an impending deluge. Once off the beaten road, and still toiling upward, they occasionally missed the track, which was lost in a plashy bog, or under ferns dripping with rain, or struck across a wild growth of blue bilberries. They crossed the morass, using the rocks as stepping-stones; the old gentleman without help, and Eva with her hand in Frank's, fearing lest her little feet should slide on the smooth green moss. She laughed gaily, skipping from stone to stone with his help; sometimes suddenly slipping and supporting herself against his shoulder, and then again going on bravely, trying the stones with her stout stick. She felt as though she need take no particular heed, now that he was at her side; that he would support her if she stumbled; and they chatted eagerly as they went, almost leaping from rock to rock.

"What sort of man is your friend, Mr. Westhove?" Eva suddenly inquired.

Frank was a little startled; it was always an unpleasant task to give any information concerning Bertie, less on account of his past life than of his present position, his quiet sponging on himself, Frank, who, though enslaved by Bertie, knew full well that the situation was strange, to say the least of it, in the eyes of the world.

"Oh he is a man who has been very unfortunate," he said evasively, and he presently added: "Has he not made a pleasant impression on you?"

Eva laughed so heartily that she was near falling into a pool of mud, if Frank had not firmly thrown his arm round her waist.

"Eva, Eva!" cried her father, shaking his head, "pray be more careful!"

Eva drew herself up with a slight blush.

"What can I say?" she went on, pursuing the subject. "If I were to speak the whole truth—"

"Of course."

"But perhaps you will be vexed; for I can see very plainly that you are quite infatuated with your friend."

"Then you do not like him?"

"Well, then, if you insist on knowing, the first day, when I made his acquaintance, I thought him insufferable. With you we got on famously at once, as an amusing traveling companion, but with him—but perhaps he has not traveled much?"

"Oh, yes, he has," said Frank, who could not help smiling.

"Well, then, perhaps he was shy or awkward. However, I began to think differently of him after that; I don't think him insufferable now."

It was strange, but Frank felt no particular satisfaction on hearing of the young lady's changed opinion; he made no reply.

"You say he has had much to trouble him. And, indeed, I can see it in his face. There is something so gentle in him, so tender, I might almost say; such soft, dark eyes, and such a sweet voice. At first, as I tell you, I found it intolerable, but now it strikes me as rather poetical. He must certainly be a poet, and have been crossed in love: he can be no commonplace man."

"No, that he certainly is not," said Frank,

vaguely, a little ill at ease over Eva's raptures; and a mingling of jealousy and regret—something like an aversion for the worldly polish, and a dull envy of the poetic graces which Eva attributed to his friend—ran through his veins like a chill. He glanced up, almost pathetically, at the pretty creature, who was sometimes so shrewd and sometimes so naive; so learned in all that bore on her favorite studies, so ignorant of real life. A dim compassion came over him, and on a sudden the gray rain-clouds weighed upon him with a pall of melancholy, as though they were ominous of some inevitable fatality which threatened to crush her. His fingers involuntarily clasped her hand more tightly.

"Here is the path once more!" cried Sir Archibald, who was twenty steps ahead of them.

"Oh, yes! There is the path! Thank you, Mr. Westhove!" said Eva, and she sprang from the last stepping-stone, pushing her way through the snapping bracken to the beaten track.

"And up there is the hut with the weather-cock," her father went on. "I believe we have made a long round out of our way. Instead of chattering so much, you would do well to keep a sharp lookout for the path. My old eyes, you know—"

"But it was great fun jumping over the stones," laughed Eva.

Far above them they could now see the hut with

the tall pole of the weather-cock, and they went on at an easier pace, their feet sinking in the violet and pink blossomed heath, crushing the bilberries, dimly purple like tiny grapes. Eva stooped and picked some.

"Oh! so nice and sweet!" she exclaimed, with childish surprise, and she pulled some more, dyeing her lips and fingers blue with the juice of the berries. "Taste them, Mr. Westhove."

He took them from her soft, small hand, stained as it were with purple blood. It was true; they were deliciously sweet, and such fine ones!

And then they went on again, following Sir Archibald, often stopping, and triumphing like children when they came on a large patch where the whortleberries had spread unhindered like a miniature orchard.

"Papa, papa! Do try them!" Eva cried, heedless of the fact that papa was far ahead; but Sir Archibald was not out of sight, and they had to run to overtake him; Eva's laughter ringing like a bell, while she lamented that she must leave so many berries untouched—and such beauties!

"I dare say there will be plenty round the hut," said Frank, consolingly.

"Do you think so?" she said, with a merry laugh. "Oh, what a couple of babies we are!"

The path grew wider, and they found it easy walking up to the top, sometimes quitting the track and scrambling over the stones to shorten the way. Presently they heard a shout, and, looking up, they saw Sir Archibald standing on the cairn in which the staff of the weather-cock was fixed, and waving his traveling-cap. They hurried on, and soon were at his side. Eva knocked at the door of the hut.

"The hut is shut up," said her father.

"How stupid!" she exclaimed. "Why does it stand here at all if it is shut up? Does no one live in it?"

"Why, of course not," said Sir Archibald, as if it was the most natural thing in the world.

Frank helped Eva to climb the cairn round the pole, and they looked down on the panorama at their feet.

"It is beautiful, but melancholy," said Eva.

The long fjord lay below them, a narrow ribbon of pale, motionless water, hemmed in by the mountains, now wreathed with gray vapor, through which they gleamed fitfully like ghosts of mountains; Lauparen and Vengetinder, Trolltinder and Romsdalhorn, towering up through the envious, rolling mist, which, swelled by the coming storm, hung in black clouds from every peak and cast a gloomy reflection on the still waters. The hills were weeping—unsubstantial, motionless phantoms, sorrowing and tragical under some august and superhuman woe—a grief as of giants and

demigods; the fjord, with its township, a plot of
gardens, and roofs, and walls, and the white châlet
of the Grand Hotel—all weeping, all motionless
under the gloomy sky. A ghostly chill rose up
from the gulf to where the trio stood, mingling
with the tangible clamminess of the mist, which
seemed to weigh on their eyelids. It was not
raining, but the moisture seemed to distil on them
from the black unbroken rack of clouds; and to
the westward, between two cliffs which parted to
show a gleaming strip of ocean, a streak was visible
of pale gold and faint rose-color—hardly more
than a touch of pink, a sparkle of gold—a stinted
alms of the setting sun. They scarcely said another
word, oppressed by the superhuman sadness which
enwrapped them like a shroud. When Eva at last
spoke her clear voice sounded far away—through
a curtain.

"Look, there is a glint of sunshine over the sea.
Here we are pining for the sun. Oh, I wish the
sun would break through the clouds! It is so dismal here—so dreary! How well I understand
Oswald's cry in Ibsen's 'Ghosts' when he is going
mad: 'The sun, the sun!' Men might pray for sunshine here and get no more than that distant gleam.
Oh, I am perished!"

She shivered violently under the stiff, shining
folds of her waterproof cloak; her face was drawn
and white, and her eyes looked large and anxious.

She suddenly felt herself so forlorn and lonely that she instinctively took her father's arm and clung to him closely.

"Are you cold, my child; shall we go home?" he asked.

She nodded, and they both helped her down the heap of stones. Why, she knew not, but suddenly she had thought of her mother, who was dead, and wondered whether she had ever felt thus forlorn in spite of her father's fondness. But when they came in sight of the hut again, she said, as if it had just occurred to her:

"Papa, there are some names cut in the door; let us cut ours too."

"But, child, you are so cold and pale—"

"Never mind; let us cut our names; I want to," she urged, like a spoiled child.

"No, Eva—what nonsense!"

"Oh, but I do want to," she repeated coaxingly, but the old man would not give in, grumbling still; Frank, however, pulled out his pocket-knife.

"Oh, Mr. Westhove, do cut my name; nothing but Eva—only three letters. Will you?" she asked softly.

Frank had it on his lips to say that he would like to cut his own name with hers, although it was so long, but he was silent; it would have sounded flat and commonplace in the midst of this mournful scenery. So he carved the letters on the door, which was like a traveler's album. Eva stood gazing out to the west, and she saw the three streaks of gold turn pale, and the rose-tint fade away.

"The sun, the sun!" she murmured, with a shudder, and a faint smile on her white lips and in her tearful eyes.

A few heavy drops of rain had begun to fall. Sir Archibald asked if they were ever coming, and led the way. Eva nodded with a smile, and went up to Frank:

"Have you done it, Mr. Westhove?"

"Yes," said Frank, hastily finishing the last letter.

She looked up, and saw that he had cut "Eva Rhodes," and in very neat, even letters, smoothly finished. Below he had roughly cut "Frank," in a great hurry.

"Why did you add 'Rhodes'?" she asked, and her voice was faint, as if far away.

"Because it took longer," Frank replied simply.

Fate

CHAPTER VII

THEY got back to the Grand Hotel in a torrent of rain, a deluge poured out of all the urns of heaven; muddy to their waists, wet to the skin, and chilled to the bone. Eva, after a hot supper, was sent off to bed by her father, and the three men—Sir Archibald, Frank, and Bertie—sat in the drawing-room, where a few other visitors, all very cross at the bad weather, tried to solace themselves with illustrated papers or albums. The old gentleman took a doze in an easy-chair. Frank gazed pensively at the straight streaks of rain, which fell like an endless curtain of close steel needles, thrashing the surface of the fjord. Bertie sipped a hot grog, and looked at his shiny slippers.

"And did you not miss my company on your excursion?" he asked, addressing Frank with a smile, just to break the silence that reigned in the room.

Westhove turned to him in some surprise, as if roused from a dream; then, with a frank laugh, he briefly answered:

"No."

Bertie stared at him, but his friend had already

turned away, lost in thought over the patter of the rain; so Bertie at last took up his book again, and tried to read. But the letters danced before his eyes; his ears and nerves still thrilled uncomfortably under the remembrance of that one short, astounding word which Frank had fired into the silence like a leaden bullet. It annoyed him that Frank should take no further notice of him.

Frank stood unmoved, looking out at the mountains, scarcely visible through the watery shroud; what he saw was their walk back from Moldehoï; the meandering downward path through the tall, dripping bracken; the pelting rain streaming in their faces as from a watering-pot; Eva, closely wrapped in her wet mackintosh, and clinging to his arm as if seeking his protection; behind them her father, carefully feeling the slippery, moss-grown stones with his walking-stick. Frank had wanted to wrap her in his own thick waterproof coat, but this she had positively rejected; she would not have him made ill for her sake, she said, in that far-away voice. And then, when they were at home again, after they had changed their clothes and dined, and laughed over their adventure, Sir Archibald was afraid lest Eva should have taken cold.

Frank remembered at this moment a fragment of their conversation; his asking her, a little surprised in spite of himself, "Have you read Ibsen's

'Ghosts'? You spoke of Oswald when we were up on Moldehoï."

As it happened, he had himself read "Ghosts," and he did not think it a book for a young girl; she had noticed his surprise, and had blushed deeply as she replied:

"Yes, I have read it. I read a great deal, and papa has brought me up on rather liberal lines. Do you think that I ought not to have read 'Ghosts'?"

She herself had seen no harm in it, had not perhaps fully understood it, as she candidly confessed. He had not ventured to tell her that the study of such a drama of physiological heredity was, to say the least, unnecessary for a young girl; he had answered vaguely, and she had colored yet more deeply, and said no more.

"She must have regarded me as a prig of a schoolmaster!" thought he, ill at ease. "Why should she not read what she likes? She does not need my permission for her reading; she is grown up enough. She must have thought me a pedantic owl."

"Frank!" said Bertie again.

"What?" said Frank, startled.

"We leave this place to-morrow morning, I suppose?"

"Yes, that was our plan. At least if the weather improves."

Fate

"What is the name of the next outlandish spot we are going to?"

"Veblungsnaes; and from thence to Romsdal and Gudbrandsdal."

"And the Rhodeses?"

"They are going to Bergen."

"To-morrow?"

"I don't know."

And he stood once more lost in thought; the gray, wet atmosphere without cast a gloom on the scene within; and in his soul, too, reigned the deepest gloom. What was the use of fostering warm feelings when a few days of sympathetic companionship could only end in parting? This was always the case with friendly traveling acquaintance, and was it not so throughout life, with every one—everything—we love? Was it worth while to care for anything? Was not all love a great delusion, by which men blinded themselves to their disgust with life?

Fate

CHAPTER VIII

DECEMBER in London. Cold and foggy. White-Rose Cottage wrapped in mist; in the back room a blazing fire.

But Robert van Maeren was no longer in the blissful mood to enjoy this luxury, as we have hitherto known him; moreover, he now regarded it as quite a matter of course, which came to him by right, since he was a creature of such refined feeling, so slight and fragile, and did not feel himself born to endure poverty and want. Still, he had known misery, the slavery of hired labor, to which he had bent his back with crafty subservience; still, he had felt the gnawings of hunger, the bitterness of squalid beggary. But all this seemed long ago, and as vague as a dream, or as the vanishing lines of the London streets out there, dimmed and blurred by the pall of fog; as indistinct as our dubious impressions of a former state of existence. For, after his metamorphosis, he had determined to forget—he had forced himself to forget; never for an instant to recall his sufferings, or to think of the future. He hated the past as an injustice, a disgrace, an ineradicable

238

stain on the superficial spotlessness of his present
life; he had persuaded himself that all those things
which he had now hidden, buried, forever ignored, had indeed never happened. And he had
succeeded in this effacement of his life in America; it seemed wiped out of the annals of his
memory.

Why, now, must those years rise slowly before
him, like ghosts out of the grave of oblivion?
What had they to say to him now? Nearer and
nearer, till, year by year, month by month, day by
day, they passed before him, dancing in the flames
at which he sat staring, like a dance of death of
the years. They grinned at him from skulls, with
hollow eyes and pallid faces, distorted by a crafty
smile; the dead years which beckoned to him,
wearing filthy rags, and poisoning his cigar with
their foul odor! He saw them, he smelt them; he
shuddered with their chill—there, in front of the
fire; he felt their hunger, in spite of the dinner
that awaited him. Why was it that the future,
which he no less persistently ignored, was beginning to hang over him as an omen of evil, which
each day, each hour, brought nearer and nearer
irresistibly, inevitably?

That future must perhaps be such as the past
had been.

Yes, something was impending. There he sat,
sick with alarms, cowardly, spiritless, effete.

Something was in the air; he felt it coming nearer, to overwhelm him, to wrestle with him for life or death in a frenzy of despair; he felt himself tottering, sinking; he was torn from the ease and comfort of his present life, cast out into the streets, without shelter, without anything! For what had he of his own? The clothes he wore, the shoes on his feet, the ring on his finger were Frank's. The dinner to come, the bed upstairs, were Frank's. Thus had it been for a year past; and if he were to go with all he possessed, he would go—naked, in the winter.

And he could not again be as he had been in America, tramping for work day after day. His body and mind alike were enervated, as by a warm bath of luxury; he had become like a hothouse plant which is accustomed to the moist heat, and perishes when it is placed in the open air. But it hung over him, cruel and unrelenting; not for an instant did the threat relax, and in his abject weakness he feebly wrung his white hands, and two tears, hot with despair, rolled down his cheeks.

Struggle for existence! He was incapable of such a battle; his energy was too lax for that—a laxity which he had felt growing on him as a joy after his fight for life, but which now had made him powerless to screw himself up to the merest semblance of determination.

Fate

And before him he saw the fateful chain of events passing onward—some so infinitely small —each detail a terrible link, and all leading on to catastrophe. Strange that each one was the outcome of its predecessor! the future the outcome of the past! If, after his failure from sheer idleness at Leyden, his father had not placed him as clerk in the office of a Manchester house, he would probably never have known certain youths, his fellow clerks, fashionable young rakes, and fierce "strugglers for existence"; still scarcely more than boys, and already the worse for dissipation. If he had never known them and yet, how pleasantly had they borne him along, merely by humoring his natural bent!—he might, perhaps, not have played such underhand tricks with the money belonging to the firm, that his patron, out of sympathy and regard for his father, had shipped him off to America. That was where he had sunk deepest, swamped in the maelstrom of more energetic fortune-hunters. If only he had been less unlucky in America, he would not have found himself stranded in London in such utter destitution, or have appealed to Westhove for help.

And Frank—but for his suggestion, Frank would never have gone to Norway, never have met Eva. Oh, that journey to Norway! how he cursed it now; for Frank might, perhaps, not have fallen in love, and never have thought of marriage. And now—only yesterday Westhove had called at Sir Archibald's house, where the two friends had been made very welcome after their acquaintance in Norway, and had come home engaged to Eva. Frank would marry, and he, Bertie? Where was he to go? What was to become of him?

He was painfully conscious of the fatality of life, of the injustice of the dispensations of fortune; and he discerned that his own immediate difficulties owed their origin to a single word. One single word: Norway!—Norway, Eva, Frank's falling in love, Frank's engagement and marriage, and his own shipwreck—how horribly clearly he saw every link of the chain of his own life in each word! One word, uttered under a foolish impulse: Norway! And it had irretrievably wrought the happiness of two other persons at the cost of his own. Injustice! Injustice!

And he cursed the impulse, the mysterious, innate force which more or less prompts every word we speak; and he cursed the fact that every word uttered by the tongue of man remains beyond recall. What is that impulse? Something obscurely good, an unconscious "better self," as men declare, which, though deeply and mysteriously hidden, dashes ahead like an unbroken colt, treading down the most elaborate results of careful thought? Oh, if he had but held his tongue! Why Norway?

Fate

What concern had he with that one fatal, fateful land, above all others? Why not Spain, Russia, Japan, good God! Kamchatka, for aught he cared; why especially Norway? Idiotic impulse, which had unlocked his miserable lips to pronounce that luckless name; and oh, the injustice of fate, of life, of everything!

Energy? Will? What could will and energy do against Fate? They were words, empty words. Be a cringing fatalist, like a Turk or Arab, and let day follow day; never think, for behind thought lurks impulse! Fight? Against Fate, who forges her chains blindly, though surely, link upon link?

He threw himself back in his chair, still feebly wringing his hands, and the tears trickled again and again down his cheeks. He saw his own cowardice take shape before him; he stared into its frightened eyes, and he did not condemn it. For he was as Fate had made him. He was a craven, and he could not help it. Men called such a one as he a coward: it was but a word. Why coward, or simple and loyal and brave, or good and noble? It was all a matter of convention, of accepted meaning; the whole world was mere convention, a concept, an illusion of the brain.

There was nothing real at all—nothing!

And yet there was something real: misery and

poverty were real. He had felt them, wrestled with them hand to hand; and now he was too weak to fight them again, too delicate, too refined! He *would* not face them again. Then, leaning back with his pallid head resting against the cushioned back of his chair, his deep-set black eyes clouded with the venom of these reflections, he was aware of a gentle, pleasant electric current thrilling through him—a current of Will. Fatality had willed to bring Frank and Eva together; well, he—a mere plaything of fate—would will, that—

Yes. He would will to part them.

And before his very eyes, as it seemed, that purpose rose up, cold and rigid, an evil and mysterious form, like an incarnation of Satanic malignity.

It looked at him with the eye of a Sibyl, of a Sphinx; and, as compared with the Titanic cruelty of that image, his former visions sank into nothingness—the Dance of Death of the years, the continuity of Fatality, and his cursing of it all. These now vanished, and he only saw that figure, like a ghost, almost tangible and almost visibly solid in the dusk, against the dying glow of the fire. The gloomy, questioning gaze of those eyes hypnotized his soul; his instinct fell asleep under its crushing power. . . . Friendship! gratitude! They, too, were mere words.

Fate

There was nothing real in life but conventionality and—poverty. And then there was that image —there, in front of the fire—with its staring, fixed gaze, petrified to an embodiment of silent, irresistible, infernal magnetism!

CHAPTER IX

THAT night—he saw Frank no more, for he had stayed to dine with Sir Archibald Rhodes—that night Van Maeren could not sleep; the wildest fancies kept him wide awake. Illusions and schemes whirled through his fevered brain; strange voices buzzed in his ears, hissing like an angry sea.

He saw himself sitting with Eva in a cab, passing through the gloomiest and foulest parts of London. Squalid figures stood in their way, and came close to Eva. He laughed as he saw her dragged away by men with brutal faces, and then come back to him, with her clothes torn, sobbing because she had been insulted. A fearful headache hammered in his brain, and he groaned with a painful effort to control the wild extravagance of his fancy. He got up, rubbing his eyes, as if to drive away the melodramatic vision, and wrapped his burning head in a wet, cold towel. He involuntarily looked in the glass; and, in the subdued glimmer of the nightlight, his face stared back at him as pale as death, drawn and

246

Fate

haggard, with hollow, sunken eyes, and a gaping mouth. His heart beat violently, as if it were rising into his throat, and he pressed it down with both hands.

After drinking a glass of water he lay down again, forcing himself to be calm. Subtler fancies now crowded his mind, like fine threads caught athwart and across—webs mingled in a maze like an inextricable tangle of lace; and his imagination worked out the intricacies of wearisome intrigues, as though he were a poet who, during a night of lucid sleeplessness, constructs a drama, and, not content with its plot, goes through it again and again, to master the great conception in his mind before writing it out.

Now he saw the orgies of a past day repeating themselves below in the sitting-room. He saw the skating-rink, and Frank and himself drinking champagne, and laughing and singing. But suddenly the door opened, and Sir Archibald came in with Eva on his arm. Sir Archibald cursed Frank with tremendous words and vehement gestures, and Frank hung his head; but Eva threw herself between them, with words of anguish and imploring hands. And it was all the last scene of the fourth act of an opera. The singing in his ears, and the dreadful throbbing in his aching head, were like the thunder of a full orchestra, excited to the utmost by the beat of an energetic conductor, and the loud, strident crash of brass instruments.

Bertie moaned, and tossed from side to side, compelling himself to picture less violent scenes. Now it was like a modern comedy. Eva, at his suggestion, was suspiciously watching Annie, the maid and housekeeper at White-Rose Cottage. Eva was jealous, and then a grand catastrophe— Eva finding Annie in Frank's arms.

Sick with thinking, bewildered by his own imaginings, he drove away the chaotic vision. Exhaustion overcame him; his frenzy was worn out, though his head was still burning, throbbing, bursting; although acute pain shot through his brain, from his brows to his neck, as if he were being scalped; although the blood in his temples leaped furiously in his veins, with rhythmical torture.

And in the immediate torment of physical suffering, his pride, which was to defy Fatality, collapsed like a tower crumbling into ruins. His imagination became vacancy; he forgot his terrors of the future. He lay motionless, bathed in clammy sweat; his eyes and mouth wide open; and the indecision of exhaustion cast a softened light on all his fancies—mere delirious dreams, which could never bear the faintest resemblance to reality.

Things must go on as they might, he lazily

thought; the future was still remote; he would think no more about it; he would let himself go with the chain of events, link by link; it was madness to double his fists against Fate, which was so strong—so omnipotent.

CHAPTER X

THE following days passed quietly enough, though a vague fear still hung over Bertie's head. He bowed that head without further thought, but still with a dull ferment in the depths of his heart, below the superficial calm.

Then one day he went with Frank to the Rhodeses, and Eva, taking his hand, said:

"We shall be good friends, shall we not?"

And after she had spoken he heard her voice still ringing in his ears like little bells. He mechanically let his velvety eyes rest on hers, and smiled, and allowed her to lead him to a sofa, and show him designs for furniture and patterns of curtains for their new home—her home and Frank's. Frank himself sat a little way off, talking to Sir Archibald. He looked at them, sitting side by side, like brother and sister, on the softly cushioned settee—their heads bent together over the rustling pages of the pattern-book, their hands meeting from time to time. And his brows were knit in a frown of displeasure.

And yet he laughed, and said to Eva:

Fate

"Bertie will be of the greatest use; he has far better taste than I."

And he felt as though he had spoken the words in spite of himself, or had meant to say something quite other than this compliment, but could not help it. All the time he was talking politics to Sir Archibald his eyes rested on them, magnetically attracted by their familiar manner.

There was a sisterly gentleness in Eva, an emanation of sympathy for her lover's friend, a somewhat romantic interest in the mystery of Van Maeren's fine dark eyes and insinuating voice, and a compassion for the deep Byronic sorrows which she attributed to him—something like the esthetic pathos of a sentimental reader over the inexplicable woes of a hero of romance.

It was to her a poetic friendship, which very harmoniously supplemented her love for Frank Westhove; a kind of love of which in her girlish enthusiasm she had never imagined the existence, and of which, if she could have suspected it, she would certainly never have thought herself capable: a calm, peaceful, and true affection, practical, almost homely, without the faintest tinge of romance; a love, not blind to her lover's faults, but faithful to him in spite of them, like a mother's for her undeserving child. She perceived his indolence over every voluntary effort, his indecision over every serious question, his vacil-

lation between this and that; and did not blind
herself to all this weakness. But it was this very
weakness which had gained her heart, as a pleasing
contrast with the cool, uneffusive, sober affection
of her father, who spoiled her indeed, but never
so much as she herself desired.

Then there was another contrast which charmed
her even more, which had filled her heart with
an admiration that had become a passion; the
contrast in Frank himself, of his mild, yielding
character with the robust vigor of his stalwart
person. She, woman as she was, found something
adorable in the fact of this splendidly strong
youth, with his broad chest and shoulders, his great
mane of fair hair and powerful neck—this man,
whose suppleness and ease in lifting and moving
things betrayed constant practise in the use of his
limbs—being so feeble in determination, and so
gentle in demeanor. When she was alone and
thought of him so, she could not help smiling,
though the tears came into her eyes—tears of happiness—for this contrast made her happy. It was
very strange, she thought, and she could not understand it; it was a riddle; but she did not try to solve
it, for it was a riddle that she loved, and as she
thought of it, with smiling lips and tear-dimmed
eyes, she longed only to have her arms round his
neck—her own Frank's.

She did not idealize him; she never now

thought of platonic twin-souls in superhuman ecstasy; she took him as he was, a mere man; and it was for what he was that she worshiped him, calm and at rest in her worship. Although she knew that the romantic side of her nature could never find fulfilment—such as it now did through her sisterly regard for Bertie—she had no regret for it in her abounding love for Frank. And since her nature found completion in the enjoyment of the moment, she was pleased and quite satisfied, and felt such a sunny glow in her and about her as deserves to be called true happiness.

This was her frame of mind now, as she looked through the patterns with Bertie, while Frank sat chatting with her father. There was the man she loved, here her brother-friend. This was all good; she never could wish for anything more than to be thus happy in her love and her friendship. She looked at Bertie with a protecting and pitying smile, and yet with a touch of contempt at his slight, boyish figure, his white hands and diamond ring, his little feet in patent leather shoes, hardly larger than her own; what a dapper little mannikin he was. Always spotlessly precise in dress and manner, with an appealing cloud of melancholy over his whole person.

As he glanced up at her, consulting her about some detail in one of the prints, Bertie detected this smile on Eva's face, ironically patronizing and at the same time kind and sisterly; and knowing that she liked him, he could to some extent read its meaning; but he asked her:

"What are you smiling at?"

"At nothing," said she; and she went on, still smiling affectionately: "Why did you never become an artist, Bertie?"

"An artist?" said Van Maeren, "what next?"

"A painter, or an author. You have great artistic taste—"

"I!" he repeated, much surprised, for he really did not know that he possessed very remarkable esthetic feeling, an exquisiteness of taste worthy of a woman, of a connoisseur; and her words set his own character before him in a new light. Does a man never know himself and what really lies in him?

"I could do nothing," he replied, somewhat flattered by Eva's speech; and in his astonishment, candid for once in spite of himself, he went on: "I should be too lazy."

He was startled by his own words, as though he had stripped himself bare; and he instinctively looked across at Frank to see if he had heard him. Vexed at his own thoughtlessness, he colored and laughed to hide his annoyance, while she, still smiling, shook her head reproachfully.

CHAPTER XI

WHEN, a little later, Eva was alone with her lover, and she showed him the patterns which his friend had preferred, Frank began: "Eva—"

She looked at him inquiringly, beaming with quiet happiness.

There was a turmoil in his brain: he wanted to speak to her about Bertie. But he suddenly remembered his promise to his friend never to reveal anything of his past life. Frank was a man who simply regarded a spoken word as inviolable, and he suddenly perceived that he could not say what he had on his tongue. And yet, he remembered his uncomfortable sensations when, on the top of Moldehoï, Eva had so innocently expressed her change of opinion in his friend's favor. Had he not then felt as though the black clouds were an omen of evil hanging over her head? And had he not experienced the same shudder as he saw them sitting side by side on the sofa, as if a noose were ready to cast round her neck? It was an instinctive dread, springing up unexpectedly, without anything to lead up to it.

255

Ought he not to speak, to tell her what Bertie was? But he had promised—and it was foolishly superstitious to allow such an unreasoning terror to have any influence on his mind. Bertie was not like ordinary men; he was very lazy, and lived too contentedly at the expense of others—a thing that Westhove could not understand, and over which in his good nature he simply shook his head with a smile—but Bertie was not wicked. So he was concealing nothing from Eva but that Bertie had no money. Still, he had meant to say something; something was seething in his brain. Eva was looking at him wide-eyed; he must speak. So he went on, embarrassed in spite of himself, coerced by a mysterious force which seemed to dictate the words:

"I was going to say—perhaps you will think me silly—but I do not like, I do not think it right—"

She still looked at him with her surprised eyes, smiling at his hesitancy. It was this very indecision which, in her eyes, was so engaging a contrast to his stalwart frame; she sat down on his knee, leaning against him, and her voice sounded like a poem of love:

"Well, what, Frank? My dearest Frank, what is it?"

Her eyes smiled in his; she laid her arms round his neck, clasping her hands, and again she asked:

"Tell me, foolish boy, what is the matter?"

Fate

"I do not like to see you always—that you should always—sit so—with Bertie."

The words forced their way against his will; and now that they were spoken it seemed to him that he had meant to say something quite different. Eva was amazed.

"Sit so with Bertie!" she repeated. "How do I sit with Bertie? Have I done anything I ought not? Or—tell me, Frank, are you so horribly jealous?"

He clasped her closer, and, kissing her hair, he muttered: "Yes, yes! I am jealous."

"But of Bertie—your best friend, who lives with you? You can not surely be jealous of him!"

She burst out laughing, and, carried away by her own mirth, fairly shook as she sat there, on his knee, with her head against his shoulder.

"Of Bertie!" she said, still gasping. "How is it possible? Oh, oh, of Bertie! But I only think of him as a pretty boy, almost a girl. He is so tiny, and has such neat little hands. Oh, oh! What! jealous of Bertie?"

"Do not laugh so!" he said, with a frown. "I really mean it—you are so familiar with him—"

"But he is your dearest friend!"

"Yes, so he may be—but yet—"

She began again to laugh; she thought him most amusing; and at the same time she loved him all the better for being so sullen and jealous.

Fate

"Silly fellow!" she said, and her fingers played with his fair, golden-tinted mustache. "How foolish—oh! how foolish you are!"

"But promise me—" he began again.

"Of course, if it will make your mind easy, I shall keep more at a distance. But I shall find it very difficult, for I am so accustomed to Bertie. And Bertie must not be allowed to guess it; thus your friendship will remain unbroken. I must still be good friends with him. No, no! I tell you I must be kind to him. Foolish boy that you are! I never knew that you could be so silly!" And she laughed again very heartily, shaking his head in her engaging merriment, and tousling his thick hair with her two little hands.

Fate

CHAPTER XII

FRANK had of late begun to think of Bertie as an intolerable burden. Though he himself did not understand why, he could not bear to see Eva and his friend together, and their intimacy brought this about almost every day. Eva had rightly perceived that she could hardly behave to Bertie otherwise than oho had done hitherto. Meanwhile he had to put up with great coolness from Frank. After one of his escapades, which had lasted three days, this coolness was very conspicuous. Westhove, who usually made very pressing inquiries on his return from these mysterious absences, on this occasion said not a word. And Bertie vowed to himself that this should be the last of these disappearances.

But then came the discussion, which Van Maeren had so greatly dreaded; in a confidential moment his friend spoke of his impending marriage, and asked Bertie what plans he had for the future.

"For you know, dear old fellow," was Frank's kind way of putting it, "that I will with pleasure do my best to help you. Here, or in Holland, I have a few connections. And so long as you have nothing, of course I shall not leave you out in the cold; on that you may safely reckon. But I shall be leaving White-Rose Cottage: Eva thinks it too much out of the way, and, as you know, prefers Kensington. But we have had good times together, haven't we?"

And he clapped Bertie on the shoulder, grateful for the life of good-fellowship they had enjoyed within those walls, and feeling a little compassion for the poor youth who took so kindly to the good gifts of wealth, and who had, alas! no wealth to procure them with. However, he penetrated no further into Bertie's state of mind; he had always had a turn for a Bohemian existence: he had known luxury after living in misery; now life must be a little less easy for him again. That was all.

Bertie, on his part, horrified by the heartless villainy of his first reflections, allowed himself to slide on day by day, with no further thought of his various plots. He sometimes even had a naive belief that at the last moment fortune would look on him with favor: his Fatalism was like a form of worship, giving him strength and hope.

However, a moment came when he thought all hope lost; the danger was pressing and imminent.

"Bertie," said Westhove, who had just come home in some excitement, "to-morrow you can find some employment to suit you, I think. Tayle

—you know, our friend at the club—tells me that he wants to find a secretary for his father, Lord Tayle. The old man lives on his place, up in Northumberland; he is always ailing, and sometimes tiresome, still, it seems to me that you will not easily get such another chance. You will have a salary of eighty pounds, and live in the house of course. I should have spoken of you to Tayle at once, but that you begged me long ago—"

"Then you did not mention my name?" said Bertie, hastily and almost offended.

"No," replied Frank, surprised at his tone. "I could make no overtures till I had spoken to you. But make up your mind at once, for Tayle has two other men in his eye already. If you can decide at once I will go back to Tayle this minute: my cab is waiting." And he took up his hat.

Eighty pounds, and a position as secretary, with free quarters at the Castle! How the splendor of such an offer would have dazzled Bertie not so very long since, in America. But now—

"My dear Frank," he said, very coldly, "I am very much obliged for your kind intentions, but, pray, take no trouble on my account. I can not accept the place. Dismiss your cab—"

"What!" cried his friend, in utter amazement. "Will you not at least think it over?"

"Thank you very much. If you have nothing better to offer me than to become the servant of

the father of a man with whom I have been intimate as an equal, I can only say, Thank you for
nothing. I am not going to shut myself up in a
country-house, and scribble for an ailing, fractious
old man, for a pittance of eighty pounds a year.
And what would Tayle think of me? He has
·always known me as your friend, and we have been
familiar on that footing; and now he is to see me
his father's hired menial! I can not say that you
have much delicate feeling, Frank."

His brain was in a whirl while he spoke; never
before had he assumed such a haughty tone in
addressing Frank, but it was like a cry of despair
rising up from the ruins of his false pride.

"But, good God, man! what do you expect?"
exclaimed Westhove. "You know all my friends,
and it is only through my friends that I can hope
to help you."

"I will take no help from any one like the men
of our own club, nor from any one to whom you
have introduced me as their equal."

"That certainly makes the case a difficult one,"
said Westhove, with a sharp laugh, for great wrath
was rising up in him. "Then you have nothing
to say to this?"

"Nothing."

"But what on earth do you want?" said Frank,
indignantly.

"For the moment, nothing."

"For the moment—well and good; but by and by?"

"That I will see all in good time. And if you can not be more considerate—"

He stopped short, startled by his own voice. He was speaking loudly—as it would seem with domineering vehemence, but in fact only with the energy of despairing indolence and pride at bay. The two men looked at each other for a few seconds, each suddenly feeling as though he had a store of buried grievances against the other—grievances which had accumulated in spite of the friendly intimacy of their lives, and which they were on the point now of flinging in each other's teeth as foul insults.

But Van Maeren checked his outburst. He recollected himself, or he had not forgotten himself. He smiled and held out his hand:

"Forgive me, Frank," he said, humbly, with that voice like beaten gold, and that mitigating smile; "I know you meant well. I can never, no, never, repay you for all you have done for me. But this place I can not really accept. I would rather be a waiter, or the conductor of a tram-car. Forgive me if I seem ungrateful."

So they made it up. But Westhove thought this pride on his companion's part ridiculous, and was vexed that the whole affair must remain a secret from Eva. He would have liked to consult her on

Fate

the subject. And it was with a deeper frown and more scowling glance that he watched those two, Bertie and Eva, as they sat side by side in the evening in the subdued light of the blue-shaded lamp, chatting like brother and sister. It was like some covert dishonesty. It was all he could do to keep from proclaiming aloud that Bertie was a parasite, a low fellow, from tearing them apart, from snatching them away from their blissful smiling and guileless intimacy as they discussed furniture and hangings.

CHAPTER XIII

AFTER this ineffectual attempt to help Van Maeren his friend took no further trouble, expecting that when the case became urgent Bertie himself would ask his assistance. But Bertie's refusal led Frank to perceive for the first time the false position in which he had placed his companion, both with regard to himself and to his associates; his kindness to a friend out of luck in allowing him to live for a year as a man of fortune struck him now—seen in the light of an attachment which had purified, renovated, and transformed his whole nature—as indescribably preposterous, as trampling on every law of honor and veracity; an unjustifiable mockery of the good faith of the world he lived in. Formerly he had thought all this very amusing, but now he felt that it was mean, base, to have enjoyed such amusement as this. And he understood that he had himself encouraged the growth, as of some poisonous weed, of Van Maeren's false pride, which now forbade him to accept a favor from any one of their boon companions.

The days glided by, and Westhove could not

Fate

shake off the sense of self-reproach, which, indeed,
grew upon him as time went on. Van Maeren
cast a shadow over the happiness of his love. Eva
saw that some dull grief made him silent; he
would sit brooding for many minutes at a time—
his brows knit and a deep furrow across his
forehead.

"What ails you, Frank?"

"Nothing, my darling."

"Are you still jealous?"

"No. I will cure myself of it."

"Well, you see, it is your own fault; if you had
not always sung the praises of Bertie as your best
friend I should never have become so intimate with
him."

Yes, it was his own fault; that he saw very
clearly.

"And are you satisfied with me now?" she
asked, laughing.

He, too, laughed. For indeed it was true; for
Frank's sake she had now suddenly changed her
behavior to Bertie; she would rise and quit the
sofa where they sat while he was yet speaking; she
sometimes contradicted him, reproached him for
his foppishness, and laughed at him for his dainty
little hands. He looked at her in amazement,
fancied she meant it for flirtation, but could not
understand what she would be at. One evening,
for hour after hour she pestered him with petty

266

annoyances, pin-pricks, which she intended should reassure Frank and not wound Bertie too deeply. The conversation presently turned on heraldry, and Sir Archibald wanted to show the two men the blazoned roll of his family tree. Frank rose, ready to follow him to his study, and Bertie did the same. Eva felt a little compunction, thinking she had carried her teasing rather far this time, and she knew that her father's pedigree would not interest him in the least.

"Leave Bertie here, papa," said she. "He knows nothing about heraldry."

And, at the same time, to comfort Frank, who dared not betray his jealousy, she added lightly, with a mollifying twinkle of her long eyelashes:

"Frank will trust us alone together, I dare say!"

Her voice was so simple, her glance so loving, that Frank smiled and nodded trustfully, though annoyed at seeing Bertie sit down again.

As soon as they were alone Bertie began:

"For shame, Eva, how could you torment me as you have been doing?"

She laughed and blushed, a little ashamed of herself for treating him so to please Frank. But Bertie's face was grave, and with an appealing gesture he folded his hands, and said beseechingly: "Promise me that you will not do so again."

Fate

She gazed at him in surprise at his earnest
tone:

"It is only my fun," said she.

"But a form of fun which is suffering to me,"
he replied in a low voice.

And still she looked at him, not understanding.
He sat huddled up, his head on his breast, his eyes
fixed before him, and his brown hair, which waved
a little over his forehead, clinging to his temples,
which were damp with perspiration. He was evidently much agitated. He had no idea what
might come of this dialogue, but he was aware
that his tone had been solemn, that these first
words might be the prelude to a very important
interview. He felt that these few minutes were
destined to become a precious link in the chain of
his life, and he waited with the patience of a fatalist for the thoughts which should take shape in his
brain, and the words which should rise to his lips.
He kept an eye on himself, as it were, and at the
same time spun a web about Eva, as a spider
entangles a fly in the thread it draws out of its
bowels.

"You see," he went on slowly, "I can not bear
that you should torment me so. You think less
well of me than you used. But if I have little
hands, I can not help it."

She could not forbear a smile at the intention-
ally coquettish tone he had assumed, an affectation

of spoiled-childishness which she saw through at once. But she replied, nevertheless:

"Well, I beg your pardon for teasing you. I will not do so again."

He, however, had risen from his chair, and, pretending not to see the hand she held out, he silently went to the window, and stood there, looking out on the park-like greenery of Kensington Gardens, dimmed with mist. She sat still, waiting for him to speak; but he said nothing.

"Are you angry, Bertie?"

Then he slowly turned round. The gray daylight fell through the muslin curtains, and gave a pallid look—a hue of Parian china—to his delicate features. Very gently, with a deep, melancholy smile, he shook his head in negation. And to her romantic fancy the sadness of that smile gave him a poetic interest as of a youthful god or a fallen angel; the celestial softness of a sexless mythological being, such as she had seen in illustrated books of verse; a man in form, a woman in face. She longed to invite him to pour out his woes; and at this moment it would scarcely have surprised her if his speech had sounded like a rhythmical monologue, a long lament in blank verse.

"Bertie, my dear fellow, what is the matter?"

There he stood speechless, in the pale slanting light, knowing that the effect must be almost theatrical. And she, sitting where it was darker, could see that his eyes glistened through tears. Much moved, she went up to him; she took his hand, and made him sit down by her side.

"Speak, Bertie, have I vexed you? Can you not tell me?"

But again he shook his head, with that faint smile. And at last he said huskily:

"No, Eva, I am not vexed. I can be vexed no more. But I am very, very sad because we must so soon part, and I care for you so much—"

"Part! Why? Where are you going?"

"Indeed, I do not myself know that, sweet girl. I shall remain till you are married, and then I must go, to wander hither and thither quite alone. Will you sometimes think of me, I wonder?"

"But why do you not stay in London?"

He looked at her. He had begun this conversation without knowing whither it might lead him, abandoning himself to chance. But now, with this look which her eyes met in response, there suddenly blazed up in him a little diabolical flame. He knew now what he was driving at; he weighed every word he uttered as if they were grains of gold; he felt himself very lucid, very logical and calm, free from the painful, incoherent agitation of the last few minutes. And he spoke very slowly, in a mournful, hollow voice like a sick man:

Fate

"In London! No, Eva, I can not remain here."

"Why not?"

"I can not, dear girl. I can not, not with any decency. It is impossible."

The hypocrisy of his eye, the languor of his tone, his assumption of inconsolable grief, distilled into her mind a vague suspicion like an insidious poison —the suspicion that it was on her account that he could not remain in London, because he would have to meet her as his friend's wife. It was no more than a suggestion. The wordless despair which seemed to exhale from him inspired the inference. But her mind rebelled against it; it was a mere suspicion and groundless. He went on, still very slowly, considering every word as if with mathematical accuracy. "And when I am gone and you are left with Frank, always with him, will you be happy, Eva?"

"Why, Bertie?" She paused. It would be almost cruel to say "Yes," in the security of her happiness, in the face of his pain.

"Why do you ask?" she said, almost timidly.

He gazed into her face with the deep, soft, misty blackness of his fine eyes. Then he bent his head, and they filled with tears, and he clutched his hands as if they were cold.

"Why—why?" Eva insisted.

"Nothing, nothing. Promise me that you will

be happy. For if you were not happy I should be heartbroken."

"What should hinder my being happy; I love Frank so dearly?" she exclaimed, though still fearing lest she should hurt his feelings.

"Yes; and so long as you are happy all is well," he murmured low, still rubbing his hands.

Then, on a sudden, while her inquiring gaze still rested on his face, he said: "Poor child!"

"What—why poor child?" she asked in dismay.

He seized her hands, his tears dropped on her fingers.

"Oh, Eva, Eva! God, who can read my heart— If you—oh! I feel such pity, such great, passionate pity for you. I would do I know not what—I would give my life if I—if you . . . Poor, poor child!"

She was standing up now, trembling, and as pale as death; her fingers clutched the table-cover, which slipped as she pulled it, and a glass vase, in which a few flowers were fading, was upset; the water trickled over the velvet cloth in great silvery beads. She let it flow into pools, staring at it with wide, terrified eyes, while he covered his face with his hands.

"Bertie," she cried, "oh, Bertie! Why do you speak thus? What is it all? Tell me. Tell me everything. I must know. I desire you to speak out."

Fate

His reply was a gesture—a perfectly natural gesture of deprecation, with no touch of theatrical insincerity, a gesture as though he would retract his words, and had said something he should have kept to himself; then he, too, rose, and his face had changed; its expression was no longer one of suffering or of pity, but of cool decision.

"No, no. There is nothing to tell, Eva."

"Nothing! And you could exclaim, 'Poor child!' And you pity me! Good God, but why? What is this—what evil threatens me?" She had Frank's name on her lips, but dared not utter it, and he was conscious of this.

"Nothing, really and truly, nothing, dear Eva. I assure you, nothing. I sometimes have the most foolish thoughts, mere fancies. Look, the vase has fallen over."

"But what were you thinking then—what fancies?"

He wiped the water off the table-cloth with his pocket handkerchief, and replaced the flowers in the glass.

"Nothing; nothing at all," he murmured, huskily; he was tremulous with nervousness, and his tone was deeply compassionate, as if his words were meant to shroud some awful secret. Then, as he said no more, she sank on the sofa and broke into uncontrolled and passionate sobs, scared by the undefinable terror which rose up in her soul.

"Eva, dear Eva, be calm!" he entreated her, fearing lest some one should come into the room. And then—then he knelt down close by her, taking her hands, and pressing them tenderly.

"Look at me, Eva. I assure you; I swear to you there is nothing wrong—nothing at all, but what exists in my own imagination. But, you see, I care for you so fondly: you will let me say so, won't you? For what I feel for you is only guileless, devoted friendship for my friend's bride and my own little sister. I love you so truly that I can not help asking myself, Will my dear Eva be happy? It is a foolish thought, no doubt; but in me it is not strange, because I am always thinking of those I love. You see, I have known so much sorrow and suffering. And when I see any one I care for so truly as I do for you—see her so full of confidence in life and of fair illusions, the thought comes over me, terrible, but irresistible: Will she be happy? Is there, indeed, any such thing as happiness? Oh, I ought not to say such things; I only darken your outlook, and give you pessimistic notions; but sometimes when I see you with Frank, my heart is so full! For I love Frank, too. I owe so much to him, and I should so gladly see him happy with some woman—with some one— Still, I can only say, trust wholly in Frank. He loves you, though he is a little fickle, a little capricious in his feelings; but he adores you. The delicate shades of a woman's nature are above his comprehension, perhaps, and he is apt to carry his light-heartedness a little too far—still, he means no harm. He is so candid, so honest; you know always so exactly what he is at. And so, Eva, dear Eva, never let any misunderstanding come between you—always be open with each other; will you not, my child. Oh, my poor Eva!"

And he, too, sobbed low in his mysterious anguish, which was not altogether a pretense, for he was really in despair at the prospect before him. She looked down on him in dismay, greatly distroooed by hio wordo, from which she inferred something which he would not reveal: each word a drop of subtle venom, and the germ of strange doubts, which shot up like poisonous weeds.

"Then there is nothing to tell?" she said once more, in a weary tone of entreaty, clasping her hands.

"No, dear Eva, nothing at all. Only I am worn out, you see—quite an old man—and so I worry myself sometimes about you two. When I am far away—far from London—will you be happy? Tell me, Eva, will you be happy? Promise me, swear to me that you will."

She gently nodded in the affirmative, with a sigh of regret that he must leave London—regret for what he had suggested, worst of all for what he had left unsaid: the mystery, the terror! He, meanwhile, had risen; holding out his hands to her, and shaking his head, as though over the follies of man, he said, with his most pathetic smile:

"How silly you must think me, to torment myself so about nothing. I ought not to have said so much; perhaps I have saddened you with it all. Have I?"

"No," she replied with a gentle smile, shaking her head. "No, not really."

He let himself drop into a chair, sighing deeply.

"Alas! such is life!" he murmured, with a fixed gaze full of sinister significance. She made no answer, her heart was too full.

By this time it was dark. Van Maeren took his leave. Frank alone had been asked to stay to dinner.

"Have you forgiven me?" he asked, very humbly, with his most insinuating and romantic air, as the last rays of daylight shed an ethereal glow on his face.

"For what?" she said, but she was silently weeping.

"For having distressed you, even for a minute?"

She nodded, and rose, trembling, exhausted, and tottering.

"Oh, yes; you gave me a great fright. But you will not do so again, I beg."

"Never," he murmured.

He kissed her hand; a courteous caress he was

accustomed to bestow, with a touch of foppery like an eighteenth century marquis; and he went away.

She was left alone. Standing there, in the middle of the room, she closed her eyes, and she felt as though a mist had fallen and enwrapped her. And in that mist she saw Moldehoï and the spectral fjord gleaming between the two ranges of protecting mountains, and far away, in the west, those three thin bars of gold. And suddenly she felt, as she had never felt before, so forlorn, so lonely, in the midst of the cloud, without even a thought of Sir Archibald and Frank, remembering nothing but her long dead mother. A weight pressed on her brain, like the icy palm of a giant's hand; dusky gloom closed in upon her, and suddenly the living warmth within her was chilled as with a deadly frost. She felt as if she were standing in vast space, and through it—invisible, intangible, and yet sensibly and undeniably real—she was aware of a coming horror, rolling dully on like distant thunder. She stretched out her hands, feeling for some support. But she did not fall senseless; she recovered herself; and found that she was still in the middle of the room, now almost dark, a little tremulous, and with a feeble sensation about the knees. And she could not but think that there was something yet—something which Bertie had concealed from her.

Fate

CHAPTER XIV

Next day she thought it all over once more. What was it? What was it? Would Bertie have pitied her so if there really had been nothing in it but his own pessimistic fears for her happiness? Or was he not indeed hiding something? And had it anything to do with Frank?

And then Frank came, and she often saw him sit quite still for a time, with a frown on his brow.

"What is the matter?" she asked. And he replied just as usual:

"Nothing, sweetheart."

And they chatted together, at first a little constrained, but soon quite happy again in their plans and dreams, forgetting what weighed on their minds. Eva would laugh brightly, and perch herself on Frank's knee, and play with his mustache. But if Bertie came in, something seemed at once to come between them; a shadow which parted them.

It was when the friends were alone together that they were most ill at ease. Then Westhove could only long to turn Van Maeren out of doors at once, without the smallest perceptible cause, like a mangy hound. He pictured Bertie as he had seen him standing shivering in his wretched raiment that snowy night. Now he was such a dandy, and nothing was too good for him; and he was irreproachable; he did not even go off for a few days at a time, wandering obscurely like a cat. He was always "interesting," with his halo of melancholy; and since the scene over the secretaryship, he often assumed a reproachful tone in his voice and expression when speaking to Frank.

Eva, when left to herself, was deeply wretched. Chaotic doubts tortured her soul, doubts which, for the moment, she could set aside, but which would force themselves on her as soon as she thought of Bertie's sympathetic smile and strange compassion for her. Oh! what was it? What was it? She had often meant to talk it over with Frank, but when she was on the point of beginning the subject, she did not know what to say. That Bertie pitied her? It could be nothing but his own pessimism which, in its universal humanity, regarded the world as worthy of pity, since it seemed created to be wretched.

Should she ask Frank whether he had any silent grief—if he had anything to trouble him? This she did once or twice, and the answer was always the same:

"Nothing, dearest!"

What then, oh, what was this horror? Alas!

she could get no further; she stood as it were blind-fold in an enchanted circle, which she could not overstep, and her hand felt all round, but could grasp nothing. If she resolutely banished such thoughts they came back again persistently. They overwhelmed her afresh, they repossessed themselves of her brain, suggesting endless doubts; and ending always, always, in the same question which was the invariable outcome of these miserable cogitations:

"What can it be? Is there anything at all?"

And never an answer.

She had once again questioned Bertie; but he had only smiled, with that terrifying smile of woe, and had implored her not to rack her brain over anything which he might have inconsiderately let drop as the natural outcome of his melancholy temper. Otherwise, he should henceforth always be afraid of speaking to her with any frankness; he must weigh his words, and their confidential intimacy as brother and sister would be at an end. And her own feeling in the matter was full of dubious half-lights, in which no outline was distinct, no color decided—a confusion of shadowy gray tints which dimmed the clear brightness of her love with increasing gloom, fatiguing her spirit by their indefiniteness, their non-existence in actual life, and their intangible semblance of reality, like a dream.

Fate

Once, however, the dream took substance; once she touched—she saw—she heard—something. But was that it?

They were coming out of the Lyceum. The crowd streamed forth, slowly shuffling, pushing impatiently now and then, shoulder to shoulder. And in the crush, close to her, Eva saw the flaming red plush opera-cloak of a tall, stout woman, and under a babyish "cherry-ripe" hat a face, rose, white and black, with a doll-like smile, which suddenly leaned across her to address Frank. The brim of the hat rested on a mass of yellow curls, a scent of musk and rice-powder greeted her nostrils, and, like a blow in her own face, she heard the words:

"Hallo! good-evening, Frank; how are you, old boy?"

She started and shrank back, looking hastily first at the rouged face and then at Frank; she saw his flashing look of rage, nor did the tall woman's confusion escape her notice—a damsel of the skating-rink—though the stranger drew back at seeing a lady on Frank's arm; she had evidently at first seen him over Eva's head in the crowd, and she now vanished, disconcerted by her own blunder in addressing a man who had a lady with him.

But she shot a glance of amazed inquiry at Van Maeren who was close behind. Bertie might have warned her; for it was Bertie who had whispered three words under the "cherry-ripe" hat, with a nod toward the front, saying: "There goes Frank."

She was vexed with herself; but she really had not seen the young lady.

When they reached home, Sir Archibald, who had observed nothing, was bidding them goodnight at the door, but Frank exclaimed: "I beg your pardon—but I must speak to Eva—I beg of you—"

It was already late, but Sir Archibald was no stickler for etiquette.

They were alone, looking at each other with anxious eyes, but neither spoke. Frank began hurriedly, stumbling over his words as if he were eager to forestall any evil suspicion she might entertain.

"Eva, believe me, Eva; you must believe me; it was nothing. You must not think anything of —of what happened just now."

In a few brief words he told of a former acquaintance—a young man's acquaintance—of the skating-rink. This was all at an end, it was a thing of the past; she must know that every man had a past. She knew that—surely?

"A past," she echoed coldly. "Oh! every man has a past? But we—we have no past."

"Eva, Eva!" he cried, for through the irony of her tone there pierced such acute pain that he stood dismayed and helpless, not knowing how to comfort her.

"Tell me only this much," she went on, going close up to him and looking into his face with that strange stare. She laid her hands on his shoulders and tried to read his inmost soul through his eyes. And she slowly said, expecting to hear her own doom in the first word he should utter:

"It is at an end?"

He fell on his knees before her where she had dropped on a chair, rigidly upright, as if she were frozen; he warmed her resisting hands in his grasp —and he swore that it was. His oath rang true; truth was stamped on his face; and she believed him. He besought forgiveness, told her that she must never think of it again, that all men—

"Oh, yes," she nodded her comprehension. "I know, I understand. Papa has brought me up on rather liberal lines."

He recollected that phrase; she had used it once before. And they both at once remembered Moldehoï and the black clouds. Eva shuddered.

"Are you cold, dearest?"

But she shook her head, still with a strange light in her eyes. He would have clasped her in his arms, but she drew back, and he felt himself rebuffed, almost rejected. He could not understand her. Why no kiss, why no generous reconciliation, if she understood so well, if she had been so liberally trained? But she was perhaps a little upset; he would not be too urgent. It would no doubt blow over.

When he was gone, Eva, in her own room, shivered and her teeth chattered as if she had an ague. And she began to cry bitterly, miserably, with deep despairing sobs, for grief that she lived, that she was a rational being—a woman—above all, that she had ever loved; that the world existed, that everything was so mean, so base—a mud-heap! She loathed it all. She felt as if she had never really understood any of the books she had read; neither the "Faery Queen" nor "Ghosts"—especially "Ghosts"; never understood anything she had learned under her father's "rather liberal" training. The white-feathery down of her illusions was blown into space; a rough hand had rubbed away the bloom from her most secret and inmost soul; the sacred innocence of her maidenhood had been dragged in the gutter. For the first time the peace of her great but reasonable love for Frank came into violent collision with the romance of her girlish dreams, and the balance of the two feelings was destroyed—of the practical and the romantic side of her character.

CHAPTER XV

AFTER that conversation with Eva, Bertie felt as though he were living in a more subtle atmosphere, wandering in a labyrinth full of mysterious ways of craft and cunning, in which he must walk very circumspectly if he did not wish to lose himself. He knew very well what he had been driving at; he wanted to instil into Eva suspicions of Frank's constancy. Did she not herself know her lover to be fickle, almost capricious? Had not his hints been well chosen? Had he not sown the seed of doubt? He did not know. He saw nothing to reassure him in the regular, monotonous routine of everyday life, in which subtle shades of manner so often escape even the keenest observer. Eva had, indeed, once asked him about that Something; but after that, in appearance at least, their intercourse had been on the old footing again. He saw no difference in Eva—none in Frank; so Eva could have said nothing to her lover and asked him no questions.

Before that afternoon Bertie had known hesitancy, had felt some disgust at his own heartlessness, some horror of his own monstrous selfishness.

But that talk with Eva had been the first step on a downward path, where it was now impossible to turn back. A singular lucidity of thought dawned in his brain, as though his brain were a crystal mirror, in which his ideas were reflected in a vivid light. Never yet had he felt himself so keenly alert, so clearly logical; never had he aimed so true at an object in view, with the precision of a needle. The clearness of his mind was so perfect that in a naive perception of his own baseness— a lucid moment of self-knowledge which once flashed on him, to his surprise, for no more than a second—he wondered that he should not apply so much talent and ingenuity to a nobler purpose.

"Why did you never become an artist?" he could hear Eva asking him.

But he only smiled; the practical weariness of life rose up before him; his own indolence, his catlike love of physical ease. No, no, he could not help himself; so it must be. The first step was taken. It was Fate!

Then, that evening as they came out of the theatre, that woman who belonged to their past life, his own significant nod, and his words, "There goes Frank." Was not all this, too, a fatality? Did not Fate strew such trivial incidents as these in the path of those who burned incense at her shrine and paid her due worship, to be utilized by them as benefits—infinitely small

links, which they must themselves weld into the
chain? Did not Fate give men the illusion of
free will, and a semblance of truth to the lie which
says that they by their own energy can coerce the
course of circumstance? No more than a word,
a nod—"There goes Frank!"—and then, for the
rest, trust to the chance— Chance! What is
chance?—that the smart damsel of the skating-
rink should overlook Eva—tiny, dainty Eva—lost
in the crowd.

Had the result been such as he had counted on?
Had he guessed the purpose of Fate? Yes, he
thought, in some small degree; why else should
Frank have craved an interview with Eva at so
late an hour And so, in that atmosphere of finely
spun cunning, in that labyrinth of wiles, he no
longer regarded himself as base, heartless, selfish.
Words—mere words! It was folly to consider
things too closely; he dismissed all scruples, and
if they would sometimes force themselves on him
he would argue with himself: Who could tell
whether it was not a good thing if Frank should
not marry? He was not a man to marry—no,
really; he was changeable, capricious, and incon-
stant; he would not make a wife happy.

Still, Van Maeren could see at once that this was
self-deception; and he would laugh to himself,
shaking his head, at finding himself so droll, so
singular. Life was as nothing; nothing was worth

troubling one's self about; but this introspection, this self-study, looking into one's own mind, juggling with one's own thoughts—that was really interesting, that was an amusing occupation, while lying at full length on a comfortable sofa.

And yet he seldom enjoyed any repose of mind. The web of his scheming was perpetually being wearily woven in his mind. His interviews with Eva were a fatiguing effort—sometimes a long discourse, sometimes only half utterances—for he had constantly and precisely to weigh every word. Still, this weariness was never to be detected in his air and manner, or in the phrases which fell from his lips, so apparently unpremeditated that they seemed alive with natural impulse. They were, in fact, the outcome of theatrical and carefully elaborated pessimism; they were lamentations over the ills of life, pity for Eva, wrapped in mysterious regrets; and amid all this melancholy, accusations against Westhove—mere trifles, passing hints, amounting to nothing but for the tone and accent—accusations of levity, inconstancy, caprice, fickleness. But at the slightest outry on Eva's part he was ready to contradict himself, fencing cleverly enough, now with himself, and now with Eva, with all the feints of a master of the foils, just touching her lightly—a prick here and a prick there—drawing a tiny drop of blood at each hit.

And to Eva it seemed that her soul, after having

been dragged through a gutter, was bleeding to death under these pin-pricks. It was a very sensible pain when she hopelessly compared the reality with her dreams, as they grew more vague and faded away, when she argued with herself in the cold light of reason, and asked herself, "Why am I so wretched? Because Frank is a young man like other young men; because Bertie is a pessimist, and despairs of my ever being happy?" And then she would shrug her shoulders; her trouble was intangible, had paled to a thin cloud, and vanished. She had always been very happy; Bertie's dejection was sickly nonsense; she should be happy again. But, notwithstanding that her common sense thus dissipated the pain, it constantly returned in spite of reason and argument; returned persistently, like an object tossed on a wave, which comes and goes, comes and goes.

She could endure it no longer, and one day when she ventured to look honestly into her own heart, she saw that she did indeed doubt Frank, and the truth of his statements about that woman. Longing for some certainty, she asked Bertie—his friend:

"Tell me, Bertie—that Something of which you once spoke to me; that mystery: what is it?"

"Oh, nothing, my dear girl, absolutely nothing."

She gazed at him with penetrating eyes, and went on in a strange, cold tone:

"Well; but I know; I have guessed."

Bertie was startled. What was she thinking? what had she got into her head?"

"Yes, I have guessed it," she repeated. "Frank does not love me; he loves—he loves that woman —that creature of the Lyceum. He has always loved her; is it so?"

Bertie said nothing, but stared before him; that was the easiest and best reply.

"Bertie, tell me, is it so?"

"No, it is not so," he answered, dully. "What a foolish notion to have got into your head. What made you think of such a thing?" But there was no ring of conviction in his voice; he spoke mechanically, as though in absence of mind, as if he were thinking of something else.

"Does he ever see her now?" she went on, feeling as if she were defiling herself with her own words; as if her lips were dropping slime.

"Why, of course not. What are you thinking of?"

She leaned back with a sigh, and tears glistened in her large eyes. He was silent for a minute, studying her out of the corner of his eye. Then, as if to mitigate his too feeble repudiation of the suspicion, he went on reproachfully:

"Really, Eva, you must not think such things of Frank. It is not nice; you must have some confidence in the man you are to marry."

"Then it is not the truth?"

"Certainly not. He never sees her now."

"But does not he think of her still?"

He gave her a long, deep, enigmatical look. His eyes were like black velvet darkness; she could not read their meaning.

"Fie!" said he, reprovingly, and he shook his head.

"That is no answer," she said, urgently. And again he fixed that dark gaze on her.

"Good God! answer me!" she cried, her heart wrung to the very core.

"How can you expect me to know Frank's feelings?" he dared to murmur. "I don't know—there!"

"Then it is so?" she moaned, clutching his hands.

"I don't know," he repeated, and, freeing himself from her grasp, he turned away and rose.

"He loves her; he can not live without her; he is that creature's slave, as you men sometimes are to such women; and though he sees her no more, out of respect for me, he thinks of her and talks of her to you—and that is why he is so silent and grave when he is here. Is it so?"

"Good Heavens! I do not know," he groaned, with mild impatience. "How should I know?"

"But why then does he pretend to love me? Why did he ask me to marry him? Because once, for a moment in Norway, he fancied he could do without her? Because he meant to live a new life, and now finds that he can not?" She clasped her hands with a gesture of anguish.

"Good God, Eva! say no more—say no more. I do not know, I tell you—I know nothing about it—nothing."

He sank back in his chair with a sigh of exhaustion. She said no more; the tears streamed from her eyes like rain impossible to be restrained.

CHAPTER XVI

AND in her misery she thought she had been very clever and cunning, and that she had guessed rightly; while, in truth, as guileless as a child, she had been as it were hypnotized by his magnetic gaze, and had spoken the very words he had intended she should utter.

She felt nothing of this, she saw him still as her brother-friend, fragile, affectionate, and unhappy, dreading to wound her, anxious to screen her from the truth for fear of hurting her, and yet not crafty enough to conceal it when she pressed him too closely. This was how he appeared to her. Not for an instant did she suspect that she was as a fly wrapping itself closer and closer in the spider's toils.

Bertie himself, after this scene, failed to see clearly that he had pulled the wires; that he had been the first to taint her confidence with the poison of suspicion; that he had brought about the catastrophe as they came out of the Lyceum; that he had compelled Eva to follow the clue he had chosen to suggest. Dimness shrouded the clearness of his mental vision, as a breath clouds

a mirror; the lucid crisis of his faculties was past.
This was all the outcome of circumstances, he
thought; no human being of his own free will
could work such things out— How easily everything had come about, how simply, without a
hitch! It was because Fate had so willed it and
had favored him—he had no part in it. Nor was
this self-deception: he really thought so.

In the evening after their last interview, Eva
went, very late, to seek her father in his study,
where he sat reading his books on heraldry. He
supposed she had come to bid him good-night, as
usual; but she sat down facing him, very upright,
and with a set face like a sleep-walker.

"Father, I want to speak to you."

He looked at her in surprise. In the Olympian
peace of his genealogical studies, in the calm,
emotionless existence of a hale old man, who finds
a solace for advancing years among his books, he
had never discerned that a drama was going on
close beside him, played by three beings whom he
saw every day. And he was startled at his daughter's rigid face and tone of suppressed suffering.

"Are you ill, my child?"

"Oh, no, I am quite well. But I want to ask you
something. I want to know if you will speak to
Frank?"

"To Frank?"

"Yes. To Frank. The other evening as we were

coming out of the Lyceum——" And she told him the whole story, sitting straight up in her chair, with that strange look in her face, and a husky, subdued voice; all about the yellow-haired woman, and her own suspicions and distrust. It was wrong of her to doubt Frank, but really she could not help it. She would fain have quoted Bertie as evidence, but Bertie had after all said nothing definite, so she did not see how she could bring him into court, and did not therefore mention his name.

Sir Archibald listened in dismay. He had never suspected what was going on in his daughter's mind; he had always supposed that everything was as clear as the sun at noon.

"And—what then?" he asked in some embarrassment.

"And then—I want you to speak to Frank. Ask him pointblank whether he still loves this woman, who has played some part in his past life; whether he can not bear to give her up; whether that is the reason he is always so silent and gloomy when we see him here. Get him to speak out. I would rather hear my doom than live in this dreadful suspense. And to you, perhaps, he will clear it all up, so that things may go on as they were before. Say nothing of my distrust; if it is not justified by the facts it might make him angry. It is too bad of me to suspect his truth, and I have tried to bring

myself to a better mind; but I can not succeed.
There is something in it, I know not what. There
is something in the air about me—oh! what, I
know not—which whispers to me: 'Do not trust
him, do not trust him.' I can not understand what
it is, but I feel it in me, all about me! It is a voice
in my ear; sometimes an eye which gazes at me.
At night, when I can not sleep, it looks down on
me; it speaks to me; I feel as if I were going crazy.
Perhaps it is a spirit! But do you speak to him,
papa. Do that much for your child. I am so
very, very unhappy."

She knelt at his feet and laid her head on his
knees, sobbing bitterly. He mechanically stroked
her hair, but he did not in the least understand.
He loved his child, but his affection was more a
matter of tender habit than of sympathetic intelligence. He did not understand her; he thought her
foolish and fanciful. Was it for this that he had
given her a first-rate education, let her read all
kinds of books, and made her know the world as
it was—stern, practical, and selfish, a struggle in
which each one must endeavor to conquer and secure a place and a share of happiness, by sheer
calm determination? He had his own corner in it,
with his books and his heraldry; why did she let
herself be a victim to nervous fancies? For it was
all nerves—nothing but nerves! Cursed things
were nerves! How like her mother she was, in

spite of her liberal education! Dreamy, romantic, full of absurd imagination. He speak to Frank? Why—what about—what was he to say? The lady at the Lyceum; this woman or that, to whom he had bowed? That might happen to any one. Eva was very absurd not to see that it might. And as to his talking it over with Frank—why, the young man would think that his future father-in-law was a perfect fool. There were thousands of such women in London. Where was the young man who had no acquaintance among them? And the picture of disturbed peace, of an unpleasant discussion, which would destroy an hour or perhaps a day of his Olympian repose and tear him from his studies, rose up in his brain, a terror to his simple-minded selfishness.

"Come, Eva, this is sheer folly," he good-humoredly grumbled. "What good do you think I can do? These are mere sickly fancies."

"No, no. They are not sickly fancies; not fancies at all. It is something—something quite different. There is something in me, around me—beyond my control."

"But, child, you are talking nonsense!"

"When I try to think it out, it goes away for a little while; but then it comes back again."

"Really, Eva, you must not talk so foolishly. After all, what is this story you have told me; what does it all mean? It comes and it goes, and it stays away, and then again it comes and goes."

She shook her head sadly, sitting on the floor at his feet in front of the fire.

"No, no," she said, very positively. "You do not understand, you are a man; you do not understand all there is in a woman. We women are quite different. But you will speak to him, will you not, and ask him all about it?"

"No, Eva; that I certainly will not. Frank might very well ask me what business it was of mine. You know as well as I do that every man has, or has had, acquaintance among such women. There is nothing in that. And Frank strikes me as too honorable to have anything to do with one of them now that he is engaged to you. I know him too well to imagine that. It is really too silly of you—do you hear: too silly!"

She began to sob passionately, and moan in an overpowering fit of grief. She wrung her hands, rocking herself from side to side, as if suffering intolerable torments.

"Oh, papa!" she entreated. "Dear papa, do, do! Do this for your child's sake, your little Eva. Go to him, talk to him. I am so unhappy, I can not bear it, I am so wretched! Speak to him; I can not speak of such a matter. I am only a girl, and it is all so horrible, so sickening. Oh, papa, papa, do speak to Frank!"

Fate

She tried to lean coaxingly against his knees, but he stood up; her tears angered him and made him more obstinate. His wife had never got anything from him by tears; quite the reverse. Eva was silly and childish. He could not recognize his spirited daughter—always indefatigable and bright —with whom he had traveled half over the world, in this crushed creature dissolved in woe.

"Stand up, Eva," he said, sternly. "Do not crouch on the floor. You will end by vexing me seriously with your folly. What are you crying for? For nothing, pure foolish imagining. I will have no more of it. You must behave reasonably. Get up, stand up."

She dragged herself to her feet, groaning as she did so, with a white face and clenched hands.

"I can not help it," she said. "It is my nature, I suppose. Have you no pity for your child, even if you do not understand her? Oh, go and speak to him—only a few words, I implore you—I beseech you."

"No, no, no!" he cried, stamping his foot, his face quite red as if from a congestion of rage at all this useless, undefined vexation, and his daughter's folly, and weeping and entreaties, which his obstinacy urged him on no account to indulge. She however rose, looking taller in her despair; her eyes had a strange look as they gazed into her father's.

"Then you will not speak to Frank? You will not do that much for me?"

"No. It is all nonsense, I tell you. Worry me about it no more."

"Very well. Then, I must do it," she said gravely, as if pronouncing some irrevocable decision. And very slowly, without looking round, without bidding him good-night, she left the room. It was as though Sir Archibald was a total stranger, as though there were no bond of tenderness between her and her father—nothing but the hostility of two antagonistic natures. No; under their superficial affection they had had no feeling in common; they had never really known, never tried to understand each other; she had no sympathy with his old age; he had none with her youth. They were miles asunder; a desert, a pathless waste, lay between them. They dwelt apart as completely as though they were locked up in two shrines, where each worshiped a different God.

"He is my father," thought she, as she went along the passage. "I am his child."

She could not understand it. It was a mystery of nature that scarcely seemed possible. He—her father, she—his child; and yet he could not feel her anguish—could not see that it was anguish—called it folly and fancy. And a vehement longing for her mother rose up in her heart. She would have understood!

Fate

"Mamma, mamma!" she sobbed out. "Oh mamma, come back. Tell me what I can do. Come as a ghost; I will not be afraid of you. I am so forlorn, so miserable—so miserable! Come and haunt me; come, only come!"

In her room, in the darkness, she watched for the ghost. But it came not. The night hung unbroken, like a black curtain, behind which there was nothing but emptiness.

Fate

CHAPTER XVII

WHEN Frank came to call next morning, he at once saw in her face that she was greatly agitated.

"What is the matter, dearest?" he asked.

At first she felt weak. There was something so terrible—and then again so shocking—but she commanded herself; she drew herself up in her pretty self-will, which gave firmness to the child-like enthusiasm and womanly coyness of her nature, like a sterner background against which so much that was soft and tender stood out. And, feeling above all that she stood alone, abandoned by her father, she was determined to be firm.

"Frank, I have no alternative," she began, with the energy of despair. "I must talk matters over with you. Even before you answer me I am almost convinced that I am wrong, and think myself odious; but still I must speak, for I am too unhappy under this—all this. To keep it all to myself in silence is more than I can bear; I can endure it no longer, Frank. I asked papa to speak to you, but he will not. Perhaps he is right; still, it is not kind of him, for now I must do it myself."

302

Even in the excited state of mind she was in she loathed this cruel necessity; but she controlled herself and went on:

"That woman—Frank, Frank! That woman—I can think of nothing else!"

"But, dear Eva!"

"Oh! let me speak—I must speak; I see that creature always at my elbow; I smell her perfume; I hear her voice. I can not get it out of my ears." She shuddered violently, and the dreadful thing came over her again, again possessed her; the ghostly hypnotism of that eye, that whisper, that strange magnetic power which her father could not understand. The words she spoke seemed prompted, inspired by that voice; her expression and attitude obeyed the coercion of that gaze. In her inmost soul she felt those eyes as black as night.

"Oh, Frank!" she cried, and the tears came from nervous excitement, and the fear lest she should not have courage to obey these promptings. "I must, I *must* ask you. Why, when you come to see me, are you always so grave and silent, as though you were not happy in my society; why do you evade all direct replies; why do you always tell me that there is nothing the matter? That woman —it is because of her, because you still love her— better, perhaps, than you love me! Because you can not forget her, because she still is a part of

your life, a large part—perhaps the largest? Oh,
it is such torture, such misery—ever-present misery. And I am not meanly jealous; I never have
been. I quite understand your feeling about her
—the first-comer—though it is dreadful. But you
yourself are too silent, too sad; and when I think
it over I doubt, in spite of myself—Frank, in spite
of myself, I swear to you. But the suspicion forces
itself upon me and overwhelms me! Great God,
why must it be? But, Frank, tell me I am a sim-
pleton to think so, and that she is nothing to you
any longer—nothing at all. You never see her, do
you? Tell me, tell me."

The anguish of her soul as she spoke was elo-
quent in her face, though disfigured with grief,
and pale with the dead whiteness of a faded azalea
blossom; a convulsive pang pinched the corners of
her mouth, and her quivering eyelids; she was
indeed a martyr to her own too vivid fancy.

But he, at this moment, was incapable of seeing
her as a martyr. Her words had roused in him a
surge of fury such as he could remember having
felt occasionally as a child, lashed up as it were
by the blast of a hurricane, drowning every other
feeling, sweeping away every other thought, like
dust before the storm. It came blustering up at the
notion of his honesty being questioned, his perfect
candor, honor, and truth—like a whirlwind of
righteous indignation at such injustice; for in his

own mind he could not conceive of such a doubt, knowing himself to be honest, honorable, and true. His dark gray eyes flashed beneath his deeply knit brows; his words came viciously from between his set teeth, which shone large and white under his mustache, like polished ivory.

"It is inconceivable! Good God, this is monstrous! I have answered you, once for all; I have told you in plain words: 'No—no—no!' And you ask me again and again. Do you think I am a liar? Why? Have you ever seen anything in me to make you think I can lie? I say no, and I mean no! And will you have doubts; still you think and worry over it like an old woman. Why do you not take things as they are? You know the facts; why do you not believe me? I am not sad, I am not gloomy; I am quite happy with you; I love you; I do not doubt you. But you—you!— Believe me, if you go on in this way you will make yourself miserable; and me too, me too!"

She looked at him steadfastly, and her pride rose up to meet his wrath, for his words offended her.

"You need not speak to me in that tone," she answered haughtily. "When I tell you that it is against my will—you hear—in spite of myself, that I have doubts, and that this makes me miserable, you need not take that tone. Have some pity on me, and do not speak like that."

"But, Eva, when I assure you," he began again,

trembling with rage, which he tried to control, forcing himself to speak gently: "when I assure you."

"You had done so already."

"And you doubt my word?"

"Only in so far as—"

"You disbelieve me?" he roared, quite beside himself.

"Only in so far as that I think you are keeping something back," she cried.

"Something back! What, in Heaven's name?"

His friend's name was on her tongue; but as soon as she thought of Bertie, hesitancy and indecision took possession of her, for she knew not what exactly Bertie had in fact told her. It was always as though Van Maeren had enclosed her in a magic circle, a spell of silence, which made it impossible for her to mention him; and even at this juncture he was an intangible presence, his name an unutterable word, his hints a mere inarticulate jangle.

"What—what?" she gasped in bewilderment. "Oh, I do not know. If only I knew! But you are concealing something from me—and perhaps it is something about her, that woman!"

"But when I tell you that she—"

"No, no," she insisted, confirmed in her imaginings by her offended pride. "I know—I know. You men count such matters as nothing. A thing of the past; it is so all the world over, you say; and what I call something, you call nothing. And so I say there is something—that you are hiding, Frank."

"Eva, I swear—"

"Do not swear to it, for that would be a sin!" she shrieked out, wrought up, in spite of herself, to a paroxysm of insane belief in a thing of which she knew nothing certain. "For I feel it. I feel it here, in me, about me, everywhere!"

He seized her by the wrists, carried away by his rage at her rejecting his asseverations, wounded in his proud consciousness of honor and truthfulness, and amazed at the depth of her infatuated distrust.

"Then you do not believe me," he said, with an oath. "You do not believe me?" And for the second time his tone offended and enraged her. The exposure of their two antagonistic natures, with all their passions and infirmities, brought them into collision.

"No; since you will have it— No!" she cried, and she wrenched herself free from his vise-like grasp with such violence that her slender wrists cracked. "Now you know it: I do not believe you. You are hiding something from me, and it has something to do with that woman. I feel it, and what I feel is to me undeniable. That creature, who dared to speak to you, has taken root in my imagination; I feel her close to me, smell her scent, and am so intensely conscious that there is still something between you and her that I am bold to say to you: 'You lie; you lie for her sake and are cheating me!'"

With a sort of low bellow, which broke from him involuntarily, he rushed at her, clenching his fists, and she mechanically shrank back. But he seized her hands again, enclosing them in his great strong fingers, so that she felt his power through her flesh, in her very bones.

"Oh"—and it was like muttering thunder; "you have no heart—none, that you can say such things to me! You are base, mean, even to think them! 'You feel, and you feel!' Yes. It is your own petty narrowness that you feel. You have nothing in you but base and contemptible incredulity! Your whole nature is mean! Everything is at an end between us; I have nothing more to do with you. I was mistaken in you."

He flung her off, on to a sofa. There she remained, staring up at the ceiling, with wide-open eyes. At the moment she was startled rather than angry, and did not fully understand the state of things. Her overwrought brain was bewildered; she knew not what had happened.

For a minute he stood looking at her. His lips wore a sneer of contempt, and his eyes, half closed in scorn, glanced over her prostrate form. He saw how pretty she was; her graceful figure, stretched on the Turkish pillows, revealed the soft lines of its supple, girlish mold through the clinging folds of a thin pale green material; her hair, which had come loose, hung to the floor, like the red-gold fleece of some rare wild creature; her bosom heaved with spasmodic rapidity. She lay there like a ravished maid, flung aside in a fit of passion. He saw all the charms that he had forfeited; deep wrath sprang up in him, a wild longing for the happiness he had lost; but his injured honor ousted regrets and longing. He turned away and left her there.

She remained on the same spot, in the same attitude. She was full of obscure wonderment; darkness had fallen on her soul, as though, after being entrapped by falsehood, blindfolded by doubt, she had been led into a labyrinth and then suddenly released—her eyes unbound—in a dark chamber. Her soul indeed seemed to have bled to death; she could not yet know how deeply it was wounded, and in spite of her intolerable grief she still thought only of the darkness about her.

"How strange," she whispered. "But why? In Heaven's name, why?"

CHAPTER XVIII

AFTER this there was a month of peace. A sudden calm had fallen on them both, full, for both alike, of silent, bitter grief. And, with it all, the insignificant commonplace of ordinary life, and the recurring, monotonous tasks of every day.

Even Bertie found himself breathing this strange, stagnant air. He wondered greatly what could have occurred. How simply, how easily, things had worked themselves out! He? No, he had done nothing; he could have done nothing. Events had merely followed each other. What had come about was the inevitable. And the possibility of a life free from care again lay before him; an eternity of comfort and wealth with Westhove, for whom he felt his old affection revive with the glow almost of a passion, now that Frank, severed from Eva, though blaming himself indeed, needed consolation and sympathy. And Bertie's low, unctuous tones were full of sympathy. Oh, the dark melancholy of the first few days, the terrible grief of wondering, when now, his indignation cold, Frank asked himself, as Eva had asked herself, Why? Why had this happened? What had he done? What had brought it about? And he could not see, could not understand; it was like a book out of which leaves have been torn so as to spoil the sense. He could comprehend neither himself and his fury, nor Eva and her doubts. All life seemed to him a riddle. For hours together he would sit gazing out of the window, staring at the opaque dulness of the London fog, his eye fixed on that riddle. He rarely went out, but sat dreaming in White-Rose Cottage, which was lonely and quiet enough in its remote suburb. An enervating indifference possessed his stalwart frame, for the first time in his life he saw himself in a true light, and detected the vacillation and weakness deep down in his being, like a lymphatic stream traversing his sanguine physical vigor. He saw himself, as a mere child in resistance to the storm of rage, the blast of fury which had swept away his happiness. And his suffering was so terrible that he could not entirely comprehend it; it seemed too all-embracing for the human mind.

These were days of dreary gloom which they spent together; Frank too dejected to go out of doors, Bertie creeping about very softly under the pressure of a vague dread and indefinable dissatisfaction. He felt Frank's friendship reviving, and, flattered by this revival, was conscious of a sentiment of pity, almost of sympathy; he tried to rouse Frank from his moodiness, and talked of

a supper party—with ladies—on the old pattern.
He made plans for going away, here or there, for
a few days. He tried to persuade Westhove to
take to work, mentioning the names of various
great engineers who were to be found in London.
But everything fell dead against Frank's obdurate
melancholy, everything was swallowed up in the
dark cloud of his dejection, which seemed incapable of more than one idea—one self-reproach, one
grief. And the only solace of his life was always
to have Bertie at his side; a closer intimacy to
which Van Maeren himself was no less prompted,
now that he had gained his selfish ends, having no
further fear of impending poverty, and seeing always by him a consuming sorrow. Had he not
rejected the notion that he had been the cause of
it all? And had he not, during his late existence
as an idle bachelor, become so superfine a being
that he felt a craving for the vague delights of
sympathy; nothing more than sympathy, since no
great and noble love, no strong and generous
friendship could breathe in the complicated recesses of his soul, for lack of room and fresh air
in those narrow cells built up on strange fallacies,
and since love and friendship must pine and die
there, like a lion in a boudoir.

Thus it was that he could still feel for Frank,
could lay his hands on his shoulders and try to
comfort him, could find words of affection—new

on his lips—and unwonted phrases of consolation or cheering. Women, he would say, were so narrow-minded; they were nothing, they loved nothing, they were a mere delusion; no man should ever make himself miserable for a woman. There was nothing like friendship, which women could not even understand, and never felt for each other; a passion of sympathy, the noble joy of affinity and agreement. And he believed what he said, sunning himself in Platonism with catlike complacency, just as he basked in material ease and comfort, rejoicing in his raptures of friendship, and admiring himself for his lofty ideals.

But Frank's love for Eva had been, and was still, so absorbing, that he erelong saw through this effete and decrepit devotion, and thenceforward it afforded him no solace. His depression wrapped him in darker folds. He forced himself to recall exactly everything that had happened; what Eva had said, what he had replied. And he laid all the blame on himself, exonerating Eva for her doubts; he cursed his own temper, his barbarous violence to a woman—and to her! What was to be done? Parted—parted forever! It was a fearful thought that he might never see her again, that she could be nothing henceforth in his life. Could it be no otherwise? Was all lost? Irrevocably?

No, no, no; the desperate denial rose up within

him; he would triumph over circumstances; he would win back his happiness.

And she? How was she? Was she, too, suffering? Did she still doubt him, or had his vehemence, notwithstanding its brutality, made his innocence clear? But if it were so, if she no longer doubted him—and how could she?—good heavens, how wretched she must be! Grieving over her want of trust, with self-accusation even more terrible than his own—for his wrath had at any rate been justifiable, and her suspicions were not.

Was it so? Or was she, on the contrary, stricken almost to death, perhaps, by his cruelty, or filled with contempt for his lack of power to control his anger, which was like some raging wild beast? How was she? What was her mood? A passionate desire to know pierced his heart now and again like a sword-thrust; to go to her, to pray for pardon, for restoration to the happiness he had thrown away, as he had flung her from him on that sofa. She would never admit him to her presence after so great an insult. But he might write. Of course, a letter! His heart leaped with joy. What bliss to grovel, on paper, in the dust, at her feet; to humble himself in penitential prayers for mercy, and adoring words, while asserting his dignity in the pride of his truth, and his anguish under her doubts! She would hearken, as a Madonna to a sinner; he would recover his lost happiness!

Fate

And he tried to compose his letter, thrilling with the effort to find words, which still did not seem fervent or humble enough.

He spent a whole day over his task, polishing his phrases as a poet does a sonnet. And when at last it was finished he felt refreshed in spirit, with renewed hopes—a complete resurrection. He was convinced that his letter would remove every misunderstanding between him and Eva.

In the highest spirits he betook himself to Van Maeren, told his friend of the step he had taken, and all he hoped for. He spoke eagerly; his very voice was changed.

Bertie leaned back in his chair, rather grave and pale; but he controlled himself so far as to smile in answer to Westhove's smile, and he agreed in his anticipations in words to which he vainly strove to give a ring of conviction.

"To be sure, of course, everything must come right again," he muttered; and the perspiration stood on his forehead under his chestnut curls.

CHAPTER XIX

BUT an hour later, alone in his room that evening, he walked to and fro with such seething agitation as set every nerve quivering in his slight frame, as a storm tosses a rowboat. His soft features were distorted to a hideous expression of malignancy, with rage at his own impotence, and he strode up and down, up and down, like a beast in a cage, clenching his fists. Then it was for this that he had elaborated his tastes, had sharpened and polished all his natural gifts, and had directed all the powers of his mind like a battery charged with some mysterious fluid, on the secrets of a girl's love and life! A single letter, a few pages of tender words, and the whole work would be destroyed! For now, in his wrath, he suddenly saw and prided himself on the fact; he saw that he—very certainly he—had guided events to sever Frank and Eva. How could he even for a moment have doubted it?

And it was all to come to naught! Never, never! No, a thousand times, no! Awful, and infinitely far as the horizon, the perspective of life

316

yawned before him—the dead level of poverty,
the barren desert in which he must pine and perish
of hunger. And in his horror of treading that
wilderness every sinew of his lax resolve seemed
strained to the verge of snapping.

He must take steps forthwith. An idea flashed
through his brain like the zigzag of forked lightning. Yes; that was his only course; the simplest
and most obvious means, a mere stroke of villainy
—as conventionality would term it. . . . No
need here for any elaborate psychological *pros*
and *cons;* they were never of any use; they got
entangled in their own complications. Simply a
theatrical *coup.*

He took his hat and crept quietly out of the
house, with a sneer of contempt, of scorn for himself, that he should have fallen so low. It was
half-past ten. He hailed a cab, and laughed to
hear the melodramatic sound of his own voice
as he gave the driver Sir Archibald's address—
the voice of a stage traitor. Then he shrank into
a corner of the vehicle, his shoulders up to his ears,
his eyes half closed and gazing out through the
dim mystery of the night. Deadly melancholy
lurked at the bottom of his soul.

He got out near Sir Archibald's house, walked
a few yards to the door, and rang—and the minutes
he waited in the darkness before the closed house
seemed an eternity of intolerable misery, of horror,

aversion, loathing of himself. His lips were pinched into a grimace of disgust.

A man-servant opened the door with a look of surprise at the belated visitor, a surprise which gave way to an impertinent stare when he saw that Van Maeren was alone, without Westhove. He bowed with insolent irony, and held the door wide open with exaggerated servility, for Bertie to enter.

"I must speak with you at once," said Bertie, coolly, "at once and alone."

The man looked at him, but said nothing.

"You can do me a service. I need your assistance—pressingly. Can I say two words to you without being seen by any one?"

"Now?" said the servant.

"Yes, now; without delay."

"Will you come in—into the servants' hall?"

"No, no. Come out and walk up and down with me. And speak low."

"I can not leave the house yet. The old man will be going to bed in an hour or so, and then I can join you in the street."

"Then I will wait for you; opposite, by the Park railings. You will be sure to come? I will make it worth your while." The footman laughed, a loud, brazen laugh, which rang through the hall, filling Bertie with alarm. "Then you are a gentleman now? And pretty flush, eh?"

Fate

"Yes," said Van Maeren hoarsely. "Then you will come?"

"Yes, yes. In an hour or more, fully an hour. Wait for me. But if I am to do anything for you, you will have to fork out, you know; and fork out handsomely too!"

"All right, all right," said Bertie. "But I hope you will not fail me. I count on your coming, mind."

The door was ruthlessly shut. He walked up and down for a very long time in the cold and damp. The chill pierced to his very marrow, while the twinkling gas lamps stared at him through the gray mist like watery eyes. He waited, pacing the pavement for an hour—an hour and a half—perishing of fatigue and cold, like a beggar without a shelter. Still he waited, shivering as he walked, his hands in his pockets, his eyes dull with self-contempt, staring out of his white face at the dark square of the door, which still remained shut.

CHAPTER XX

WHEN, after a few days of anxious expectancy, Frank still had no answer from Eva, he wrote a second time; and although the first bloom of his revived hopes was already dying, he started whenever the bell rang, and would go to the letter-box in the front door; his thoughts were constantly busy with picturing the messenger who was walking up the road with his happiness—wrapped up in an envelope. And he would imagine what Eva's answer might be: just a few lines—somewhat cool, perhaps—in her large bold English hand, on the scented, ivory-laid paper she always used, with her initials crossed in pink and silver in one corner.

How long she took to write that answer! Was she angry? Or could she not make up her mind how to word her forgiveness; was she elaborating her letter as he had elaborated his? And the days went by while he waited for that note. When he was at home, he pictured the postman coming nearer and nearer, now only four—three—two doors away; now he would ring—and he listened; but the bell did not sound, or, if it did, it was not by reason of the letter. When he was out, he would be electrified by the thought that the letter must be lying at home and he hurried back to White-Rose Cottage, looked in the letter-box, and then in the sitting-room. But he never found it, and the intolerable emptiness of the place where he looked for it made him swear and stamp with rage.

Twice had he written—two letters—and yet she gave no sign! And he could think of no cause in his ardent expectancy which made him regard it as the most natural thing that she should reply at once. Still he lived on this waiting. The reply must come; it could not be otherwise. His brain held no other thought than: It is coming—it will come to-day. All life was void and flat, but it could be filled by just one letter. Day followed day, and there was no change.

"I have had no answer yet from Eva," he said, in a subdued tone to Bertie, as feeling himself humiliated, disgraced by her determined silence, mocked at in his illusory hopes.

"Not yet?" said Bertie; and a mist of melancholy glistened in his black velvety eyes. A weight indeed lay on his mind; he sighed deeply and frequently. He really was unhappy. What he had done was so utterly base. But it was all Frank's fault. Why, now that he was parted from Eva, could he not forget his passion; why could

he not find sufficient comfort in the sweets of
friendship? How delightful it might have been
to live on together, a happy pair of friends, under
the calm blue sky of brotherhood, in the golden
bliss of perfect sympathy, with no woman to disturb it. Thus he romanced, consciously working
up his friendly, compassionate feeling toward
Frank to a sort of frenzy, in the hope of comforting himself a little, of forgetting his foul deed, of
convincing himself that he was magnanimous;
nay, that in spite of that little deception, he now
more than ever since he was sunk in the mire,
really longed for a high ideal. It was all Frank's
fault. And yet, was Frank to blame because he
could not forget Eva? No, no. That was all
fatality. No one was to blame for that. That was
the act of Fate.

"Yes, that is certain!" thought he. "But why
have we brains to think with, and why do we feel
pain, if we can do nothing to help ourselves? Why
are we not plants or stones? Why should this
vast, useless universe exist at all? And why, why
did nothingness cease to be? How peaceful, how
delightfully peaceful, that would be!"

He stood, as it were, before the sealed portals of
the great Enigma, suddenly amazed and horrified
at himself. Good God! How had he come to this;
how was it that nowadays he was always thinking
of such things? Had he ever had such notions

in America, when he was toiling and tramping in his daily slavery? Had he not then regarded himself as a gross materialist, caring for nothing but plenty of good food and unbroken peace? And now, when he had long experience of such material comforts, now he felt as though his nerves had been spun finer and finer to mere silken threads, thrilling and quivering under one emotion after another, vibrating like the invisible aerial pulsations which are irresistibly transmitted, with a musical murmur, along the telephone wires overhead. How had he come by all this philosophy, the blossom of his idle hours? And in his bewilderment he tried to recall his youth, and remember whether he had then had this predisposition to thought, whether he had then had any books which had impressed him deeply; tried to picture his parents, and whether this might be hereditary. And he—he—had handed round coffee-cups in New York! Was he not after all happier in those days and freer from care? Or was it only that "distance lent enchantment to the view," the distance of so few years?

CHAPTER XXI

WHEN Frank, after a few days of death-in-life patience, had still received no answer, he wrote to Sir Archibald. Still the same silence. He poured out his grief to Bertie in bitter complaint, no longer humble, but full of wrath like an enraged animal, and yet half woful at the ill-feeling shown by Eva and her father. Was it not enough that he had three times craved forgiveness? Had Eva cared for him in fact so little, that when he groveled at her feet she could find no word even to tell him that all was at an end?

"I can not now remember all I said," he told Bertie, as he paced the room with long, equal, and determined steps. "But I must have been hard upon her. God help me, I can never govern my speech! And I seized her, I recollect, so, by the arms. And then I came away. I was too furious. I ought not to have done it; but I can not keep cool, I can not."

"Frank, I wish you could get over it," said Bertie soothingly, from the depths of his arm-chair. "There is nothing now to be done. It is very sad that it should have happened so, but you must throw it off."

"Throw it off! Were you ever in love with a woman?"

"Certainly."

"Then you must know something of it— But you could never love any one much; it is not in your nature. You love yourself too well."

"That may be; but at any rate I love you, and I can not bear to see you thus, Frank. Get over it! They seem to have taken the whole business so ill that there is nothing more to be done. I wish you would only see that, and submit to the inevitable. Try to live for something else. Can there be no other woman in the world for you? Perhaps there is another. A man does not perish so for love. You are not a girl—girls do so."

He gazed at Frank with such a magnetic light in his eyes that Westhove fancied there was a great truth in his words; and Bertie's last reproof reminded him of his vacillation, his miserable weakness, which lay beneath his manly and powerful exterior like an insecure foundation. Still he clung to his passionate longings, his vehement craving for the happiness he had lost.

"You can not possibly judge of the matter," he retorted impatiently, trying to escape from Van Maeren's eye. "You never *did* love a woman, though you may say so. Why should not every-

Fate

thing come right again? What has happened after all? What have I done? I fell into a violent, vulgar rage? What then? Is that so unpardonable in the person you love? But perhaps —I say, can I have addressed the letters wrongly?"

During a few seconds there was a weight of silence in the room, an atmosphere of lead. Then Van Maeren said—and his voice had a tender, coaxing tone:

"If you had written but once, I might think it possible; but three letters, to the same house—it is scarcely possible."

"I will go myself and call," said Westhove. "Yes, yes, I will go myself."

"What are you saying?" asked Bertie dreamily. He was still under the influence of that heavy moral atmosphere; he had not quite understood, not grasped the idea. "What was it you said?" he repeated.

"I shall go myself and call at the house," Frank reiterated.

"At what house? Where?"

"Why, at the Rhodeses'—on Eva. Are you daft?"

But Bertie rose to his feet, and his eyes glittered in his pale face like black diamonds with a hundred facets.

"What to do there?" he said with a convulsive effort in his throat to keep his voice calm

326

Fate

"To talk to her and set matters straight; I can not bear it. It has gone on too long."

"You are a fool!" said Van Maeren shortly.

"Why am I a fool?"

"Why are you a fool? You have not a grain of self-respect. Do you really think of going there?"

"Yes, of course."

"I consider it absurd," said Bertie.

"All right," said Frank, "pray think so. I myself can see that it is very weak of me. But, good God! I can hold out no longer. I love her so; I was so happy; life was so sweet; and now; now, by my own fault! I do not care what you think it. Absurd or not, I mean to go all the same."

In his distress of mind he had thrown himself into a chair, and every muscle of his features was quivering with agitation. But he went on:

"I do not know what it is that I feel; I am so unhappy, so deeply, deeply wretched. Never in my life had I known what it was to feel so content, in such harmonious equilibrium of soul as when I was with Eva; at least so it seems to me now. And now it is all at an end, and everything seems aimless. I no longer know why I live and move and eat and have my being! Why should I take all that trouble, and then have this misery into the bargain? I might just as well be dead. You see, that is why I mean to call there. And

if things do not come right then, well, I shall
make an end of myself! Yes, yes, I shall make
an end of myself."

Crushed by the burden of life, he lay back in
his chair, with his features set, his great limbs
stretched out in their useless strength, all his
power undermined by the mysterious inertia which
gnawed it away like a worm. Before him stood
Van Maeren, drawn to his full height in the energy
of despair, and his flashing eyes darting sparks of
fire. He laid his tremulous hands on Westhove's
shoulders, feeling their massive breadth, heavy and
strong. A reaction electrified him with something
like defiance; he scorned this man of might in his
love-sickness. But above all, oh, above all, he felt
himself being dragged down to the lowest deep;
and it was with the tenacity of a parasitic growth
that he clung to Frank, setting his fingers into his
shoulders.

"Frank," he began, almost hoarsely, "just listen
to me. You are making yourself ill. You talk
like a fool, and then you cry out just like a baby.
You must get over it. Show a little more pluck.
Do not mar your whole life by these foolish lamentations. And what about, when all is said and
done, what about? All because a girl has ceased
to love you. Do you place your highest hopes of
happiness in a girl? They are creatures without
brains or heart; superficial and vain, whipped up

to a froth—mere windy nothingness. And you would kill yourself for that? Heaven above, man! It is impossible— I do not know what it is to love a woman, eh? But you do not know what trouble and misery are. You fancy that all the woes on earth have come upon you. And it is nothing, after all, but a little discomfort, a little wounded conceit perhaps—it will be no worse. If I had made away with myself at every turn of ill-luck, I should have been dead a thousand times. But I pulled through, you see. How can you be such a coward? Eva has shown you very plainly that she does not want to have anything more to say to you; and you would seek her once more! Suppose she were to show you the door? What then? If you do such a thing, if you go to her, you will be so mean in my eyes, so weak, so cowardly, so childish, such a fool, such a damned fool, that you may go to the devil for aught I care!"

He cleared his throat as if he were actually sick, and turned away with a queer, light-headed feeling in his brain.

Westhove said nothing, torn in his mind between two impulses. He was no longer clear as to his purpose, quite bewildered by the false voice in his ear—in his soul. There was something factitious in Bertie's speech, a false ring which Frank could not detect, though he was conscious of it; and the voice of his own desires rang false too, with jarring, unresolved chords, which jangled inharmoniously against each other. He had completely lost his head, but he sat silent for some time, till at length he repeated, with sullen obstinacy:

"All right. I do not care a pin. I shall go all the same."

But Bertie began again, with honeyed smoothness this time, seating himself on the floor, as was his wont when he was out of luck, on the fur rug before the fire, resting his throbbing head against a chair.

"Come, Frank, get this out of your mind. You never meant that you would really go. You are at heart too proud and too brave to think of it seriously. Pull yourself together. Have you forgotten everything? Did not Eva tell you that she did not believe your word, that you were false to her, that you still were friends with that other girl, and that she knew it? To tell you the truth, I observed from the first how suspicious she was, and I did not think it becoming in a young lady; I did not think it quite—quite nice— To be sure, that evening at the Lyceum, it did look as if there was something in it. Still, when you assured her that it was at an end, it seems to me quite monstrous that she did not believe you then. You can not possibly mean what you say when you speak of seeking her again. Of course it makes no difference to me; go by all means, for what I care;

but I should regard it as such folly, such utter folly—"

And still Frank sat speechless, lost, with the bewildering jangle still in his brain.

"And you will take the same view of it if you only think it over. Think it over, Frank."

"I will," said Frank, gloomily.

Bertie went on, flattering his manly courage, and it sounded like bells in Frank's ears: pride, pluck; pride, pluck: only the bells were cracked. And yet the jingle soothed him. Did he at this moment love Eva? Or was it all over, had she killed his love by her doubt? Pride, pluck; pride, pluck. He could not tell—alas! he could not tell.

With a movement like a caress, Bertie crept nearer, laid his head on the arm of Westhove's chair, and clasped his hands about his knees, looking, in the dusk and firelight, like a supple panther; and his eyes gleamed like a panther's, black and flame-colored.

"Speak, Frank; I can not bear to see you like this. I care for you so much, though perhaps it does not seem so to you just now, and though I have my own way of showing it. Oh, I know very well that you sometimes think me ungrateful. But you do not know me; I am really devoted to you. I never loved my father, nor any woman, nor even myself, as I do you. I could do anything in the world for you, and that is a great deal for me to say. I say, Frank, I will not have you look so. Let us leave London; let us travel, or go to live somewhere else—in Paris or Vienna. Yes, let us go to Vienna—that is a long way off; or to America, to San Francisco; or to Australia—wherever you choose. The world is wide, and you may see so many things that you will get fresh ideas. Or let us make an expedition to the interior of Africa. I should enjoy seeing such a savage country, and I am stronger than I look; I am tough. Let us wander about a great deal, and go through a great deal—great bodily fatigue. Don't you think it must be splendid to cut your way through the impenetrable bush? Oh, yes, let us bathe our souls in nature, in fresh air, and space, and health."

"Well, well," Frank grumbled, "we will go away. We will travel. But I can not do it comfortably: I have very little money. I spent so much last year."

"Oh, but we will be economical; what need have we of luxury? I, at any rate, can do without it."

"Very well," Frank muttered again. "We will do it cheaply."

Then they were silent for a time. In the twilight, Frank by some slight movement touched one of Bertie's hands. He suddenly grasped it, squeezed it almost to crushing, and said in a low voice:

"Good old fellow! Dear, good fellow!"

CHAPTER XXII

CAN he have gone there? thought Van Maeren as he sat at home alone the next evening, and did not know with what purpose Westhove had gone out. Well, he would sit up for him; there was nothing else to be done. Just a few days to arrange matters and then they would be off, away from London. Oh, what a luckless wretch he thought himself. All this villainy for the sake of mere material comfort, of idleness, and wealth, which, as he was slowly beginning to discover, had all become a matter of indifference to him. Oh! for the Bohemian liberty of his vagabond life in the States, free, unshackled; his pockets now full of dollars and again empty, absolutely empty! He felt quite homesick for it; it struck him as an enviable existence of careless independence as compared with his present state of vacuous ease and servility. How greatly he was changed. Formerly he had been unfettered indeed by conventional rules, but free from any great duplicity; and now, his mind had been cultivated, but was sunk in a depth of baseness. And what for? To enable him to hold fast that which no longer had any value in his

333

eyes. No value? Why, then, did he not cut his way out of his own net, to go away, in poverty; and write a single word to Frank and Eva to bring them together again? It was still in his power to do this.

He thought of it, but smiled at the thought; it was impossible, and yet he could not see wherein the impossibility lay. But it *was* impossible, it was a thing which could not be done. It was illogical, full of dark difficulties, a thing that could never come about for mysterious reasons of Fatality, which, indeed, he did not clearly discern, but accepted as unanswerable.

He was musing in this vein, alone that evening, when Annie, the housekeeper, came to tell him that some one wanted to speak with him.

"Who is it?"

She did not know, so he went into the sitting-room, where he found Sir Archibald's footman, with his big nose and ugly, shifty, gray eyes, like a bird's, twinkling in his terra-cotta face, which was varied by blue tracts of shorn whisker and beard. He was out of his livery, and dressed like a gentleman, in a light overcoat and a felt hat, with a cane and gloves.

"What brings you here?" said Van Maeren, shortly, with a scowl. "I have always told you that I would not have you come to the house. You have no complaint to make of me, I suppose?"

Fate

Oh, no, he had no complaint to make, he had only come to call on an old friend—such a swell! Bertie would remember the times they had had in New York. They had been waiters together, pals at the same hotel. Rum chance, eh, that they should run up against each other in London? It was a small world; you were always running up against some one wherever you might go. You couldn't keep out of any one's way; in fact, if it was God's will you should meet a feller you couldn't keep out of that feller's way, and then you might sometimes be able to do him a good turn. . . . There had been some letters written —and he scraped his throat—inconvenient letters. Sixty quid down for two letters to the young woman, that was the bargain. Life was hard; to get a little fun now and then in London cost a deal of money. And now there was a third letter, in the same hand—dear, dear, whose could it be now?—addressed to the old man. He did not want to be too hard on an old pal, but he had come just to ask whether that letter too was of any value. He had it with him.

"Then give it here," stammered Van Maeren, as pale as death, holding out his hand.

Ay, but thirty sovs. was too little, a mere song. This letter was to the old man, and was worth more, and, to tell the truth, his old friend was hard up, desperately hard up. Bertie was a gentleman who could throw the money about, and he had a noble heart. He would never leave an old pal in the lurch. The devil's in it, we must help each other in this world. Say a hundred?

"You are a rascal!" cried Bertie. "We had agreed on thirty pounds. I have not a hundred pounds; I am not rich."

Well, of course he knew that; but Mr. Westhove, no doubt, gave his friend sixpence now and then, and Mr. Westhove was made of money. Come, come, Mr. Van Maeren must think it over; he really should do something for an old pal, and a hundred pounds was not the whole world after all.

"I have not a hundred pounds at this moment, I assure you," said Bertie, huskily, from a parched throat, and shaking as if in an ague fit.

Well, he would come again then, by and by. He would take great care of the letter.

"Hand over the letter. I will give you the money another time."

But his "old pal" laughed cheerfully. No, no—given is given. They might trust each other, but it should be give and take—the letter for the hundred pounds down.

"But I will not have you coming here again. I will not have it, I tell you."

All right. There was no difficulty on that score. His swell friend might bring it himself. To-morrow?

Fate

"Yes, to-morrow without fail. And now go; for God's sake, go!"

He pushed his demon out of the house, promising him, to-morrow—to-morrow evening. Then he called up Annie, and vehemently asked her whether she knew the man.

"Who was the fellow?" he roughly inquired, like a gambler who plays a high trump at a critical point of the game.

She, however, did not know, and was surprised that Mr. Van Maeren should not have known him. Had he been troublesome?

"Yes, a beggar, a regular beggar."

"He was dressed quite like a gentleman, too."

"Be more careful for the future," said Bertie, "and let no one into the house."

Fate

CHAPTER XXIII

HE sat up that evening till Frank came home. As he sat alone he wept; for hours he sobbed passionately, miserably, till, in the slightly built little villa, Annie and her husband might have heard him, till his head felt like a drum, and bursting with throbbing pain. He fairly cried in irrepressible wretchedness, and his sobs shook his little body like a rhythm of agony. Oh, how could he get out of this slough? Kill himself? How could he live on in such wretchedness? And again and again he looked about him for a weapon; his hands clutched his throat like a vice. But he had not the courage—at least not at that moment, for as he clenched his fingers an unendurable pain mounted to his already aching head. And he wept all the more bitterly at finding himself too weak to do it.

It was one in the morning. Frank must surely come in soon.

He looked in the glass, and saw a pale, purple-gray face with swollen, wet eyes, and thick blue veins on the temples pulsating visibly

338

under the transparent skin. Frank must not see him thus. And yet he must know—and he must ask—

He went up to his room, undressed, and got shivering into bed; but he did not go to sleep. He lay listening for the front door to open. At half-past two Westhove came in. Good God! If he had gone to the Rhodeses'. No, no, he must have been at the club; he went straight upstairs to bed. Annie and her husband locked up the house; there was a noise of bolts and locks, the clank of metal bars.

Half an hour later Bertie rose. Now it would be dark in Frank's room—otherwise he would have seen that purple pallor. Out into the passage. Tap. "Frank."

"Hallo! Come in."

In he went. Westhove was in bed; no light but the night-light; Bertie, with his back to the glimmer. Now, would Frank mention the Rhodeses? No. He asked, What was up? And Van Maeren began.

There was an urgent matter he must lay before his friend—some old debts he had remembered, which he must pay before they went away. He was so vexed about it; it was really taking advantage of Frank's kindness. Could Frank give him the money?

"My dear fellow, I have run completely dry.

I have only just enough left to pay for our passage to Buenos Ayres. How much do you want?"

"A hundred pounds."

"A hundred pounds! I assure you I do not know where to lay my hand on the money. Do you want it now, on the spot? Can you not put it off? Or can you not do with a bill?"

"No. I must have money down, hard cash."

"Well, wait a bit. Perhaps I can find a way— Yes, I will manage it somehow. I will see about it to-morrow."

"To-morrow morning?"

"Are you in such a deuce of a hurry? Well, all right; I will find it somehow. But now go to bed, for I am sleepy; we made a night of it. To-morrow I am sure I can help you. And, at any rate, I will not leave you in a fix; that you may rely on. But you are a troublesome boy. Do you hear? Only the other day you had thirty pounds, and then, again, thirty more!"

For a minute Van Maeren stood rigid, a dark mass against the dim gleam of the night-light. Then he went up to the bed, and, falling on his knees, laid his head on the coverlet and fairly sobbed.

"I say, are you ill? Are you gone crazy?" asked Westhove. "What on earth ails you?"

No, he was not crazy, but only so grieved to take advantage of Frank's good nature, especially if his friend was himself in difficulties. They were such shameful debts—he would rather not tell him what for. Debts outstanding from a time when for a few days he had disappeared. Frank knew, didn't he?"

"Old sins to pay for, eh? Well, behave better for the future. We will set it all right to-morrow. Make no more noise, and go to bed. I am dead sleepy; we all had as much as we could carry. Come, get up, I say."

Van Maeren rose, and, taking Westhove's hand tried to thank him.

"There, that will do—go to bed, I say."

And he went. In his own room he presently, through the wall, heard Frank snoring. He remained sitting on the edge of his bed. Once more his fingers gripped his throat—tighter—tighter. But it hurt him—made his head ache.

"Great God!" he thought. "Is it possible that I should be the thing I am?"

CHAPTER XXIV

A LIFE of wandering for two years and more, of voyages from America to Australia, from Australia back to Europe; painfully restless, finding no new aims in life, no new reason for their own existence, no new thing in the countries they traversed or in the various atmospheres they breathed. A life at first without the struggle for existence, dragged out by each under the weight of his own woe; with many regrets, but no anxiety as to the material burden of existence. But presently there was the growing dread of that material burden, the unpleasant consciousness that there was no more money coming out from home, month after month; disagreeable transactions with bankers in distant places, constant letter-writing to and fro; in short, the almost total evaporation of a fortune of which too much had long since been dissipated in golden vapor. Then they saw the necessity of looking about them for means of subsistence, and they had taken work in factories, assurance offices, brokers' warehouses, and what not, simply to keep their heads above water in this life which they found so aimless and wretched.

Fate

They had known hours of bitter anguish, and many long days of poverty, with no escape, and the remembrance of White-Rose Cottage. Still, they had felt no longing for White-Rose Cottage again. Gradually yielding to indifference and sullen patience, their fears for the future and struggles to live were the outcome of natural, inherited instinct, rather than of spontaneous impulse and personal desire.

And even in this gloomy indifference Van Maeren had one comforting reflection, one delicate pleasure, exquisite and peculiar, as a solace to his oolf contempt; the consolation of knowing that now that Westhove had known some buffeting of fortune, now that they had to work for their bread, he had never felt impelled to leave his friend to his fate or desert him as soon as the game was up.

The impulse to abandon Frank had never risen in his soul, and he was glad of it; glad that, when it occurred to him afterward as a possibility, it was merely as a notion, with which he had no concern, and which was no part of himself. No; he had stuck by Frank; partly perhaps as a result of his cat-like nature and because he clung to his place at Frank's side; but not for that alone. There was something ideal in it, some little sentiment. He liked the notion of remaining faithful to a man who had not a cent left in the world.

They had worked together, sharing the toil and the pay with brotherly equality.

Two long years. And now they were back in Europe; avoiding England and returning to their native land, Holland—Amsterdam and The Hague. A strange longing had grown up in them both to see once more the places they had quitted so long before, bored by their familiarity, to see the wider world; to drag home their broken lives, as though they hoped there to find a cure, a miraculous balm, to console them for existence. They had scraped together some little savings, and might take a few months of summer holiday by thriftily spending their handful of cash. So they had taken lodgings in a villa at Scheveningen—a little house to the left of the Orange Hotel, looking out over the sea; and the sea had become a changeful background for their lazy summer fancies, for they did not care to wander away amid the bustle of the Kurhaus and the sands. Frank would sit for hours on the balcony, in a cane chair, his legs on the railing, the blue smoke of his cigar curling up in front of his nose; and then he felt soothed, free from all acute pain, resigned to his own uselessness; though with a memory now and again of the past, and of a sorrow which was no longer too keen. And then, stiff with sitting still, he would play a game of quoits or hockey, or fence a little with Bertie, whom he had taught to use the foils. He looked

full of health, was stouter than of yore, with a fine
high color under his clear, tanned skin, a mild
gravity in his bright gray eyes, and sometimes a
rather bitter curl under his sheeny yellow mustache.

But Bertie suffered more; and as he looked out
over the semicircle of ocean and saw the waters
break with their endless rollers of blue and
green and gray and violet and pearly iridescence—
the vaulted sky above, full of endless cloud scenery,
sweeping or creeping masses of opaque gray or
white, silvery pinions, dappled feathers, drifts of
down-like sky-foam—he fancied that his Fate was
coming up over the sea. It was coming closer—
irresistibly closer. And he watched its approach;
he felt it so intensely that sometimes his whole being seemed to be on the alert while he sat motionless in his cane chair, with his eyes fixed on the
barren waste of waters.

Fate

CHAPTER XXV

Thus it happened that, sitting here one day, he saw on the shore below, between the tufts of yellow broom growing on the sand-hills, two figures coming toward him, a man and a woman, like finely drawn silhouettes in Indian ink against the silver sea. A pang suddenly shot through his frame, from his heart to his throat—to his temples. But the salt reek came up to him and roused his senses with a freshness that mounted to his brain, so that, in spite of the shock, it remained quite clear, as if filled with a rarer atmosphere. He saw everything distinctly, down to the subtlest detail of hue and line: the silver-gray curve of the horizon, like an enormous glittering, liquid eye, with mother-of-pearl tints, broken by the tumbling crests of the waves, and hardly darker than the spread of sky strewn with a variously gray fleece of rent and raveled clouds; to the right, one stucco façade of the Kurhaus, looking with stupid dignity at the sea out of its staring window-eyes; further away, by the water's edge, the fishing boats, like large walnut-shells, with filmy veils of black netting hanging from the masts, each boat with its little flag playfully waving and curling in the breeze; and on the terrace and the strand, among a confused crowd of yellow painted chairs, a throng of summer visitors like a great stain of pale water-color, in gay but delicate tints. He could see quite clearly—here a rent in the red sail of a boat, there a ribbon fluttering from a basket-chair, and again a seagull on the shore swooping to snatch something out of the surf. He noted all these little details, minute and motley trifles, bright specks in the expanse of sky and ocean, and very visible in the subdued light of a sunless day. And those two silhouettes—a man and a woman—grew larger, came nearer, along the sands till they were just opposite to him.

He knew them at once by their general appearance—the man by a peculiar gesture of raising his hat and wiping his forehead, the lady by the way she carried her parasol, the stick resting on her shoulder while she held the point of one of the ribs. And, recognizing them, he had a singular light-headed sensation, as though he would presently be floating dizzily out of his chair, and swept away over the sea. He fell back, feeling strangely weary, and dazzling sparks danced before his fixed gaze like glittering notes of interrogation. What was to be done? Could he devise some ingenious excuse and try to tempt Frank to leave the place, to flee? Oh! how small the world was! Was it for this that they had wandered over the globe, never knowing any rest—to meet, at their very first halting-place, the two beings he most dreaded? Was this accident or Fatality? Yes, Fatality! But then—was he really afraid?

And in his dejection he felt quite sure that he was afraid of nothing; that he was profoundly indifferent, full of an intolerable weariness of self-torture. He was too tired to feel alarm; he would wait and see what would happen. It must come. There was no escape. It was Fatality. It was rest to sit there, motionless, inert, will-less, with the wide silver-gray waters before him, waiting for what might happen. To struggle no more for his own ends, to fear no more, but to wait patiently and forever. It must come, like the tide from the ocean; it must cover him, as the surf covers the sands—and then go down again, and perhaps drag him with it, drowned and dead. A wave of that flood would wash over him and stop his breath— and more waves would follow—endlessly. A senseless tide—a fruitless eternity.

"I wish I did not feel it so acutely," he painfully thought. "It is too silly to feel it so. Perhaps nothing will come of it, and I shall live to be a hundred, in peace and contentment. Still, this is undeniable, this is a fact: they are there! They are here! But—if It were really coming I

should not feel it. Nothing happens but the unexpected. It is mere nervous weakness, overtension. Nothing can really matter to me; nothing
matters. The air is lovely and pleasantly soft;
there floats a cloud. And I will just sit still, without fear, quite at my ease. There they are again!
The seamews fly low— I will wait, wait—
Those boys are playing in that boat; what folly!
They will have it over!"

He looked with involuntary interest at their an-
tics, and then again at the gentleman and lady.
They were now full in sight, just below him; and
they went past, knowing nothing, without a gesture, like two puppets.

"Ah! but *I* know," thought he. "They are here,
and It has come in their train perhaps. But it may
go away with them too, and be no more than a
threat. So I shall wait; I do not care. If it must
come it must."

They had gone out of sight. The boys and their
boat were gone too. The shore in front of him was
lonely—a long stretch of desert. Suddenly he was
seized with a violent shivering—an ague. He
stood up, his face quite colorless, his knees quaking. Terror had suddenly been too much for
him, and large beads of sweat bedewed his forehead.

"God above!" thought he, "life is terrible. I
have made it terrible. I am afraid. What can I

do? Run away? No, no; I must wait. Can any harm come to me? No, none! None, none— There they were both of them, she and her father. I am really afraid. Oh! if it must come, great God! only let it come quickly!"

Then he fancied his eyes had deceived him; that it had not been those two. Impossible! And yet he knew that they were there. Terror throbbed in his breast with vehement heart-beating, and he now only marveled that he could have looked at the boat with the boys at all, while Sir Archibald and Eva were walking down on the shore: would it not be upset? That was what he had been thinking of the boat.

CHAPTER XXVI

A WHOLE fortnight of broiling summer days slipped by; and he waited, always too weary to make the smallest effort to induce Frank to quit the place. It might perhaps have cost him no more than a single word. But he never spoke the word —waiting, and gradually falling under a spell of waiting, as though he were looking for the mysterious outcome of an interesting *dénouement*. Had they already met anywhere? Would they meet? And if they should, would anything come of it? One thing inevitably follows another, thought he; nothing can ever be done to check their course.

Westhove was in the habit of remaining a great deal indoors, leading a quiet life between his gloomy thoughts and his favorite gymnastics, not troubling himself about the summer crowd outside on the terrace and the shore. Thus the fortnight passed without his becoming aware of the vicinity of the woman whom Van Maeren dreaded. Not a suspicion of premonition thrilled through Frank's mild melancholy; he had gone on breathing the fresh sea air without perceiving any fragrance in the atmosphere that could suggest her presence.

351

Fate

He did not discern the prints of her little shoes on the level strand below the villa, nor the tilt of her parasol passing under his eyes, as he sat calmly smoking with his feet on the railings. And they must often have gazed at the selfsame packet steaming into the narrow harbor, like a colored silhouette cut out of a print, with its little sails and flag of smoke, but their eyes were unconscious how nearly they must be crossing each other, out there over the sea.

After these two scorching weeks there came a dull, gray, sunless day, with heavy rain stored in the driving black clouds, like swollen water-skins.

Frank had gone for a walk on the shore, by the edge of the wailing, fretting sea; the basket-chairs had been carried higher up, and were closely packed and almost unoccupied. There was scarcely any one out. A dismal sighing wind swept the waters; it was an autumn day full of the desolation of departed summer joys. And as he walked on, his ears filled with the moaning breeze, he saw her coming toward him with waving skirts and fluttering ribbons, and—Great Heaven! it was she!

It was as though a mass of rock had been suddenly cast at his breast with a giant's throw, and he lay crushed and breathless beneath. A surge of mingled joy and anguish struggled through his pulses, thrilled his nerves, mounted to his brain.

Fate

He involuntarily stood still, and almost unconsciously exclaimed, in a tone inaudible, indeed, at any distance, and drowned in the wind:

"Eva! My God! Eva!"

But the distance was lessening; now she was close to him, and apparently quite calm; because she had already seen him that very morning, though he had not seen her; because she had gone through the first emotion; because she had walked that way, in the wind, close by the villa into which she had seen him vanish, in the hope of meeting him again. The question flashed through his mind whether he should greet her with a bow, as a stranger—doing it with affected indifference, as though unmoved by this accidental meeting and forgetful of the past. And in spite of his tremulous excitement he could still be amazed at seeing her come straight toward him, without any hesitation, as if to her goal. In an instant she stood before him, with her pale, earnest face, and dark eyes beaming with vitality; he saw her whole form and figure, absorbed them into himself, as though his soul would devour the vision.

"Frank," she said, softly.

He made no reply, shivering with emotion, and scarcely able to see through the mist of tears which dimmed his eyes. She smiled sadly.

"Will you not hear me?" she said, in her low, silvery voice.

He bowed, awkwardly muttering something, awkwardly putting out his hand. She gently grasped it, and went on, still in that subdued tone like an echo:

"Do not be vexed with me for addressing you. There is something I should like to say to you. I am glad to have met you here in Scheveningen by mere chance—or perhaps not by mere chance. There was some misunderstanding, Frank, between you and me, and unpleasant words were spoken on both sides. We are parted, and yet I should like to ask your forgiveness for what I then said."

Tears choked her; she could scarcely control herself; but she concealed her emotion and stood calmly before him; brave as women can be brave, and with that sad smile full of hopeless submission, without affectation, candid and simple.

"Do not take it amiss; only let me ask you whether you can forgive me for having once offended you, and will henceforth think of me more tenderly."

"Eva, Eva!" he stammered. "You ask me to forgive? It was I—it was I who—"

"Nay," she gently interrupted, "you have forgotten. It was I—do you forgive me?" And she held out her hand. Frank wrung it, with a sob that choked in his throat.

"Thank you. I am glad," she went on. "I was in the wrong; why should I not confess it? I own it frankly— Will you not come and see papa? We are living in a *hôtel garni*. Have you anything to do? If not, come now with me. Papa will be very pleased to see you."

"Certainly, of course," he muttered, walking on by her side.

"But I am not taking you from any one else? Perhaps some one is waiting for you. Perhaps now—by this time—you are married."

She forced herself to look at him with her faint smile—a languid, pale courtesy which parted her lips but sadly; and her voice was mildly blank, devoid of any special interest. He started at her words; they conveyed a suggestion which had never occurred to him; a strange idea transferred from her to him; but it took no root, and perished instantly.

"Married! Oh, Eva—no, never!" he exclaimed.

"Well, such a thing might have been," said she, coolly.

They were silent for a while; but in a few moments, Eva, touched by the tone of his last words, could no longer contain herself, and began to cry gently, like a frightened child, sobbing spasmodically as they walked on, the tears soaking her white gauze veil.

In front of their hotel she stopped, and, controlling herself for a moment, said:

"Frank, be honest with me: do you not think it

odious of me to have spoken to you? I could not make up my mind what I ought to do; but I so much wanted to confess myself wrong, and ask you to forgive me. Do you despise me for doing such a thing which, perhaps, some other girl would never have done?"

"Despise you! I despise you?" cried he, with a gulp. But he could say no more, for some visitors were coming toward them—though but few were out on this windy and threatening day. They went a little further, hanging their heads like criminals under the eyes of the strangers. Then they turned into the hotel.

CHAPTER XXVII

Sir Archibald received Frank somewhat coolly, though civilly. Then he left them together, and Eva at once began:

"Sit down, Frank. I have something to tell you."

He obeyed in some surprise; her tone was business-like, her emotion was suppressed, and she seemed to be prepared to make some clear and logical statement.

"Frank," said she, "you once wrote a letter to papa, did you not?"

"Yes," he nodded sadly.

"You did?" she exclaimed eagerly.

"Yes," he repeated. "Two to you and one to Sir Archibald."

"What! and two to me as well?" she cried in dismay.

"Yes," he nodded once more.

"And you had no answers," she went on, more calmly. "Did you ever wonder why?"

"Why?" he echoed in surprise. "Because you were offended—because I had been so rough—"

357.

"No," said she, very positively. "Simply and solely because we never received your letters."

"What?" cried Westhove.

"They never reached us. Our servant William seems to have had some interest in keeping them back."

"Some interest?" repeated Frank, dully, bewildered. "Why?"

"That I do not know," replied Eva. "All I know is this: our maid Kate—you remember her —came crying one day to tell me that she could not stay any longer, for she was afraid of William, who had declared that he would murder her. I inquired what had happened; and then she told me that she had once been just about to bring up a letter to papa—in your handwriting. She knew your writing. William had come behind her when she was close to the door, and had snatched it from her, saying that he would carry it in; but instead of doing so he had put the letter into his pocket. She had asked him what he meant by it; then they had a violent quarrel, and ever since she had been afraid of the man. She had wanted to tell me a long time ago, but dared not for fear of William. We questioned William, who was rough and sulky, and considered himself offended by our doubts of his honesty. Papa had his room searched to see if he had stolen any more letters or other things. Nothing, however, was to be found, neither stolen articles nor letters. Not even the letter to papa, which seems to have been the last of the three you wrote."

"It was," said Frank.

"Of course papa dismissed the man. And—oh, what was it I wanted to tell you?—I can not remember— So you wrote actually three times?"

"Indeed, I did; three times."

"And what did you say?" she asked, with a sob in her throat.

"I asked you to forgive me, and whether— whether all could not be the same again. I confessed that I had been wrong—"

"But you were not."

"Perhaps not. I can not tell now. I felt it so then. I waited and waited for a word from you or your father. And none came."

"No, none!" she sighed. "And then?"

"What could I have done?"

"Why did you not come yourself? Oh! why did you never come near us?" she wailed reproachfully.

He was silent for a minute, collecting his thoughts; he could not remember it all.

"Tell me, Frank?" she said softly. "Why did you not come yourself?"

"I can not remember exactly," he said, dully.

"Then you did think of it?"

"Yes, certainly," said he.

"Then how was it that you never came?"

Frank suddenly broke down; he gulped down his tears with difficulty, a gulp of anguish.

"Because I was heart-broken, because I was so wretched, so unspeakably wretched. I had always taken rather cynical views of women, and love, and so forth; and then when I met you it was all so new, so fresh to me, I felt myself a boy again; I was in love with you, not only for your beauty, but for everything you said and did; for being what you are, always so calm and sweet. Good God! I adored you, Eva— Then there was that change: that doubt, that dreadful time. I can not remember it all now; and I felt so forlorn and broken-hearted. I could have died then, Eva, Eva!"

"You were so miserable? And you did not come to me?"

"No."

"But, good heavens, why not?"

"I wanted to go to you."

"And why did you not do it, then?" Again he sat lost in thought; his brain seemed clouded.

"Ah, yes! I think I remember all about it now," he said slowly. "I wanted to go—and then Bertie said—"

"What did Bertie say?"

"That he thought me a fool for my pains; a coward, and a cur, and a fool."

"But why?"

"Because you had disbelieved my word."

"And then?"

"I thought perhaps he was right and I did not go."

She flung herself on a sofa in utter woe, weeping passionately.

"Then it was what Bertie said?" she cried reproachfully.

"Yes; nothing else," he said, mournfully. "God in heaven! that alone."

They were both silent. Then Eva sat upright again, shivering; her face was white and bloodless, her eyes fixed with a dull, vacant glare, like weathered glass.

"Oh, Frank!" she cried—"Frank, I am so frightened! It is coming!"

"What, what?" he asked in alarm.

"I feel it coming upon me!" she moaned, panting. "It is like the sound of distant thunder, droning in my ears and in my brain. Great Heavens! It is close to me! Frank, oh, Frank! It is above me, over me. The thunder is over my head!" She shrieked and fought the air with her arms as if to beat something off, and her slender frame was convulsed as from a series of mysterious electric shocks. Her breath came rattling in her throat. Then she tottered, and he thought she would have fallen. He clasped her in his arms.

Fate

'Eva, Eva!" he cried.

She allowed him to drag her to the sofa without making any resistance, happy in his embrace in spite of her hallucination; and there she remained, sitting by him, with his arm round her, cowering against his breast.

"Eva! come, Eva, what is it that ails you?"

"It has passed over," she murmured, almost inaudibly. "Yes, it is gone now—it is gone. It has come over me so often lately; it comes roaring on, slowly and stealthily, and then it breaks over my head, shaking me to the core; and then it goes away, dies away—away— I am in such terror of it; it is like a monster which comes bellowing at me, and it frightens me so! What can it be?"

"I can not tell; overwrought nerves, perhaps," he said, consolingly.

"Oh! hold me close," she said, caressingly; "hold me tightly to you. When I am alone after it is past, I am left in such deadly fear; but now— now I have you—you once more. You will not cast me from you again; you will protect me, your poor little Eva, will you not? Ah! yes, I have you back now. I knew, I felt, I should have you back some day; and I have made papa come to Scheveningen every summer. I had an idea that you must be somewhere in Holland—at The Hague or at Scheveningen; and that if we were ever to meet again it would be here. And now it has happened,

and I have you once more.   Hold me tightly now
—in both arms—both arms.   Then I shall not be
frightened."

She clung more closely to his breast, her head
on his shoulder; and then, in a voice like a child's:

"Look," she said, holding out her wrist.

"What?" asked he.

"That little scar.   You did that."

"I did?"

"Yes; you clutched me by the wrists."

He felt utterly miserable, in spite of having
found her again, and he covered the line of the
scar with little kisses.

She laughed quietly.

"It is a bracelet!" she said lightly.

CHAPTER XXVIII

PRESENTLY, however, he started up.

"Eva," he began, suddenly recollecting himself, "how—why—?"

"What is it?" she said, laughing, but a little exhausted after her strange fear of the fancied thunder.

"Those letters. Why did William?—what could they matter to William? Not mere curiosity to see what was in them?"

"He would not have snatched that last one so roughly from Kate, if that had been all. No, no—"

"Then you think he had some interest?"

"I do."

"But what? Why should he care whether I wrote to you or no?"

"Perhaps he was acting for—"

"Well?"

"For some one else."

"But for whom? What concern could my letters be of anybody's. What advantage could it be to any one to hinder your getting them?"

She sat up and looked at him for some time

without speaking, dreading the question she must ask.

"Can you really think of no one?" she said.

"No."

"Did no one know that you had written?"

"No one but Bertie."

"Ah! Only Bertie," said she, with emphasis.

"But Bertie—no! Surely?" he asked her, indignant at so preposterous a suspicion.

"Perhaps," she whispered, almost inaudibly. "Perhaps Bertie."

"Eva! Impossible. Why? How?"

She sank back into her former attitude, her head on his breast, trembling still from the impression of the thunder she had heard. And she went on:

"I know nothing; I only think. I have thought it over day after day for two years; and I have begun to find a great deal that seems mysterious in what had never before been puzzling, but, indeed, sympathetic to me—in Bertie. You know we often used to talk together, and sometimes alone. You were a little jealous sometimes, but you had not the smallest reason for it, for there never was anything to make you so; we were like a brother and sister. We often talked of you— Well, afterward I remembered those talks, and it struck me that Bertie—"

"Yes? That Bertie—"

"That he did not speak of you as a true friend

should. I am not sure. While he was talking it never occurred to me, for Bertie had a tone, and a way of saying things. I always fancied then that he meant well by us both, and that he really cared for us, but that he was afraid of something happening—some evil, some catastrophe, if we were married. He seemed to think that we ought not to marry. When afterward I thought over what he had said that was always the impression. He really seemed to think that we—that we ought never to be married."

She closed her eyes, worn out by this effort to solve the enigmas of the past, and she took his hand and stroked it as she held it in her own. He too tried to look into that labyrinth of the past, but he could discern nothing. His memory carried him back to their last days in London; and he did recall something: he recollected Van Maeren's stern tone when he, Westhove, had said he should call at the Rhodeses'; he remembered Bertie's urgent haste to get out of London and wander about the world. Could Bertie—? Had Bertie any interest? —But he could not discern it, in the simplicity of his unpractical, heedlessly liberal friendship, which had never taken any account of expenses, always sharing what he had with his companion because he had plenty and the other had nothing; he could not see it, since he had never thought of such a possibility in his strange indifference to everything that approached money matters—an indifference so complete as to constitute a mental deficiency, as another man is indifferent to all that concerns politics, or art, or what not—matters which he held so cheap, and understood so little and could only shake his head over it, as over an abracadabra. He looked, but saw not.

"You see, I fancied afterward that Bertie had been opposed to our marrying," Eva repeated dreamily; and then, bewildered by the mystery which life had woven about her, she went on: "Tell me, Frank, what was there in him? What was he, who was he? Why should you never tell me anything about him? For I discovered that too, later, during those two years when I thought out so many things."

He looked at her in dismay. Bitter self-reproach came upon him for never having told her that Bertie was poor, penniless, and dependent on his friend's bounty. Why was it he had never told her? Was it out of a sense of shame at being himself so careless, so foolishly weak about a concern in which others were so cautious and prudent? So foolishly weak—careless to imbecility. And still he looked at her in dismay.

Then a suspicion of the truth flashed across his mind like the zigzag glimmer of distant lightning, and he shrank from its lurid gleam.

"Eva," he said, "I will go to Bertie—"

Fate

"To Bertie?" she shrieked. "Is he here?"

"Yes."

"He! here! Oh, I had never thought of that. I fancied he was away, far away—dead perhaps. I did not care what had become of him. Great God! Here! Frank, I implore you, Frank, leave him; do not go near him."

"But, Eva, I must ask him."

"No, Frank—oh, Frank, for God's sake, do not go. I am afraid—afraid. Do not go."

He soothed her gently with a soft, sad smile which just lifted his yellow mustache; with grave fondness in his honest eyes; he soothed and petted her very gently, to reassure her.

"Do not be afraid, my darling. I will be quite calm. But still I must ask, don't you see? Wait for me here; I will return in the evening."

"Can you really be calm? Oh, you had better not go—"

"I promise you I will be quite calm, quite cool." And he embraced her fondly, closely, with passionate fervor.

"Then you are mine once more?" he asked.

She threw her arms round his neck, and kissed his lips, his eyes, his face.

"Yes," she said, "I am yours. Do what you will with me."

"Till we meet again," then said he; and he quitted the house.

Fate

Eva, left alone, looked about her with a shudder, as if seeking the evil she dreaded. She was afraid—afraid for herself and for Frank, but chiefly for Frank. In an instant her fears had risen to intolerable horror. She heard her father's step in the passage: she recognized his shuffling tread. It was impossible for her to meet him just then; she snatched up a cloak and wrapped it about her, pulling the hood over her head, as she rushed out of doors.

It was raining heavily.

Fate

CHAPTER XXIX

FRANK found Van Maeren at home. And Bertie saw at once that it had come. He read it in Frank's drawn face, heard it in the thick utterance of his voice. And at the same time he felt that the lax springs of his determination were trying to brace themselves in despair, in self-defense, and—that they failed.

"Bertie," said Westhove. "I want to speak to you, to ask you something."

Bertie made no reply. His legs quaked. He was sitting in a large cane chair, and he did not move.

"I have just met Eva," Frank went on, "and I went with her to see her father. Sir Archibald tells me that they have been here some weeks—"

Still Bertie spoke not; he gazed up at Frank with his deep, black eyes, and their brilliancy was overcast by distress and fear. Frank stood in front of him, and he now passed his hand over his brow in some confusion. He had at first purposed to tell his story, and then, quite calmly, to ask a question; but something, he knew not what, in Bertie's cat-like indolence, roused his anger, made him furious with him for the first time in all the years he had known him. He was angry that Bertie could stay there, half lying down languidly at ease, his graceful hand hanging over the arm of the lounge; and he did not detect that his attitude at this moment was assumed merely to conceal an all too overwhelming agitation. And Frank's intention of telling a logical tale and asking a plain question suddenly collapsed in rage, giving way to a mad desire to know at once—at once—

"Listen to me, Bertie. You remember the three letters that I wrote before we left London. Eva tells me that they were kept back by their servant, William. Do you know anything about it?"

Bertie was silent, but his eyes were fixed on Frank with dull, anxious entreaty.

"No one knew of the existence of those letters but you. Have you any suspicion why it should be to William's interest to suppress them, then?"

"No. How should I?" said Bertie, scarcely above his breath.

"Come, come—speak out!" cried Westhove, quivering in every muscle. "You must know something about it, that is quite clear. You must. Speak out."

All thought of self-defense melted away under the vehemence of Frank's tone. Bertie hardly had **any** curiosity even to know what had occurred to betray William's complicity; and he felt that it would be easiest now to give himself up completely, without reserve, since that which he had been dreading for weeks had come upon him, inevitably and fatally; since whatever was to happen would happen inevitably and fatally; and in his weakness he was conscious of the horrible pathos, the hopeless pity of his being what he was—of things being as they were.

"Well, then," he muttered, dejectedly, "I do know."

"What do you know?"

"It was I who—"

"Who did what?"

"Who bribed William not to deliver the letters."

Westhove looked at him in dumb astonishment; darkness clouded his sight; everything was in a whirl; he did not hear, did not understand, forgetting that the truth had already flashed across his brain.

"You! You!" he gasped. "My God! but why?"

Van Maeren got up; he burst into tears.

"Because—because—I don't know. I can not tell you. It is too vile."

Westhove had seized him by the shoulders: he shook him, and said in a hoarse roar:

"You damned villain, you will not tell me why? You will not tell me? Or must I shake it out of your body? Why? Tell me this instant!"

"Because, because," sobbed Van Maeren, wringing his white hands.

"Tell me—out with it!"

"Because I wanted to stay with you, and because if you married I should have had to go. I was so fond of you, and—and—"

"Speak out! You were so fond of me—and then—"

"And you were so kind to me. You gave me everything. I foresaw that I should have to work for my living again, and I was so well off where I was. Frank, Frank, listen to me; hear what I have to tell you before you say anything, before you are angry. Let me explain; do not condemn me till you know. Oh, yes, it was base of me to do what I did, but let me say a word; and do not be angry, Frank, till you know everything. Frank, try to see me as I am. I am as God made me, and I can not help it; I would have been different if I could—and I only did what I could not help doing. Indeed, I could not help it; I was driven to it by a power outside me. I was so weak, so tired; I could rest with you; and though you may not believe me, I loved you, I worshiped you. And you wanted to turn me out, and make me work. Then it was—then I did it. Hear me, Frank, let me tell you all. I must tell you all. I made Eva believe that you did not really love her; I made her doubt you, so that everything was broken off between you. And the letters, I stopped them— It was all my doing, Frank, all, all; and I hated myself while I did it, because I was not different from what I am. But, I could not help it. I was made so— And you do not understand me. I am such a strange mixture that you can not understand. But try to understand me and you will, Frank; and then you will forgive me—perhaps you will even forgive me. Oh, believe me, I beseech you, I am not wholly selfish. I love you with all my soul, so truly as one man hardly ever loves another, because you were so good to me. I can prove it to you; did I not stick by you when you had lost all your money in America? If I had been selfish, should I not have left you then? But I stayed with you, I worked with you, and we shared everything, and were happy. Oh, why did not things remain as they were? Now you have met her, and now—"

"Have you done with words!" roared Frank. "So you did this, you wrecked all that life held for me! God in heaven! is it possible? No, you are right; I do not understand you!" he ended with a venomous laugh, his face crimson and his eyes starting with rage. Bertie had dropped crouching in a heap on the ground, and sobbed aloud.

"Oh, but try to understand," he entreated. "Try to see a fellow-creature as he is, in all his comfortless nakedness, with no conventional wrappings. My God! I swear to you that I wish I was different. But how can I help being what I am? I was born without any option of my own; I was endowed with a brain and I must think; and I think otherwise than I gladly would think, and I have been tossed through life like a ball— like a ball. What could I do, thus tossed, but try to keep my head up? Strength of will, strength of mind? I do not know whether you have any; but I have never, never, never felt such a thing. When I do a thing it is because I must, because I can do no otherwise; for though I may have the wish to act differently the strength and energy are not there! Believe me, I despise myself; believe that, Frank; and try to understand and to forgive."

"Words, words! You are raving," growled Frank. "I do not know what all your talk means. I can understand nothing at this moment; and, even if I could, at this moment I would not. All I understand is that you have ruined me, that you have destroyed my whole life's joy, and that you are a low scoundrel, who bribed a servant to stop my letters, out of gross, vile, unfathomable selfishness. Bribed him? Tell me, rascal, wretch, coward—bribed him!—with what, in Heaven's name? Tell me with what you bribed him."

"With, with—" but Van Maeren hesitated in abject fear, for Westhove had collared him by the waistcoat, as he groveled on the floor, and shook him again and again.

"By thunder, you villain, you bribed him with my money—with my own money! Tell me—speak, or I'll kick it out of you!"

"Yes."

"With my money?"

"Yes, yes, yes." Frank flung him down with a yell of contempt, of loathing of such a thing as he.

But Van Maeren was experiencing a reaction from his self-abasement. The world was so stupid, men were stupid, Frank was stupid. He did not understand that a man should be such as he, Bertie, was; he could not understand; he bellowed out in his brutal rage, like some wild beast without brains or sense. He, himself, had brains; happier was he who had none; he envied Frank his lack of them!

He sprang up with one leap.

"Yes, if you will have it! Yes, yes, yes!" he hissed it hard. "If you don't understand, if you are too idiotic to take it in— Yes, I say! Yes, yes, yes! I bribed him with your money, that you were so kind as to give me the very last day when we were leaving London. You gave me a hundred pounds, to pay William—do you remember? To pay William!— You do not understand? Well— you don't understand! You are a stupid brute without brains. Ay, and I envy you for having none. There was a time when I had none; and

do you know how I came by them? Why, through
you. There was a time when I toiled and worked,
and never thought and never cared. I ate all I
earned, and when I earned nothing I went hungry.
And I was happy! It was you—you who fed me
on dainties, and gave me wine to drink; and it was
you who clothed me, so that I had not to work,
but had nothing to do but to think, think, in my
contemptible idleness all day long. And now I
only wish I could crack my skull open and throw
my brains in your face for having made me what
I am, so finikin and full of ideas! You don't understand? Then perhaps you will not understand
that at this moment I feel no gratitude for all you
have done for me—that I hate you for it all, that
I despise you, and that you have made my life infinitely more wretched than I have made yours!
Do you understand that much, at any rate, eh?
That I despise you and hate you, hate you?"

He had entrenched himself behind a table, sput-
tering out this volley of words in a paroxysm of
nervous excitement; he felt as though every fibre
of his frame was ready to crack like an over-
strained cord. He had got behind the table, because Westhove was standing before him, at the
other side now, his eyes staringly white and blood-
shot in his purple face; his nostrils dilated, his
shoulders up, his fists clenched, ready, as it seemed,
to spring upon him. Westhove was waiting, as it

appeared, till Van Maeren had spit out in his face all the foul words he could find.

"Yes, I hate you!" Bertie repeated, "I hate you!" He could find nothing else to say.

Then Frank let himself go. With a bellow like a wild beast, a sound that had nothing human in it, he sprang over the table, which tilted on its side, and came down with all the weight of his impetus on Bertie, who fell under him like a reed. He seized his foe by the throat, dragged him over the legs of the table, into the middle of the room, dropped him with a crack on the floor, and fell upon him, with his bony, square knee on Bertie's chest, and his left hand holding his neck like a vise. And a hard, dry feeling, like a thirst for sheer brutality, rose to Westhove's throat; with a dreadful smile on his lips he swallowed two or three times, fiendishly glad that he had him in his power, in the clutch of his left hand, under his knee. And he doubled his right fist and raised it like a hammer, with a tigerish roar.

"There, there, there!" he growled; and each time a sledge-hammer blow fell on Bertie. "There, there, there!"—on his nose, his eyes, his mouth, his forehead—and the blows resounded dully on his skull, as if on metal. A red mist clouded Westhove's sight; everything was red—purple, scarlet, vermilion. A blood-stained medley circled round him like whirling wheels, and through that strange crimson halo a distorted face grinned up at him under the pounding of his fist. The corners of the room swam in red, as if they were full of tangible red terror, whirling, whirling round him—a purple dizziness, a scarlet madness, a nightmare bathed in blood; and his blows fell fast and steadily—"there!—there!—there!"—and his left hand closed tighter on the delicate white throat below that face—

The door flew open, and she, Eva, rushed up to him through the red mist, parting it, dispelling it by the swift actuality of her appearance.

"Frank, Frank!" she screamed. "Stop, I entreat you! Stop! You are murdering him!"

He let his arm drop, and looked at her as in a dream. She tried to drag him back, to get him away from the battered body, to which he clung in his fury like a vampire.

"Leave him, Frank, I beseech you; let him stand up. Do not kill him. I was outside, and I was frightened. I did not understand, because you were speaking Dutch. Great Heavens! What have you done to him? Look, look! What a state he is in!"

Frank had risen to his feet, dazed by that red frenzy; he had to lean on the table.

"I have given him what he deserved—I have thrashed him, and I will do it again!"

He was on the point of falling on the foe once

more, with that devilish grin on his face and that brutal thirst still choking him.

"Frank, no! Frank!" cried Eva, clinging to him with both hands. "For God's sake be satisfied! Look at him! oh, look at him!' '

"Well, then, let him get up," Frank snarled. "He may get up. Get up, wretch, at once; get up!"

He gave him a kick—and a second—and a third —to make him rise. But Van Maeren did not move.

"Great God! only look at him," said Eva, kneeling down by the body. "Look—don't you see?" She turned to Frank, and he, as if awaking from his dream of blood, did see now, and saw with horror. There it lay: the legs and arms convulsed and writhing, the body breathlessly still in the loose, light-hued summer suit; and the face a mask of blue and green and violet, stained with purplish blood, which oozed from ears and nose and mouth, trickling down, clammy and dark, drop by drop, on to the carpet. One eye was a shapeless mass, half pulp and jelly; the other stared out of the oval socket like a large, dull, melancholy opal. The throat looked as though it had a very broad purple band round it. And as they stood gazing down at the features it seemed that they were swelling, swelling to a sickening, unrecognizable deformity.

Fate

Out of doors the storm of rain had not ceased. There they stood, staring at the horror that lay bleeding and motionless on the ground before them; a leaden silence within, and without the falling torrent, an endless, endless plash.

Eva, kneeling by Bertie's side, and shuddering with terror, had felt his heart, had listened with her ear against the breathless trunk—close to the dreadful thing, to make sure—and she had got up again quaking, had very softly stepped back from it, her eyes still directed on it, and now stood clinging against Frank, as if she would become one with him in her agony of fear.

"Frank," she gasped. "God have mercy! Frank! He is dead! Let us go—let us go; let us fly!"

"Is he dead?" asked Westhove, dully. His mind was beginning to wake—a faint dawn like murky daybreak. He released himself from her grasp; knelt down, listened, felt, thought vaguely of fetching a doctor, of remedies; and then he added huskily, certain, indeed, of what he said, but quite uncertain of what he should do:

"Yes, he is dead—he is dead. What can I—?"

Eva still hung on to him, imploring him to fly, to escape. But his mind was gradually getting clearer, daylight shining in on his bewilderment; he freed himself from her embrace, and tried to go; his hand was already on the door-handle.

381

"Frank, Frank!" she shrieked, for she saw that he meant to abandon her.

"Hush!" he whispered, with a finger on his lips. "Stay here; stay and watch him. I will come back."

And he went. She would have followed him, have clung to him in an agony of terror, but he had already shut the door behind him, and her trembling knees could scarcely carry her. She sat down by the body, shivering miserably. There it was—the swollen, bruised, and purple face, sad, and sickening in the diffused afternoon light which came in obliquely through the curtain of rain. Every breath stuck in her throat; she was dying for air, and longed to open the window, being closer to that than to the door.

But she dared not; for outside, through the dim square panes, she saw the tragical sky covered with driving slate-colored piles of cloud, and the rain falling in a perfect deluge, and the sea dark and ominous as an imminent threat, the raging foam gleaming through a shroud of pouring water.

"Molde, Molde!" she exclaimed, icy-cold with terrible remembrance. "It is the sky of Molde, the fjord of Molde! That was where I first felt it. O God! Help, help!"

And she fell senseless on the floor.

CHAPTER XXX

SINCE that day of terror two years had elapsed, years of silent endurance for them both; each suffering alone. For they were parted; with only the solace of a brief meeting now and then, when she could go and see him where he was spending those two years, the days slowly dragging past, in the prison among the sand-hills.

He had given himself up at once to the police of Scheveningen, as if he were walking in his sleep, and had been taken to the House of Detention. He had stood his trial—it had lasted six weeks, a short time, his lawyer had said to comfort him, because there was no mystery to clear up; the murder was proved to a demonstration, beyond the shadow of a doubt, to be the result of a quarrel. This was evident also from the evidence of Miss Rhodes, who had stated that the criminal himself had not at first understood that his friend was dead, for that he had immediately after kicked him two or three times to rouse him, thinking he was only in a state of collapse; and that this had taken place in her presence. The trial was watched with

interest by the public; and their sympathy was
aroused when the purchase of the letters came out
through the evidence of Sir Archibald and his
daughter, confirmed by William, whose presence
was secured by diplomatic interference. There
were no difficulties; six weeks settled everything.
Frank was sentenced to two years' imprisonment,
and the case was not taken to a higher court.

He had spent the time, day after day, in a wak-
ing dream of gloomy lucidity, with always, always
the sinister vision of that writhing body, and the
horror of that dreadful battered face before his
eyes. He had felt it glide over the pages of his
book when he tried to read, among the letters he
traced when he tried to write—what he scarcely
knew, fragments of an account of his travels
through America and Australia—a melancholy
employment and full of pain, since every word
reminded him of the murdered man who had been
his constant companion. And when he did nothing, but gazed in dreary reverie out of the window
of his cell, there, just below, and not very far away,
he could see the villa where they had dwelt together and where he had done the deed, with a
glimmer of the sea, a shining gray streak; and in
fancy he could smell the briny scent, as in the days
when he had spent hour after hour, with his feet
on the balustrade—the hours which, as they crept
on, though he knew it not, were bringing inevitable

doom on them both, every moment nearer. So it never left him; it haunted him incessantly.

Eva had entreated her father to remain at The Hague during all this terrible time, and Sir Archibald had consented, fearing for his daughter's health. Her natural sweet equanimity had given way to a fitful nervousness, which tormented her with hallucinations, visions of thunder and of blood. So they had settled in the Van Stolk Park, and all through Frank's imprisonment she had been able to see him from time to time, coming home more exhausted from each visit, in despair over his melancholy, however she might try to encourage him with hopes for the future, later on, when he should be free. She herself could hope, nay, lived only on hope; controlling her excitability under the yoke of patience, and of her confidence in something brighter which might come into her life, by and by, when Frank was free. A new life! Oh, for a new life! and her spirits danced at the thought—and new happiness! Great God! some happiness! She did not herself understand how she could still hope, since she had known so much of life and of men, and since she had lived through that fearful experience; but she would not think of it, and in the distant future she saw everything fair and good. Even her hallucinations did not destroy her hopefulness; though dreading them, she regarded them as a recurring malady of the brain, which would presently depart of itself. She could even smile as she sat dreaming in the pale light of a starlit summer evening, the calendar in her hand, on which she scratched through each day as it died, with a gold pencil-case which she had bought on purpose and used for nothing else, wearing it in a bracelet;—struck it out, with a glad, firm stroke, as bringing her nearer to the blissful future. And she would even let the days pass without erasing them severally, that she might have the joy at the end of a week of making six or seven strokes, one after another, in a luxury of anticipation.

And now, long as they had been, the days had all stolen by—all, one after another, beyond recall. The past was more and more the past, and would forever remain so; it would never come back to them, she thought, never haunt them more with hideous memories. She grew calmer; her nervousness diminished, and something like peace came upon her in her passionate longing for the happy future; for she was going to be happy with Frank.

She was now in London again with her father, living very quietly; still feeling the past, in spite of her present gladness, still conscious of what had been, in all its misery and its horror. Frank, too, was in London, in a poorly paid place as assistant overseer in some engineering works, the only opening he could find by the help of his old connections; jumping at it, indeed, in consideration of his antecedents, of which he had no cause to be proud. By and by he should get something better, something more suited to his attainments. And he took up his studies again to refresh his technical knowledge, which had grown somewhat rusty.

Sir Archibald had grown much older, and was crippled by attacks of rheumatism; but he still sat poring over his heraldic studies. Living in Holland for his daughter's sake, he had too long been out of his own circle of acquaintance and groove of habit; and though he had from time to time, in a fit of childish temper, expressed his vexation at Eva's becoming the wife of a murderer, he now agreed to everything, shrinking from the world and troubling himself about nothing; only craving to be left undisturbed in the apathy of his old age. "He knew nothing about it; old men know nothing of such things. The young people might please themselves; they always knew best and must have their own way." So he grumbled on, apparently indifferent, but glad at heart that Eva should marry Frank, since Frank, if he could be violent, was good at heart; and Eva would be well cared for, and he himself would have some one to bear him company in his own house—yes, yes, a little company.

Frank and Eva met but rarely during the week,

for he was busy even in the evenings, but they saw each other regularly on Sundays. And Eva had the whole week in which to think over the Sunday when she had last seen him, and she tried to recall every word that he had said, every look he had given her. On these treasures she lived all the week. She had never loved him so dearly as now, when crushing depression weighed on him, which she longed to lighten by the solace of her love. There was something motherly in her feeling for him, as though his sufferings had made a child of him, needing a tenderer regard than of yore. She had loved him then for the mysterious charm, as it seemed to her, of the contrast between his feeble gentleness and his powerful physique; and now it was no more than a higher development of the same charm, since she saw the stalwart, strong man suffering so pitiably under the memory of what he had gone through, and lacking the energy to rise superior to it and begin life anew. But this want of vigor did not discourage her in her hopes for the future; on the contrary, she loved him for his weakness, while regarding this as singular and incomprehensible in herself; dreaming over it in her solitude, or smiling with gladness.

For she, as a woman, in spite of her nervous, visionary temperament, could resolutely forget the past, bravely go forward to meet the future, compelling happiness to come to her by her sweet

patience and elastic constancy. Had not all the
woes of the past lain outside them both? Had
not Frank done penance enough for his fit of rage
to hold up his head again now? Oh, they would
soon have got over it completely; they would insist
on being happy, and she would cure him of everything like heart-sickness.

Thus she hoped on, a long, long time, refusing
at first to acknowledge that he grew more melancholy and gloomy, sinking into deeper and deeper
dejection under his burden. But at last she was
compelled to see it, could no longer blind herself.
She could not help seeing that he sat speechless
when she talked so hopefully, listened in silence
to her cheerful words and bright illusions, saying
nothing, and sometimes closing his eyes with a sigh
which he tried to suppress. She could not deceive
herself; her sanguine moods aroused in him only
an echo of despair.

And when one day this was suddenly clear to
her, she felt, suddenly too, that her nervous fears
had worn her out; that she was sad and ill; that
her courage, her hopes, her illusions were sinking
down, down, deeper and deeper. A bitterness as
of wormwood rose up in her, tainting everything;
she flung herself on her bed, in her loneliness,
heart-broken, in utter anguish, and cursed her life,
cursed God, in helpless woe.

CHAPTER XXXI

THEN, circumstances occurred which, in spite of all this, led to its being settled that they were to be married in quite a short time—in about six weeks. Frank had been helped by some of his old friends to obtain an appointment as engineer in a great Glasgow firm; Eva was to have her mother's fortune; there were no difficulties in the way.

Frank now always spent the whole of Sunday at Sir Archibald's house. He came to lunch, sitting as silent as ever, and after lunch they were usually left to themselves. At first the hours flew by, sped by Eva's day-dreams, though she was still, and in spite of herself, somewhat nervous; they would discuss various matters and even read together. But then for some little time minute would link itself to minute, while they did nothing but sit side by side on a deep sofa, holding each other's hands, and gazing into vacancy. And a moment came when they could no longer endure that grasp—no longer dared. The image of Bertie, with his purple, blood-stained face, would rise up between them; their hands parted—they were both thinking of the dead. Eva felt as if she had

been an accomplice in the deed. As it grew
darker intolerable misery would so overpower her
that it seemed as though she must suffocate; then
they would throw the windows open and stand for
a long, long time to refresh themselves in the cool
air, looking out over the park in the gathering
gloom. She listened in dread to Frank's breath
as it came and went.

Ay, and she was afraid of him, in spite of her
love. After all, he had committed murder; he
could do such things in his rage! Oh! if in a fit
of passion she too— But she would defend herself; with the strength of despair she would cling
to life. Had she not herself felt strong enough to
kill?— No, no. Not she, surely. She was too
timid. And, besides, she loved him so dearly; she
adored him, and soon she would be his wife! Still,
she was afraid.

The Sundays were no longer days so sweet as
to leave a treasure of memory in which she could
live through the week. On the contrary, Eva now
dreaded Sunday; she awaited it with terror. . . .
Friday—Saturday. . . . Here it was again!
There was Frank, she heard his step. And still she
was afraid, and still she loved him.

They were sitting thus one evening, hand in
hand, and silent. It was still early in the afternoon, but a storm threatened, and the gray gloom

peered in through the thick lace curtains. Eva, depressed by the heavy weather, thirsting for some comfort, suddenly, in spite of her fears, threw herself on Frank's breast.

"I can no longer endure this weather!" she wailed, almost moaning. "This dark, cloudy sky always oppresses me of late. I want to go to Italy, Frank, to the sun, the sun!"

He pressed her to him but did not speak. She began to weep softly.

"Say something, Frank," she sobbed.

"Yes; I do not like this heavy sky," he said, dully.

Again there was silence; she tried to control herself, clinging closely to him. Then she went on:

"I can not bear up against it; I believe since that rainy day which overtook us in Molde, so long ago now—five years and more—you remember—when we had met three or four times, a few days before, at Trondhjem?" She smiled and kissed his hand, remembering her youth: she was old now. "You recollect, we got home to the hotel drenched. I believe I have been ill ever since that day, that I took a bad cold which settled in me, though at first I did not feel it and said nothing about it, but which has been undermining me ever since, all this long time—"

He made no reply; he, too, had a vague recollection of something tragically painful at Molde, but he could no longer remember what. But she suddenly burst into a violent fit of weeping.

"Oh, Frank, speak! Say something," she besought him, in despair at his silence, feeling her terror grow greater in the stillness, and her heart throbbing wildly in spite of herself.

He passed his hand over his forehead, trying to collect his thoughts. Then he slowly replied:

"Yes, Eva—for I have something to say to you. Just this very day."

"What is that?" she asked, looking up through her tears, in surprise at his strange tone.

"I want to speak to you very seriously, Eva. Will you listen?"

"Yes."

"I want to ask you something—to ask you if you would not rather be free. To ask if you would not be glad that I should release you?"

She did not immediately understand him, and sat gazing at him open-mouthed.

"Why?" she said at length, shuddering, terrified lest he should understand something of what was torturing her soul.

"Because it would be so much better for you, my child," he said, gently. "I have no right to fetter your life to mine. I am wrecked—an old man—and you are young."

She clung closely to him.

"No, I am old, too," said she, with a smile, "and I will not have it. I will be true to you. I will always comfort you when you are out of heart. And so, together, we will both grow young again, and both be happy."

Her voice was as sweet as balm; to give him strength she felt something of her old illusions reviving in her. She would cling to him whatever the cost: she loved him.

He clasped her tightly to his breast, and kissed her fondly. For the moment she felt no fear; he was so unhappy.

"You are a dear, good girl," he whispered in a husky, trembling voice. "I do not deserve that you should be so good to me. But, seriously, Eva, think it over once more. Consider again whether you would not be unhappy, nay, wretched, if you had to be with me always. There is yet time; we have our future lives in our hands, and I can not spend mine with you, Eva, only to make yours more miserable than I have done already. So, for your sake, for your happiness, I would gladly give you back your word."

"But I will not have it!" she moaned, desperately. "I will not. I do not understand you. Why should you give me back my word?"

He took her hands caressingly in his own, and looked in her face a long time, with a sad smile under the gold-colored mustache.

Fate

"Why? Because you—because you are afraid of me, my darling."

A spasm shot through her whole frame, like an electric shock; wildly she looked at him, and wildly protested:

"It is not true, Frank; I swear it is not true! Great God! Why do you think that? What have I done to make you think it? Believe me, Frank; take my word. I swear to you by all that is holy; there. I swear to you it is not true. I am not afraid of you."

"Yes, yes, Eva, you are afraid of me," he said, calmly. "And I understand it; it must be so. And yet I assure you, you should have no cause to be. For I should be a lamb in your hands; I would lay my head in your hands; your pretty, cold, white hands, and sleep like a child. You should do with me whatever you would, and I would never be angry with you, for I could never be so again, never again. I would lie at your feet; I would feel your feet on me, on my breast, and lie so still —so calm and blessed!"

He had fallen on his knees before her, with his head in her lap, on her hands.

"Well, then," she said, gently, "if that is the case, why should I ever be afraid of you since you promise me this? And why do you talk of releasing me from my word?"

"Because I can not bear to live on, seeing you

so unhappy; because you are unhappy with me, as I can see; and because you will be even more so when we are together, later—always."

She quivered in every fibre. A strange lucidity came over her. She saw all that had happened as if mirrored in crystal.

"Hear me, Frank," she said, in a clear, bright voice. "Remain where you are and listen to me; listen well. I mean to be true to you, and we shall be happy. I feel that we shall. What has occurred that we should always be miserable? Nothing. I repeat it—nothing. Do not let us spoil our own lives. I doubted you once; you have forgiven me. That is all at an end. You discovered that Bertie was a scoundrel, and you killed him. That, too, is ended. Nothing of all this can matter to me now. I will never think of it again. It has ceased to exist so far as I am concerned. And that is all, Frank. Consider, reflect—that is all. Nothing else has happened. And that is not much. We are young and strong; we are not really old. And I tell you we can live a new life, somewhere, together; somewhere, a long way from London. A new life, Frank, a new life! I love you, Frank. You are everything to me. You are my idol, my husband, my darling, my child, my great child."

She clasped his head passionately to her bosom in a rapture, her eyes sparkling, and a flush tinging the azalea whiteness of her cheeks. But his eyes met hers with a look of anguish.

"You are an angel, Eva; you are an angel. But I can not claim you. For, listen now to me. The real truth—"

"Well, what is the truth?"

"Bertie was not a scoundrel. He was nothing but a man, a very weak man. That is the truth. Listen to me, Eva; let me speak. I thought a great deal—at Scheveningen—among the sand-hills—you know. I thought over everything I could remember of what he had said to me in those last moments, in self-defense; and by degrees all his words came back to me, and I felt that he had been in the right."

"In the right? Oh, Frank! I do not know what he said in self-defense; but now, still, shall Bertie's influence come between us to part us?" she cried, in bitter despair.

"No, it is not that," he replied. "Make no mistake; it is not Bertie's influence which divides us; it is my guilt."

"Your guilt?"

"My guilt, which rises up before me from time to time, reminding me of what I have done, so that I can not forget it, shall never forget it. Let me tell you. He was right in what he said at last. He was a weak creature, he said, flung into life without any strength of will. Was that his fault? He despised himself for having done so mean a thing about those letters. But he had not known what else to do. Well, and I forgive him for being weak, for he could not help it; and we are all weak—I am weak, too."

"But you would never have done such a thing?" cried Eva.

"Because I, perhaps, am different. But I am weak all the same. I am weak when I am angry. And then—then in my fury, I was utterly, utterly weak. This is the truth. This is what is crushing me; and, broken as I am, I can not be your husband. Oh, what would I not give to have him still alive! I was fond of him once, and now I could say to him that I do understand—that I forgive him."

"Frank, do not be so foolish—so foolishly good," she exclaimed.

"Oh, it is not foolish goodness," he said, with a melancholy smile. "It is philosophy."

"Well, then," she cried, in a hard, rough tone, "I am no philosopher; I am not foolishly good; I do not forgive him for being a villain, and for making us miserable. I hate him, hate him, dead as he is. I hate him for coming between us, and haunting us now that you have killed him, and for the diabolical influence he still brings to bear on you and on me. But, I say, I will not have it," she shrieked despairingly, starting to her feet, but still clinging to him. "I tell you that I will not lose you for the second time. I swear that if you try to leave me here, I will stand, holding you fast in my arms, clasping you to me till we both are dead. For I will not let him part us; I hate him! I am glad you murdered him, and if he were living now, I would do it myself. I would kill him, strangle him, strangle him!" She clenched her hands as if she gripped his throat, and held Frank in her embrace as though he were her prey.

Out of doors it was growing darker every minute.

He gently released himself, supporting her, indeed, for he felt that she was tottering in her overtension of energy and courage. She was staring out at the weather with her sunken gray eyes, and she shivered from head to foot. He led her back to the sofa, made her sit down, and again knelt before her in more passionate devotion than ever.

"Eva!" he whispered.

"Oh, look at the clouds!" she cried. "It is pouring a deluge."

"Yes," said he. "What does that matter?—I love you."

"I can not bear up against such weather," she moaned. "It oppresses me and frightens me—oh, it terrifies me so! Protect me, Frank, shelter me; come close!"

She drew him to her on the sofa, and, opening his coat, nestled against him.

"I am so frightened. Hold me tightly—wrap your coat round me. Oh, do not let it come upon me! Lord have mercy, and do not let it come over me again, I beseech Thee!"

It was the visionary thunder she prayed to be spared. And she threw both arms round her lover, clinging to him as if to hide herself. So she remained, while he held her close; when, presently, twisting her fingers into his waistcoat-pocket, she murmured:

"What is this? what have you here?"

"What have you found?" he said, in alarm.

"This, in your waistcoat-pocket?"

"Nothing—a little vial," he muttered. "Some drops for my eyes. I have been troubled by my eyes lately."

She took out the vial. It was a tiny, dark blue bottle, with a cut-glass stopper and no label.

"For your eyes?" she said. "I did not know—"

"Yes, really," he answered. "Give it me."

But she held it hidden in her two hands, and laughed.

"No, no; I will not give it you. Why are you so uneasy? I shall not break it. Does it smell? I want to open it, but the stopper has stuck."

"Eva, I entreat you give it me," he implored her, and the perspiration stood on his brow. "It is nothing but drops for the eyes, and it has no scent. You will spill it, and it stains."

But she put her hands behind her back.

"It is not for the eyes, and you have nothing the matter with yours," she said positively.

"Yes—really—"

"No; you are deceiving me. It is—it is something else—is it not?"

"Eva, give it to me."

"Does it take effect quickly?" she asked.

"Eva, I insist. Give it me!" he repeated, angry now, and at his wits' end.

He threw his arm round her, and tried to seize her wrists; but he only grasped one empty hand, while the other flung the vial over his head on the floor. There was a little clatter of falling glass, and before he could rise she had thrown her arms round him again, dragging him down among the cushions.

"Let it lie there," she murmured with a smile. It is broken. I have broken it for you. Tell me, why did you carry that about with you?"

"It is not what you fancy," he replied, still on the defensive.

"So much the better— Why did you have it?"

He sat silent for a moment. Then, yielding to her insistence, he said:

"To take it—when all was at an end between us—in the evening, of course."

"And now you can not do so."

"Perhaps I can manage to buy some more," he said, with a gloomy laugh.

"But why is everything to be at an end between us?"

He was suddenly quite serious, mocking no more at life and death.

"For your sake, my angel; for your happiness. I beseech you, let it all be ended. Let me feel that I no longer need make you wretched. You may yet be happy; but I—I feel that everything in me hinders my ever being happy, and all happiness must begin in ourselves alone."

"And do you think I shall let you go, now that you have just told me what you would do in the evening?"

"But you are not to think that I should do it only for your sake. I always go about with that in my pocket. I have often thought of doing it; but then I have thought of you, and I lacked courage; for I know that you love me only too well."

"Not too well. I have lived in you. But for you I should never have truly lived."

"But for me you might have lived with another, and have been happy."

"No. Never with any other. That could never have been. I had to live with you. It was Fatality."

"Ay, Fatality. Bertie used to say—"

"Do not mention Bertie."

As she spoke the rain dashed against the window panes in a perfect torrent.

"It is always raining," she murmured.

"Yes—always," he mechanically repeated. She shuddered and looked in his face.

"Why do you say that?" she asked quickly.

"I do not know," said he, startled and bewildered. "I really do not know. Why, what did I say?"

They both were silent. Then she began again.

"Frank!"

"My darling."

"I will not let you leave me again. Not even for a day. I shall always be in terror for you."

"Let there be an end to everything, my child."

"No, no. Listen. Let us be together forever. Forever and ever. Let us lie down to sleep—while it is still raining."

"Eva!"

"Together. You say yourself that everything in you fails of happiness, and that nevertheless happiness must come from within. Well, it is the same with me. And yet we love each other; do we not?"

"Yes, yes."

"Then why should we remain awake in this weariful life? It is always, always raining. Give me a kiss, Frank. A good-night kiss, and let us sleep while it rains. Let me go to sleep in your arms—"

"Eva, what do you mean?" he asked, hoarsely, for he did not understand her.

"I broke the vial—broke it for you," she went on wildly. "But you can always get another!" An icy chill shot through his very marrow like a sudden frost.

"God in heaven, Eva! What do you want?" She smiled at him calmly, with a soft light in her beaming eyes, and she threw her arms round him.

"To die with you, my dearest," she whispered as in an ecstasy of joy. "What good can life do us? You were right. You can never be happy again, and I can never be happy with you. And yet I will not leave you, for you are all in all to me. Then how can we live, or why? But, oh, Frank, to die together, in each other's arms! That is the greatest bliss! A kindly poison, Frank, nothing painful. Something easy to take, that we can take together, and clasp each other, and die—die—die—" Frank shuddered with horror.

"No, Eva, no!" he cried. "You must not wish that, you can not wish that! I forbid it."

"Oh, do not forbid it," she said persuasively, falling on the floor and embracing his knees. "Let us share the same fate: that will be bliss. All about us will be rose color and gold and silver, like a glorious sunset. Oh, can you imagine anything

more beautiful? Frank, that is happiness, the
happiness we have looked for—which every one
in this world is looking for. It is Paradise! It
is Heaven!"

He was not carried away by her rapture, but
her words tempted him as with the promise of a
brief joy in this life and an unutterably peaceful
rest in death. He could say no more to dissuade
her, to check her in the heavenward flight of her
fancy; but still he reflected that there were no
means at hand, since the vial was broken.

Eva had risen, irresistibly attracted to the spot
where the vial had fallen. She stooped and
picked it up. It had fallen into the drapery of
a curtain; it was not broken, only cracked and
chipped. Not a drop had been spilled.

"Frank!" she screamed, in her frenzied gladness. "It is not broken! Look! It is whole. It
is Fate that would not allow it to be broken."

He too was standing up, quaking with an icy
chill. She had already forced out the stopper and
half emptied the vial with a mad, ecstatic smile.

"Eva!" he shrieked.

And quite calmly, smiling still, she handed it
to him. He looked at her for a moment, feeling
as if they two were already no longer of this world,
as if they were floating in a sphere of unknown
natural laws, in which strange things must come
to pass. The world, as it seemed, was about to

perish in that deluge of pouring rain. But he saw
that she stood waiting with her strange smile—and
he drank—

It was quite dark; they lay on the sofa side by
side, in each other's arms. He was dead. She
raised her head in an agony of alarm at the storm
which was raging outside, and that other storm
which was raging in her dying body. The lightning glared white and the thunder was close overhead. But louder than the echoes in the air the
thunder came rolling on toward Eva, nearer and
nearer, louder and louder, a supernatural thunder,
on the wheels of the spheres.

"It is coming!" she murmured, in the anguish
of death. "Great heavens! the thunder again!"

And she sank convulsed on the body of her lover,
hiding her head under his coat, to die there.

Then came a shuffling step in the passage outside the dark room. An old man's thin voice twice
called the name of Eva; and a hand opened the
door.